502 502
594 644
1296 0020

A PLACE IN MIND

A NOVEL BY

Dulce D. Moore

BASKERVILLE
PUBLISHERS, LTD
DALLAS · NEW YORK · DUBLIN

BASKERVILLE Publishers, Ltd.
7540 LBJ/Suite 125, Dallas, TX 75251-1008

Library of Congress Catalog Card Number: 92-070845
ISBN: 0-9627509-9-9

Manufactured in the United States of America
First Printing

"It's been a grand life in America. We have had to work hard. We have had poverty, but also the hope that if the individual man threw in enough struggle and labor, he could find his place however rough the road."
—Raymond Clapper   1941

ONE

Though I had lived in the same house nearly thirty years when Paul died, I still automatically placed myself before I was fully awake. Before the last, fading edge of my last, fading dream dissolved, before I recognized that my aging bladder needed emptying, that I wanted a cigarette, that the cat was crying to be let out into the moonset where field mice ran under last year's leaves and low-boughed birds huddled heavy with sleep and dew, I knew what town I was in, what room in which house, where every door and window was, every stick of furniture, where the car was parked, and how we were all oriented to the four directions—a leftover skill learned as a child, in order that my self, moving as it did then along a continuum of campgrounds, tourist courts, furnished apartments and wide spots at the sides of a thousand roads, might not have to keep waking up startled and strange, wondering what place it was in.

For place was of primary importance to people on the road. It was the basic topic of our conversation, the center around which all other considerations revolved, the determining factor in what we called our Luck.

And up until that autumn early in the Great Depression, a time Mama called the Red River Rampage, when we were criss-crossing the border between Texas and Oklahoma so often I couldn't keep up with which state we were in, much less which town, I had accepted place as I had accepted everything else. It was simply there, part of a pattern, each segment with its own geography, its own particular people and circumstances, its own time-distance between the place before it and the place after it.

But, my God—once into the Rampage, one dusty little town blurred into another, separated only vaguely by late suppers hurriedly eaten in the hard, white light of the Coleman lantern setting on the hood of the waiting car. We never got on the road till after everyone else had gone to bed, which generally threw us into the next camp before anyone there was up, forcing us to load and unload quietly, Mama standing on the long box to help Daddy get the tent on and off because there were no men awake to do it.

Though Mama couldn't spell him—spent half her life in a car and never learned to drive one—she did stay awake to help him stay awake, and I tried to follow her example. But I always had to give it up at some unknown point in the darkness passing by, to stumble at last, numb with sleep and motion, from the car to my cot, asking Mama, "Is it Time yet? Are we There?" Hearing her whispered, "Shh. Yes, it's Time. We're There." Fumbling for the name of "There" while she helped me undress, knowing it was lost as I fell back into sleep, waking again to wonder again where I was.

I did know I was in a campground somewhere, from an ingrained sense of season and from the scents and sounds all campgrounds made early of a morning. Daddy's Bull Durham mixed with the smell of woodsmoke and boiling coffee; pone frying, and salt pork, if someone's Luck had been good; cheap gas and thin dust rising on damp air; cars starting or trying to; the thock of a hatchet head on tent pegs; a woman calling her crew to breakfast; a man clearing his throat; kids yelling threats or promises; somebody whistling for a dog.

But what I didn't know, and what I'd become obsessed with needing to know, was where the campground was located, what name it was called by, where this move and this place belonged among all the other moves and places.

Paul never could understand why I didn't simply ask where I was if not knowing bothered me that much. But our backgrounds were so different I was never able to explain it to him. Born and raised in the same house his parents bought when they married and lived in till they died, he went through school with the same bunch of kids, attended the same church from Cradle Roll to Senior Boys, and thought camping was something you did with your scout troop on the weekend, while being on the road meant a Sunday afternoon drive down to Glen Rose and back.

More important than those differences, though, were the different ways in which we perceived our parents. He loved his. I adored mine. He saw his as ordinary, hardworking people to whom he owed, and gave, the affectionate regard of a good and dutiful son. I saw mine as images of glamour, even when they were old and ill, and that charged mixture of beauty and mystery surrounding them when they were young and strong was such a compelling force in my life as a child, I was never willing to risk a revelation of my own plain and imperfect self.

Daddy was the Provider, the master of the car, site chooser, tent raiser, fire maker, whittler and whistler, sure in the ways of men and animals, roads and rivers, towns and prairies, authority on camp protocol, story teller, old song singer, the One Who Was Never Afraid.

Mama was the Namer of Names, cook and cleaner and comforter, privy to all that was written, defender of the faith, disciple of public education, mood maker and memory keeper, the One Who Knew What Was and Was Not Nice.

So I finally quit expecting Paul to understand the lengths to which I would have gone, and did go, to pass myself off as the trooper I knew they wanted me to be, instead of the greenhorn I feared I was. And besides, I always managed to find out where we were sometime during the day, by reading the names on city limit signs and water towers, cotton gins and grain elevators, school buildings and school buses—anywhere but on a map, because if there were printed maps available to the public then, we never saw them. We got from place to place by tracing the way through Daddy's memory, or by studying the lines some gravefaced man drew in the dust with a stick or a finger, hunkered down in a circle of gravefaced men around him, watching him make a picture of his travels that showed all the outward and visible signs of roads and rivers and towns and stopping places, with all their invisible possibilities for good or bad Luck.

"We had good Luck there," he might say. "Found work four days running. There's a pretty fair camp, plenty of water. Town folks're obliging. Yep, we done all right there. I'd say give her a whirl."

Or: "We didn't have nothing but bad Luck there. Couldn't find no work nohow. Sorry camp, town people looking at us slitty-eyed, Law drifting by all the time. Nope, I'd say give that place a wide berth."

We hit about as many of the bad Luck places as we did the good. Sometimes by chance, because we'd had no warning. Sometimes through necessity, because it was on our way to somewhere else and couldn't be avoided. Sometimes by choice, because Daddy persisted in believing, for years, poor devil, that somehow his Luck would always be better than the other fellow's.

Most of the time, though, our Luck ran about average, which wasn't saying much, and before the Rampage, we always went to meet it early of a morning. Daddy liked to get into a town by mid-afternoon so he could look it over and get acquainted before he began working it. Mama liked to get in then so she could have our camp set up and functioning before supper. I never thought of it in terms of liking or disliking. When Daddy said it was time to go, it was time to go, and when he said, "Climb in, Mavis," I climbed in, over the back of his seat and into my own as I'd been doing for as long as I could remember, with no more thought of questioning it than I gave to questioning the rising of the sun.

Mama scooted in next, holding Martha May high on her

4

shoulder to keep from bumping her against the steering wheel. Then Daddy, after a last look around to be sure we hadn't left anything, got in and pulled the slipknot tight and we were off, down the camp road, over the hump, and onto the highway.

No one could get in or out on the passenger side, because that running board carried the special long box Daddy had made to hold his tripod and light stand. The rest of his equipment was stowed in the trunk, along with the jack and the tube patch and all the other paraphernalia needed to keep the car going—except for the camera itself, which rode on the seat beside me, wrapped in its black cover cloth and propped by protecting pillows.

The back door on my side couldn't be used, either, because of the rope and the boxes on the floor boards that held our household gear, stacked so that the one which served as Martha May's bed was on top, handy for her to nap in during the day.

The cots, the canvas camp stools, the tent stakes and pegs, the hatchet and extra rope, were folded inside the tent, which was lashed to the top of the car and tied so that the final knot, the famous slip, was secured to the frame between mine and Daddy's windows, where he could loosen or tighten it from inside the car.

We must have looked, to greenhorn eyes, at any rate, little different from the migrant farm workers and other lost souls floating by on the great flood of people set adrift by the Depression and the beginning of the Dust Bowl. But we had been on the road long before either of those events began to send the desperate and the destitute out to join us.

That was what a kidnapper did. And though that term had begun to be soft-pedalled the year before the Rampage, when the Lindbergh baby was stolen, it was still to be heard, mostly among old timers, as trade jargon for a traveling photographer who specialized in taking portraits of children in their homes.

Not that Daddy ever refused business from anyone,

including some whores once, he told me during one of my visits home in the weeks before he died, when we sometimes talked all night. They were 2 x 3 handouts the girls bought for favored customers, full-lengths, always a difficult pose, made more difficult because he'd never shot a nude before, or a whore, either, so far as he knew. But they paid for Santa Claus that terrible second winter in Beaumont and he had no regrets.

In boom towns, anywhere his Luck ran good, he made portraits of smiling girls to give to sweethearts, of serious young men standing by their first cars or mounted on their first motorcyles, of wedding couples, golden anniversary couples, family reunions, high school graduation classes, funeral processions, blue ribbon winners at county fairs, prized pets, proud new homes, businesses, churches, fires, floods, and when he was very young and just starting out, a public hanging.

Like so many in the vanguard of that other widespread upheaval that came after World War I, when much of a whole generation left the farms and small towns for the bigger world beyond, he had gone on the road to find a place for himself in the only way open to him—by working his way along, seeking his fortune as he went.

Jerked out of school at the end of the fourth grade, when his mother died, and put to work helping in the store, he grew up a landless, small-time grocer's son in a society where the ownership of land, not in acres, but in sections, determined wealth and position. And that society taught him very early that so long as he stayed where he was, odd jobbing around town at the lumberyard and the hotel, working as night delivery boy for one of the drugstores, extra hand for any rancher who needed one, at whatever he could pick up when he wasn't busy at the store, he would end up like his papa, an old man with nothing to show for his life but a lot of pennypinching hard work and a little two-bit business on the wrong side of the tracks.

Bankers could surmount the rule of inherited land, and

so could successful doctors and lawyers. And so could the big merchants who traded with Chicago and Kansas City, if not in position, at least in wealth. And while all the rhetoric of the time promised boys like him ways to join that blessed company without having been born into it, the smart ones knew those ways were closed to them on their own ground.

He saw his chance and grabbed it toward the end of his sixteenth year, when a kidnapper whose assistant had deserted him in Abilene, came through Angelo. Three years and a lot of miles later, he set up on his own. If he hadn't made his fortune, he had, until the Depression hit, made a good living, and he'd certainly seen a lot of what he called the world, as had we all. And if it was in a crowded old car, over bad roads, through dusty little wind-rocked towns—

"There you are," Naomi said, and letting the screen bang to behind her, popping her high-heeled mules across the porch, she brought me back to what I knew in the marrow of my bones, yet only half-believed and was determined not to think about: that time and Luck and cancer had made me a widow.

TWO

"I saw the light on in the kitchen and smelled the coffee," she said, "but I couldn't find you anywhere. It's five o'clock, Mavis, what are you doing out here in the dark? Couldn't you sleep at all?"

"I dozed some."

"Then get back to bed. You shouldn't be up at this hour."

"I come out here every morning at this time."

"At five o'clock?"

"Yes at five o'clock. Sometimes earlier. Get you a cup if you want some coffee, or go on back to bed yourself. I'm all right."

"No, I'm awake now. Got any cigs?"

"Yes, here."

"Wait till I get my coffee."

She came back out with her coffee, letting the screen bang again, and I said, "I see you're still a door slammer."

She sat down next to me on the top step and lit her cigarette and said, "And I see you're still little Miss Goody Two-shoes, sitting out here in the dark all by yourself so you won't disturb anybody."

"I told you this is something I do every day. And I had to be extra good at Grandma's, Naomi. My situation was a lot different from yours."

"That's all in your mind."

"That's where it counts."

She started to say something else, took a sip of coffee instead, and as the Cantu's rooster began crowing, for the real dawn this time, said, "Whose rooster? I didn't know people in town kept chickens anymore."

"It belongs to the Mexican family that moved into the old Bolling place, the Cantus. I'm surprised this is the first time you've heard him."

"Well, it is, I'm ashamed to admit."

"You don't have to be ashamed of sleeping till a decent hour. It's perfectly permissible."

"No, I should've been up in case you needed me. Besides, we haven't had a chance to talk since I got here. I tried to give you some time to be with Mary Fern and the boys by yourselves, but there've been so many people coming in and out—"

"Well, the worst part of that's over with. People'll pretty much go about their own business now."

"She said with a sigh of relief."

"No, no—well, yes, if you want the truth. I'm not used to crowds anymore. They wear me out."

"The house'll seem awfully empty, though, once everyone's gone."

"Oh, Mary Fern and the boys'll be here for a week when school's out, and you know Billy. He's always zipping through on the way to some deal or other. It's okay, Naomi. I'll be all right."

"I still don't like to think of you sitting out here in the dark by yourself. Not these last few mornings, anyhow. I wish you'd called me. I'd have been glad to get up."

"And I wish you'd quit worrying about it. This is a normal part of my life, something I do every day, even when it's raining. Except then Jane Long and I prowl the porch till it's time to—"

But it would never be time again for me to give Paul his medicine, or an alcohol rub, or try to coax him to eat, or ever do anything for him. And the finality of his goneness, not his death, you grasp death at once, but the total, irrevocable goneness, rushed me again, squeezing my heart till I had to bend with the pain of it.

She didn't touch me. We weren't a family of touchers. But I knew she was suffering for me and I didn't want her to. She'd had enough suffering of her own to endure. So I straightened up and lit another cigarette and didn't care if they were killing me, the sooner the better, and she said, "How quiet everything is. How beautiful. It reminds me of mornings at Home, at Grandma's. Doesn't it you? When I'd get to spend the night with you and we'd get up early and go out to the pen with her and feed the baby chicks while the stars were still out?"

I said, "Yes," but it wasn't any memory of Grandma's I was waiting for, and she said, "Why don't I fix us some breakfast?"

"In a minute. After we see the sunrise."

Then the Cantu's rooster began his last challenge to the sky turning that pure, half-light of earliest dawn, and I said, "We're going to have to stand up to see it right. That hedge has just got completely out of control. But raise up on your tiptoes and look out over it to that line of cottonwoods yonder."

It wasn't anything spectacular. Even when we'd first moved into the house and the cottonwoods along the drainage ditch were seedlings and the hedge newly planted and the houses to the east of us not built, it was pretty tame stuff compared to the thin vermillion line burning away the whole eastern edge of the world that I remembered from my childhood, when a younger, fiercer sun rose up over some great empty plain in such splendor.

"Heaven and earth are full of Thy glory, indeed," she said. "I'm sorry, Mavis, but it lifts my heart in spite of everything."

"Don't be sorry. It lifts mine, too. That's what I come out here for."

We watched till it cleared the trees and the world turned

ordinary again, and I held the screen open for her while she stood there another minute, hugging herself against a sudden chill. Then she came through the door, saying, "I may not watch the sun come up very often, but I am always glad to see daylight. God knows, I hate the darkness."

It wasn't that I didn't love Naomi. Or that I no longer sympathized with the dread of darkness she'd suffered from since Charles's plane went down in the Coral Sea. Not even forty-odd years were enough to make me forget the look on her face when she'd said, "He's buried under miles of darkness, Mavis, miles and miles."

But I also felt if she could deal with her darkness through a memory set free by that watered-down dawn she'd forced herself to share with me, she ought to be willing to let me alone so I could deal with my darkness in the memories that set me free—

When the Rampage came to an end the night we pulled out of Gould, Daddy saying, "I'm damn glad to be kissing the Red farewell forever Casoose. When we get back to Texas this time, we're staying for good."

"I can't see it's much different from Oklahoma up here," Mama said.

"I'm not talking about up here along the river. I'm talking about real Texas. Hell, the people up in these parts don't need a photographer. They need a miracle."

"I guess we could all use one of those."

"Well it ain't likely anybody around here's going to get struck by one. Besides, I figure a miracle's a lot like Luck. Part of it you got to make for yourself. And I aim to start making some for us, somehow, someway, some chance to make a little money and get back on our feet."

"That sounds like a miracle to me. I don't know, Will, this Depression just gets worse all the time. People keep saying Roosevelt's going to change things, but I haven't seen any evidence. I'm beginning to wonder if there *is* any place left that's got any real Luck in it."

11

"Why, certainly there's good places left, Fern. Plenty of them."

"We sure haven't run into any of them here lately."

"Well then, we're due for a turn of the wheel, and I don't care who gets the credit, Roosevelt or the hobgoblins. I just want us to be in a position to take advantage of it when it comes. And the first thing we got to do is get back to some bigger towns. We'll hit Childress, scout around there. Then Floydada, I reckon, Lubbock. Or we could head north and pick up Pampa, go on up to Amarillo. There ought to be some crop money still floating around."

"If anybody made a crop in this drought."

"Somebody always makes a crop. There's more than just cotton in the Panhandle, anyhow. There's wheat, milo, oil, cattle—we should've gone straight on out there when we left Texarkana last spring."

"You were so hell bent on seeing the Black Hills."

"And I'm glad we did. We won't likely ever get a chance to see country like that again."

"All I can say is, it was a long haul with a new baby. If Mavis wasn't such a trooper—"

"We raised her to be one, didn't we? And look at the education she got, seeing new places, new people, new ways of doing things. That's learning you don't get out of a book."

"Maybe so. But it was a hell of a trek to make to end up broker than we were when we started out. And it wasn't our kind of place. We'd have been strangers there if we'd stayed a hundred years."

"I never intended to settle down up there."

"You don't intend on settling down anywhere."

"Now that's where you're wrong. I been thinking about getting off the road for some time, finding us a place—"

"Uh-huh. And just where is this place we're going to do all this settling down in?"

"I don't know. There's lots of places we could do all right in."

"Not if they're in the same plight as the ones we've been hitting, there's not. I never have seen times so hard or the country look so bad. I don't know what's going to happen if the farmers don't get some rain."

Mama always took the farmers' side because her grandpa was one and that was where the happiest memories of her childhood lay. But Daddy was a town boy, and while he coveted some small piece of land as a sign he'd made his pile and knew the proper use to put it to, he was short on patience with those who made their living from it.

"I never seen a time in my life," he said, "when the damn ranchers and farmers wasn't bellyaching about something."

"They've got good cause these days. I think the whole country's drying up and blowing away."

"Hell, they've had droughts out here since heck was a pup. This one'll break like all the others. Once we get a little stake together, we'll drop on down to Snyder, hit Big Spring, maybe. Sweetwater. Might even take a look at—"

"Angelo?"

"Maybe."

"I knew it. I knew it. The minute you mentioned settling down, I knew Angelo was the place you had in mind."

"I don't see nothing wrong with that. And I don't see nothing wrong with the offer Papa's made us, either."

"I haven't forgotten what happened the last time your papa made us an offer."

"I admit things didn't work out the way we planned back then, but—"

"No, if living in niggertown and never having one red cent to rub against another wasn't part of the plan, it sure didn't."

"Take the wheel. I want to roll me a smoke."

"Roll me one, too."

The flare of the match flashed their faces across the windshield like faces seen in sudden lightning, and the smell of sulfur filled the car.

13

Daddy took the wheel back and steadied her and said, "Tell me something, Fern. Did you and Baby deliberately burn that house down?"

Mama laughed. "We sure did."

"I been afraid of that from the beginning. It was all just a little too pat the way it caught fire right when you all had it stripped out for a good cleaning. Everybody kept saying wasn't it Lucky you had Mavis out for a sunning and all the clothes and bedding airing and—that's arson, Fern."

"Well what did you expect me to do? I didn't know how else to get us out of there."

"But my God. Burning a man's house to the ground?"

"I told you I wasn't going to raise Mavis in a place like that. You should've listened to me. It wasn't a fit place for Baby, either. A fifteen-year-old girl in a neighborhood like that? If your papa had kept his end of the bargain and paid you enough for us to live somewhere else, Baby could've stayed with us and had a decent place to invite her friends— or did it make you proud to know your sister was meeting her dates downtown?"

"We could've all ended up in the pen."

Mama shrugged. "Well, we didn't."

I didn't understand why a grown man wouldn't keep his end of a bargain, a failing that quicker than any other put even a child outside the pale; or how Mama, who never did anything wrong, could do something I'd been taught since infancy was unforgivable.

For fire was more dreaded in the camps than contagious disease, and the dangers of it were drummed into children like me from the time we could sit up good. By example, by strict instruction, by a hundred horror stories, we were taught the volatility of gasoline and dry grass, of tires and canvas, the risk of people being trapped and killed, of losing everything they owned, of the prairies going up in smoke for miles around, threatening houses and stock and wildlife.

"I think I see a fire up ahead now," Daddy said.

I saw it, too, then, the smallest lick of flame, and went

dizzy with fear my own thoughts had built it till he said, "Somebody's set up camp, looks like."

"This is an awfully out of the way place for somebody to be camping," Mama said. "It's probably just some sheep-herders."

"No, too close to the road for them. Somebody's decided to give it up for the night and pulled over to have some coffee and get a little shut-eye."

"I could use a cup of coffee myself."

"You want to stop?"

"Oh, no. It's late, Will, we need to get on."

But he slowed down as we neared the car that was parked along the shallow dip of the bar ditch at a curving angle, with what looked like a little house on a trailer hooked on the back bumper making a kind of hinged semi-circle of the whole get-up. He stopped and said, "Well, I'll be hung for a horse thief. That's Ollie Ferguson's rig. I'd know it anywhere. Let's get out and say hello and get you your cup of java."

"No. Let's go on. I don't want a cup bad enough to have to be around that old reprobate to get it."

"Ollie ain't no reprobate. He may not be the Prince of Wales, but he was a top hand around Angelo when I was a boy. I watched him green-break mounts for the army many a time during the war. And he done trick riding for them moving picture people out in Hollywood till he got bunged up so bad he couldn't ride no more."

"That doesn't change the fact that he peddles dope all over the country."

"Only a little marijuana, is all, to the Mexicans and the honky-tonk crowd."

"It's still not right, selling that filthy stuff, and using those poor women the way he does, passing them and their kids off as his family to help him sneak through the Border Patrol."

"At least the women and kids eat when they're with Ollie."

"I don't approve of it."

"Well, Fern, whether you approve or not, and under the circumstances, I think you got a hell of a nerve to open your mouth about it, everybody's got to eat, even widow women and stove up cowboys."

He backed up and pulled off the road as far as he could, closing the crescent made by the Ferguson rig and putting us directly across from the fire, where I thought I'd seen some-one when we first drove up. But there was no one there now, and Mama said, "They must've already turned in."

"And left the fire burning? Ollie Ferguson ain't no greenhorn." Then he loosened the slip knot and got out and walked around to stand on Mama's side of the car, holding his hands out from his body, and yelled, "Hello, the fire! That you, Ollie?"

From someplace where we couldn't see him, a man called back, "Who's out there?"

"It's me, Will Maddox, you old stingaree."

And instead of a top hand trick riding movie star mon-ster that sold dope and did bad things to women and chil-dren, a small, skinny old man, stooped in the shoulders, limped out from behind the shadows and said, "Why hidy, Will. You all light and set a spell."

I couldn't pay attention to the talk for marvelling at the little house. It was made of board and batten, like a regular box house, and had once been calcimimed green. There was one half-sized window in the side I could see, covered with a raggedy curtain that I could feel kids behind, watching me through the torn places.

I wondered if they rode in the little house during the day, or if they only went inside it at night. I wondered where they were from and where they were going and what kind of friends they'd be if they could've come outside. It was too late to play, but we could've talked. They could've told me about the little house and I could've told them about our tent and—and then I heard Mr. Ferguson say, "Now Jennie here'll fix you all a bite of late supper, if you've a mind, or some early breakfast, either one. You name it."

"No thank you kindly," Mama said, "The coffee was plenty, and it sure hit the spot. But we need to be getting along now. This baby's heavy as lead, Will, and Mavis is falling asleep sitting up."

Daddy said, "All right, Fern," and he and Mr. Ferguson shook hands again and Daddy said, "We're much obliged, folks." Then he leaned forward and said something to Mr. Ferguson I couldn't hear, and Mr. Ferguson threw back his head and laughed, and his face looked like a warm spring day with a west wind blowing, turning him back into a true top hand, young and handsome and full of life.

THREE

"Mavis, please sit down and let me fix us some breakfast."

"I'm trying to see if Jane Long wants in."

"That cat never has failed to let you know what she wants. Now come sit down."

"I think I'll have something after while, Naomi."

"No, you'll have something right now. I'm no great shakes as a cook, but—"

"It's not that. I'm just not hungry."

"You've got to eat something anyhow. Just a few bites. Then I want you to go back to bed—no, now listen. I'll tend to the phone and the door, if there's anybody and his dog left who hasn't already called or come by—don't give me that look. I know people mean well and you appreciate their thoughtfulness and all that, but enough's enough. I want you to get some food in your stomach and a few hours rest. I'll be nice as pie, I promise."

So I sat down at the kitchen table and watched her clatter around like she was fixing dinner for an army instead of making a few pieces of toast and scrambling some eggs, and she said, "That was a real treat, sharing the dawn with you this morning. Of course, it wasn't really very dark, but—"

"It's not really very dark anywhere these days. There's too much skyglow from too many towns that've gotten too big, and too much traffic on the roads. But if it made you happy, I'm glad you could do it."

"Maybe I could get up my nerve more often if you'd move to Austin and hold my hand."

"I told you and Billy both, Naomi. I don't want to be pestered about that."

"Okay. We'll talk about it later." And before I could say I didn't want to talk about it at all, she began serving up her attempt at breakfast, pouring more coffee, saying, "And speaking of this morning—Grandma's—Home—you have those times on your mind a lot right now, don't you?"

"Well, yes, only I don't think of Grandma's as Home. I never have."

"And I've never understood why. You all lived there all that time, and—"

"About six months."

"All right, about six months. Where else did you ever live that long in one place back then?"

"Nowhere. You know that. But wherever we lived, for however short a time, we were our own family, tending to our own business and running our own lives."

"On some godforsaken stretch of road in West Texas in that damned tent."

"Well I'll tell you this, it beat the hell out of living in a house as a poor relation."

"Are you going to start that again?"

"I'm not starting anything. You're the one that brought it up."

"But whoever mistreated you? Except Lottie and Dottie, and they don't count, I hope."

"No."

"Who, then?"

"No one, exactly."

"What do you mean, no one exactly?"

"Look, Naomi, I came to realize before we left that in spite of everything, they probably did love us, in their own peculiar way. But that place wasn't Home to me then, it's not Home to me now, and it never will be Home to me."

"I wish it could be. Because it's Home to me."

"Of course it's Home to you. You were born and raised in Robb's Prairie. Your grandmother was one of Grandma's daughters. My mother was only a granddaughter, and I was—listen. I never even saw any of those people till I walked in there an eight-year-old stranger."

"You were born there the same as I was."

"And left when I was two weeks old. There's no use re-hashing all this. You inherited Aunt Hallie's place and her share of the farm, and you go back there on business a lot. I haven't even been in that county in over fifty years."

"You know I tried to give you my share of the farm. I'd deed you the income off it today, if you'd let me."

"No, no. I don't want it. I'm not ungrateful, Naomi. I appreciate everything they did for us—Grandma, Uncle Dan, Aunt Hallie, everybody. It wasn't their fault times were so hard and things in Angelo got so bad Daddy couldn't make us a living. But it sure as hell wasn't his fault, either."

"Nobody ever said it was."

"Not to our faces."

"Oh, Mavis. Don't."

"I don't hear you denying it. Not that it would make any difference if you did. I know they talked about us behind our backs. Kids always know things like that."

"But kids don't always know the reason behind things."

"They don't need to know any reasons. Knowing they're poor relations is enough. Or knowing they're taking a skinning, the way we did at Papa Maddox's, the old bastard. I hope he's roasting in Hell. No, Naomi, no matter how you cut it, we were on the outside looking in, and that's something you've got to go through yourself to understand."

"Well, I can't speak for your Grandpa Maddox, but I do think that after all these years it should've occurred to you that Grandma and Uncle Dan, and Grandmother, too, let their own fears and worries make them say things they didn't really mean. I know they loved you all, Mavis, even if it was in what you call their own peculiar way."

"And I know Mama was a slavey for Grandma and Dan the same way Daddy was one for his old man."

"All right. Let's don't argue. Let's just be glad we're still blood first cousins and permanent best friends."

"We're not really first cousins, Naomi. Our mothers were first cousins."

"Well, doesn't that make us first cousins once removed?"

"Hell, I don't know. I never did go in for all that to the umpteenth degree stuff. We can call ourselves whatever we want to, and we're 'eternal' best friends. That's the word you used, 'eternal.'"

"I guess I was an insufferable little show-off."

"Because you liked to look up words in the dictionary? I thought it was wonderful. I just wished I had one."

"Oh, lord. When happiness was curly hair and a pinto pony and a dictionary."

"No, when happiness was *wishing* for curly hair and a pinto pony and a dictionary."

"Yes . . ."

"Oh, I was happy there most of the time, and I've never forgotten that Grandma took us in when we didn't have anywhere else to go. But—losing Paul. I loved him and hated him and had a child by him and endured and enjoyed and fought through forty-five years with him. A whole life. And his death brings back all my other deaths, Mama's and Daddy's and Martha May's, because you never ever have one death at a time to survive once you lose the first person you love. You have to go through all of them, all over again, every time."

"I understand that, Mavis."

"Yes, I know, and I'm sorry. But I don't want to talk about it anymore. I'm going to take a shower and lie down awhile."

"But you haven't eaten anything."

21

"I ate some toast."

"About three little nibbles."

"That's all I wanted."

"Well, if you'll get some rest. Do you want a sleeping pill?"

"No, I don't want any more of those damned pills you and the doctor keep trying to foist off on me."

"We're not trying to foist anything off on you, Mavis. We're concerned for your health, that's all. You're not eating, you're not sleeping, and you've been under a terrible strain for a long time."

"I'm going to be okay. I'm not going to pine away or go nuts or try to hit a gas truck head on or—"

"Don't you talk like that, you hear? If I have to chain you to your bed, I will." Which was what I'd once said to her. But I didn't want to bring those days up, so I said, "I swear to you I'm going to be all right, okay?"

It took a minute, but finally she said, "Okay."

"Good. Just leave the dishes, I'll tend to them later."

"My lord, Mavis, don't you think I'm capable of washing up a handful of dishes? I fixed us a nice breakfast, didn't I?"

"Yes, Naomi, for somebody who either eats out or settles for crackers and vienna sausage, you did fine. Now I'm going to take my shower and try to nap awhile, okay?"

"Okay. I'll see you in a little bit."

Sometime while Mary Fern and I were out of the house the day Paul died, Naomi and the boys had got rid of the hospital bed and the oxygen tank, the heating pad, the medicines, all those trappings that accumulate around a long illness, turning our room, my room now, back into the way it used to be. I didn't resent it anymore, their doing what it wasn't their place to do. I was too grateful to be able to slip back into its old, familiar comfort. Just as I'd been grateful to slip back into the old, familiar comfort of the campground east of Childress, that long ago quiet and waiting hour before sunrise, when the sky behind us was beginning to pale,

22

while in front of us, toward the town, it was still dark and full of stars—

It was a fair-sized camp, well laid out, not like the miserable little huddles we'd been staying in during the Rampage. Lots of people were already up, standing close to their fires, getting their breakfasts going and warming themselves against the early morning chill. They lifted their hands to us as we went by, a couple of the men moving out to follow us as Daddy looked for a place to set up our camp.

They helped unload the tent and get it up, and before the last stake was in, their wives came over to meet Mama. They told her where the drinking water was and how much it cost, made over Martha May and smiled at me and said the school bus came by about half past seven and stopped right across the road from the camp entrance.

They didn't stay long. They had their own chores to tend to, and it wasn't good manners to take notice of how much or how little or what a person unpacked. Real visiting never began till after supper, anyhow, when whoever you were visiting didn't have to ask you to eat. Otherwise, if they didn't have enough to go around, somebody had to give you their share. So no one ever did that except total greenhorns, or someone so hungry admitting it publicly no longer mattered. Though sometimes, even proud people sent their children over to stand around till they were fed.

No big kids came over and no kids my age. I hadn't expected them to. Big kids never paid any attention to a new family coming in unless it had big kids, too, and how they handled that, I didn't know. Big kids didn't allow kids my age to meddle in their affairs.

And the rule for kids my age was, once you were old enough to go to school, it was up to you to find a place for yourself the best way you could. Everybody else had already made friends. Ways of doing things had been set, laws laid down, leaders acknowledged, followers lined up, the timid tagged, bullies in business. You made your bid and paid the price, in fear and trembling and fierce desire.

It was so late by the time we got washed up and finished breakfast and Mama got the wrinkles ironed out of my other dress, the bus was already in sight when I got to the main road. I ran for it, knowing all the kids were thinking I was a greenhorn myself, or I'd have been on time, hoping my Luck would let me make a friend somewhere in that half-formed, milling line.

One of the girls my age turned to me and said, "Hidy," but before I could answer her, the bus stopped and everybody crowded on in such a rush I knew I'd never get a seat next to her, if I got one at all, which I didn't.

I could see her, though, from where I stood holding onto a strap. She was little and wiry, what grown ups called 'feisty,' with red hair and freckles and bright, snapping eyes black as a licorice stick. She talked constantly, turning and bouncing in her seat, laughing and sticking out her tongue at the big girls who gave her dirty looks and told her to shut up. She fascinated me and horrified me and I'd have done almost anything to have her for a friend.

I lost track of her when we got off the bus, because I had to go to the principal's office to find out what room I'd be in, which turned out to be the fourth this time, and didn't see her again till dinner, having spent all of recess locating the girls' restroom and the water fountain and having to stand in line at both.

The lunchroom was so crowded it took me awhile to spot her, standing behind some other girls from the camp, still talking, hopping from one foot to the other. I made my way toward her slowly, through benches of head-dodging, shoulder-scuffling, hunching, bunching, punching bodies, through faces that laughed, sneered, simpered, and conspired, chomped, choked, spit crumbs and dribbled milk or water. She saw me, pretended not to, and turned away from my half-offered smile to say, "Hush your own mouth," to a big girl who had said, "Hush your mouth," to her.

24

I found a place off to one side and ate my pone, then stopped at the water fountain to wash it down and went outside where the other girls my age were forming tight little groups that skipped and pranced across the baked clay playground stomped out of the surrounding prairie. The big girls strolled along in their own groups, ignoring everyone else, holding their skirts down against the wind that whipped dust on across the dead grass clear out to the edge of the sky.

I could hear the thudding whack of a bat from the field behind the school where the big boys took turns hitting a ball the little boys had to chase and return, and then, in one of those sharp silences that falls when the wind drops, a girl saying, "He tried to grab my titties."

After school, I hung around the tent amusing Martha May till she got fussy and Mama said, "I think she needs a little nap. Why don't you go play?" As if it were as simple as that. But I couldn't think of an excuse I'd admit to, so I went, slow and in a roundabout way that left me room to retreat if I had to, toward the water barrels where I'd heard some girls on the bus coming home say they'd be jumping rope.

Ladies looked up from their cooking and smiled as I passed by; dogs and little bitty kids yawned; a big girl, drying her hair in the sun, looked through and beyond me to places I couldn't go; and then I heard the chanting rise and fall of

> Down by the ocean,
> Down by the sea,
> Johnny broke a bottle
> And blamed it on me.
> How many bottles did it take?

When the count began, I stopped to gather my courage, and somebody behind me said, "Hidy."

She stood there looking friendly as if she'd been nice to me at dinner instead of cutting me dead, but since I always attributed that kind of cruelty to some fault in myself I'd correct as soon as I knew what it was, I assumed whatever blame was due, and said hidy back to her.

"My name's Eileen," she said. "What's yours?"

"Mavis."

"How old are you?"

"I'll be eight next month."

"What grade are you in?"

"The fourth this time."

"How come you're in the fourth and you're not even eight yet?"

I didn't want to risk explaining it to her for fear of losing her friendship. "Well, I have to go where they tell me to."

She bent down and retied a shoe and said, "Yeah. School's dumb. I wouldn't go if the Law didn't make me. Want to jump rope?"

We got to the edge of the loose line behind the jumper, close to the flash of the turning rope and moving feet and sing-song rhythm of

> Cinderella dressed in yellow,
> Went upstairs to kiss her fellow.
> Made a mistake and kissed a snake.
> How many doctors did it take?

I heard them begin the count, saw the jumper raise a hand to push her hair out of her eyes, remembered 'Ding-dong Daddy From Dumas', and 'Eighter From Decatur', and knew the problem of placing myself was solved. It might be true that we were back in Texas for good; it might even be true we'd live in a house in Angelo for good; but it was true beyond any doubt that once learned, words strung together in rhythm and rhyme were never forgotten. They stayed in your brain forever, whether you wanted them to or not. All I had to do was put the name of whatever place we were in into a jingle, repeat it to myself a couple of times before I went to sleep, and it would sing there all night long, ready to tell me where I was before I woke up the next morning.

Right then I couldn't think of anything that rhymed with Childress except wilderness, which was an apt description if it wasn't a perfect rhyme. But I wasn't looking for perfection. All I wanted was a connection that would work. Before I could decide on how to put the two words together, though, the jumper missed, groans and laughter spilled out, the line swayed and re-assembled itself, the rope began to turn again, the next jumper running to meet it, ducking her head for an opening, moving her feet to catch the down-swing, and Eileen said, "You can jump double with me when it's my turn."

The big girl standing nearest us said, "No she can't. Everybody has to take their own turn. She came after you. She can't jump till after you."

"We came together, smart alec."

"You did not. She came last and she can't jump till last."

Eileen grabbed hold of my arm and said, "She can share my turn with me if I want her to."

"She can't either."

"She can too and I'd like to see you stop her."

I wanted to say I didn't care when I jumped, but the rope stopped and everybody made a circle around us, yelling so loud I wouldn't have been heard if I'd had the nerve to say anything. Some of the girls said the rule was a jumper could use her turn any way she wanted to. Some said that might be the rule in other camps but it wasn't in this one. The yelling got louder, pushing and shoving began, and I wished I could be far, far away. Eileen was in her element, though, out-yelling everybody else, her free hand fisted and ready to strike, her red hair standing on end.

Then the biggest girl there shut everybody up by saying, "I'm going to slap the pure D shit out of the next one of you that opens their mouth." Her face was hard with anger and power, her hands on her hips, her faded, too-tight dress mashing the lumps on her chest flat. I knew those lumps meant this would be her last season to jump rope, to assert authority over a bunch of girls, to have any desire to be around a bunch of girls. By Christmas she would be spending her time with one or two special friends, whispering a lot and looking sideways at the big boys, flouncing her hiney when she walked.

"All right, Eileen," she said, "what're you trying to stir up this time?"

"I ain't stirring up nothing. I'm just claiming my right to jump double with my best friend."

Best friend? My heart stopped in confusion, then started up again, pumping alternate beats of pride and despair.

"She's got a right to make that claim," one of the other big girls said. "It's in our rules anybody can jump double that wants to."

"That ain't in our rules no such of a thing," the mean girl said. "And I'll thank you to keep your lies to yourself, Winta Beth Boyd."

"I ain't no liar, Gladys Lambert. You take that back."

"I ain't taking nothing back. It ain't in our rules."

"Who says?"

"*I* say, and what *I* say goes."

"Oh, yeah?" Eileen said. "Where's that wrote down in the Big Book?"

"Listen here, Eileen, you little snot."

"Don't you call me names. I been in this camp longer'n you."

"Yes, and everybody's sick and tired of you, too, you ugly little dope. *I* make the rules around here, and—"

"Oh no you don't," Winta Beth said. "You ain't as high and mighty as you think you are. *I* say—"

But whatever she was going to say got lost in the screams when Gladys reached over and grabbed her hair. Pushing and shoving weren't in it then. It was slapping, hair pulling, clenched-teeth cussing, churning dust, kicking feet,

28

a swirling storm of threats, sobs, grunts, and blows, through which I saw Eileen and Winta Beth both hitting Gladys before I lost my balance from a jab in the ribs and sat down hard.

A man's voice said, "Whoa! Whoa up there! You girls cut that out right now."

Everything went quiet except for a lot of panting and snuffling and throat clearing, while the man looked at us and we looked at our feet.

"You younguns scoot on home now and help your mamas with supper," he said. "Big girls like you all. Ain't you ashamed?"

Everybody mumbled yessir and the sisters who owned the rope began winding it up and Winta Beth, surrounded by her followers, nodded a bright, hard look at Gladys, who shrugged and walked off, the last friend she had left trailing beside her.

"I guess we showed her," Eileen said.

"Yeah," Winta Beth said, "I guess we did. And you done your part like you said you would, Eileen, so you're welcome to tag along. But I ain't putting up with none of your sass, savvy?" And they all started off together, laughing and talking.

I hung there a minute watching them, waiting for them to call me to come along, too, but they didn't. And when I waved goodbye as Eileen looked back, she stared at me like she didn't know who I was, and I understood that I'd played my part, too, without even knowing it. So I headed back for the tent, walking in and out of the long shadows thrown by the setting sun, wishing wordless wishes while doves called from a stock tank somewhere and woodsmoke lay soft on the still, cool air of evening.

FOUR

I sat on the edge of the bed waiting for Naomi to finish laying the law down to me about getting the rest I was perfectly willing to try to get, if she'd just go on and leave me alone.

"Now I went ahead and pulled the plug on your phone while you were in the shower," she said, "and I'll close this door when I leave, so there's nothing to disturb you if you can get to sleep. But if you're only going to lie there and rest, please give some thought to buying that condo. I know you think I'm nagging you, but—"

"You are nagging me, Naomi."

"Because I want you to look to the future instead of the past?"

"I'm thinking about the future."

"Then why do I have the feeling you're hiding out in your childhood every chance you get?"

"I don't know why you have some of your feelings, Naomi, but I wouldn't have mentioned my childhood if you hadn't brought it up first, trying to convince me of what a wonderful damned time we were supposed to be having at Grandma's."

"I only said it was a happy time."

"And got insulted when I didn't agree one-hundred percent."

"I wasn't insulted, Mavis, I was—that's beside the

point. The point is, there's a big difference in doing a little reminiscing and in letting the past get such a hold on you you can't get beyond it. I don't want you turning into one of those little old ladies who go wandering around in a world fifty years dead."

"I don't know what I've said that would make you think something that silly."

"You don't always have to say anything for me to know what you're thinking."

"Oh, yes. You're such a mind reader."

"I've always been able to read yours pretty well."

Which was just true enough to irritate me into saying, "Are you going to let me get some rest, or are you going to stand there yapping all day?"

"I'm going to let you rest, my dear, but not without trying, and I don't care how ticked off it makes you, to get it through your thick head that not everything that's come along since the 1940's is evil. That condo could be a real paradise for you if you'd let it."

"If it meets the requirements for paradise in Texas these days, it's too phony for me—those concrete beehives with their Tidy-Bowl-blue pools and gussied up courtyards and lots of shiny little grills where people put ketchup in their barbecue sauce."

"No, the only paradise you're interested in is someplace on the road back in the dark ages."

"Well, at least there was nothing plastic about it when we were on the road."

She walked out the door saying, "I don't want to hear about it. Go to sleep."

No, back then it boiled down to any place out of the heat, the cold, the wind, the sun, the mud, the blowing dust—any place that offered rest from the elements and drinkable water. If it offered further amenities, food and music and human intercourse, like the Panhandle Paradise Cafe up ahead, so much higher on the heavenly scale it rated. And

31

though people like us couldn't afford to visit a paradise of those dimensions, we could certainly admire it from afar and see no incongruity in its name being tacked onto a weather-beaten little shack in the middle of nowhere.

We had almost passed that particular example of heart's delight on the southern outskirts of Lubbock, when Daddy slowed and turned into the parking lot and Mama said, "What are you doing stopping here?"

"Well, you see that ladder propped up there and those paint buckets stacked by the door? I want to talk to the fella doing the work, see if he needs a helper."

"You said you didn't want to take the time to work Lubbock."

"Not kidnapping, no. A town the size of Lubbock'd take me better than a week, and I want to get on in to Angelo before the bad weather hits like it's fixing to do any day now. But if I could pick up a day's work—I don't want to get into Papa's broke."

"We've got a little money."

"Damn little."

"But, Will, it's already past noon."

"Now, Fern, we can always use a couple of extra bucks, and if we drive most of the night and don't have any car trouble, we'll still get in by this time tomorrow. You all get out and stretch your legs, why don't you?"

"No, we'll just stay in the car."

Daddy got out and I could see a house behind him at the back of the cafe, with a big cat sleeping on the porch in the sunshine and a skinny little tree at the corner whipping in the wind. There was a rusty old truck in the parking lot, off to one side, and in the field beyond it a toy-sized tractor moving silently along inside its own dust cloud.

Daddy hardly finished saying, "I'll be back in a minute," when a man came running out of the cafe with a lady right behind him hitting at him with a broom. She was crying and cussing, and he kept saying, "Now, honey. Now, honey," while they ran around the parking lot twice, the man gaining all the time. When he saw he had a good enough lead, he made a break for the old truck and jumped in it and slammed the door, and the whole time he was getting it started, the lady was banging on it with the broom. Even after it got rolling, she ran swatting after it, not stopping till it rattled and bounced onto the highway and went weaving off toward town.

She yelled and shook her fist at it and threw the broom down and picked it back up and came over to the car and said, "We ain't open, mister, I'm sorry to say, and if you want the truth, we may not never be. That was my no-good husband hightailing it for town yonder, instead of helping me get our place here open for business the way he's supposed to be doing, and do you think he gives a fig? I'll tell the world he don't. He's too busy keeping his drunk going."

"Lady, I—"

"And where does that leave me? In a hell of a hole, if you'll pardon my French, that's where it leaves me. Oh, that shiftless, sorry—we could have a regular little gold mine here, all the truck traffic going by, and the buses. We been planning it and planning it, all the long time we was waiting to heir the place from his papa, who I nursed my fingers to the bone for and waited on hand and foot and putting up with his drinking fits—his—not his papa's. His papa was a teetotaler, I'll say that for him if I can't say nothing else."

"Listen, lady, I just wanted to—"

"And now we got the place and a little dab of money, and his no good, sorry brother whining around wanting his share when he done spent his share and more and can whistle for his supper for all I care, and now look at the fix I'm in.

"All that paint bought and him drunk and what am I supposed to do with that stove that won't light and my sign already up and groceries stocked and the beer truck coming and business going on by to somebody else?"

"He'll be back. He'll go on down the road apiece and cool off and come on back."

"Hah! Not him. He won't be back till he runs out of money or friends to cadge off of or the Laws get him and bring him back. I been through this too many times to—say. What about you, mister? You any good at painting and fixing things?"

"Well, I'm a pretty fair handyman. Matter of fact, the reason I stopped was to see about picking up some work, but—"

"Then let's talk terms."

"Wait a minute, now. Hold your horses. I ain't butting in between a man and his wife."

"I ain't asking you to butt in. I'm asking you to work, to help me out of this tight place I'm in." She leaned over and looked in the window and smiled at Mama and said, "Hi, hon, how you doing? I'm Francine Tucker."

"We're the Maddoxes," Mama said, and she was smiling, too. "Will and Fern, our daughter Mavis, and the baby here is Martha May."

"Proud to make your acquaintance. Gee, that's a sweet baby, and a nice little girl—why don't you all get out and come in and let me treat you to a donut and a cup of coffee and you see if you can talk that man of yours into giving me a hand. I'm desperate, girl. I'd make it right with you."

I could tell Mama wanted to, but she just said, "That's up to Will."

Francine straightened up and said, "Well, what do you say, Will? You want the job?"

"I been looking the place over, and from what you've said, I don't think there's anything here I can't handle. But I'll tell you flat out I don't want any trouble. If it'd make your husband mad—"

"I never have knowed of him getting mad because somebody else done his work for him. I been doing it for years."

"But coming in between—I never run from no lawful fight in my life, but at the same time, I ain't greenhorn enough to get in the middle of a husband-wife tangle."

"I can see you ain't no hellraiser, Will, being a family man and all, and not the kind to go looking for a rhubarb. That's one of the reasons I asked for your help. I don't need another drunk around here, or some two-bit brawler. And Lloyd, he ain't bad. There ain't a mean bone in his body. He just likes his booze, is all. Why, I expect you two'd cotton to each other right off the bat. If he come back this minute, he'd offer you a swig out of his bottle and set down and watch you work pleased as punch."

"Then I reckon we can talk turkey."

"Good. You all come on in and make yourselves at home. We got work to do."

Daddy said it would take more than the rest of that day to do everything Francine needed done, so he set the tent up between the back of the cafe and the house. While he worked on the stove, Mama helped Francine clean and straighten things, and Martha May and I sat on a quilt in front of the tent. It was quiet and out of the wind and Martha May rolled over and went to sleep before I finished the second time around on the nursery rhymes I was teaching her.

I got my shoe box out of the car, and read some of my Sunday School pamphlets over again, and dressed and undressed my Tillie the Toiler paperdoll a couple of times. Then I took out the nickel matchbox I kept cached in the bottom of the shoe box, where I hid the broken bits of colored glass I called my jewels. After I counted them to be sure they were all there, I looked out over the flat fields to where a school and a church and a few houses were strung out along a dirt road that went on out to the west of the highway till it fell off the edge of the world.

By suppertime Daddy had the ice box levelled and the stove working and the whole inside painted. We ate hamburgers and french fries at a corner table, with only the kitchen lights on, because Francine didn't want to open to the public till breakfast. She wouldn't take a nickel for anything, either, because she said she didn't know what she'd have done if Mama and Daddy hadn't come along.

35

She kept saying, "Eat up. Eat up. There's more where that come from," and Mama and Daddy would play-like groan and take another helping and she'd laugh and they'd laugh and the big beer cooler hummed and the shelves of dishes and glasses gleamed and the neon Pearl sign flickered color across the shining counter and if that wasn't paradise I couldn't have said what was.

When nobody could eat another bite, she tossed a package of ready-rolls on the table and everybody stretched and lit a cigarette, even Mama, and she said, "Well, what do you think, Fern? The honest truth, now. You think it looks okay?"

"I think it looks fine, Francine, all nice and clean and freshly painted. The stools look practically new now they've had a good scrubbing, and the chairs and tables—shoot, girl, you'll make a mint here."

"It does look pretty spiffy, don't it? I just wish you all would stay. A worker like Will ought to be able to find plenty of jobs around, and you've got such good ideas, Fern. I never would've thought up half the things you did to make the place look so high class. You and me could run this little baby like nobody's business, and I'd tell that Dora to go back where she come from if you'd say the word."

Dora was her sister-in-law who was married to the whining brother and wasn't going to be anything but a pain in the neck, she said, but she had to have a cook so she could work the front. "You all could keep your tent right where it's at, if you want, or I could scout around and find you a nice little house."

Daddy shook his head. "I got my own business, Francine, and a partnership in another one waiting for me in Angelo."

"Well, I might be willing to talk partnership myself in a few months. What do you say, Fern? I'm going to have a real little moneymaker here."

Mama laughed. "I say one partnership in the family's enough. We're obliged, girl, but I reckon not."

"Okay, only don't never say you wasn't asked. And if you change your mind—no, you all know your own business. I'm just grateful I'll be ready to open up in the morning, which I sure didn't think I was going to be able to do. How long do you think it'll take you to paint that outside, Will?"

"I'll get the first coat on by sometime after noon tomorrow, but your husband'll have to put the second one on."

"You can't stay long enough to finish it up yourself?"

"No, we got to get back on the road. That's oil paint for the outside there. It won't dry fast like this white wash I used inside, and we can't wait around no two or three days."

"Speaking of this inside. What about all these damp places? I'd sure be obliged if you'd bring your cot in here and sleep, so you could keep a eye on things. That way, we could leave both doors open and let the wind blow through and it'd all be dried out by morning and I wouldn't have to worry about being robbed. And Fern, you and the kids could stay in my spare room. That'd be fun. Come on, girl, what do you say? I mean if Will don't mind you all splitting up for the night. I would like to be sure my customers won't be rubbing spots off of the wall and getting white marks all over their clothes."

"I don't mind," Daddy said. "You gals do what you want to."

"It's all right with me," Mama said, "but the girls and I'll stay in the tent—no, Francine, I've got everything handy there and it'll be easier for me that way. But I would appreciate it if we could all have an honest to goodness bath in that big tub in your pretty bathroom."

I said 'Lubbock, Lubbock/three men in a tubbock,' a couple of times after I said my prayers, but I still had trouble getting to sleep in the tent made strange by Daddy's absence. Mama kept fussing with her covers and Martha May had to nurse, something she hadn't needed to do at night in a long time, and the vacant place where Daddy's cot belonged so disturbed the picture of the tent the way it had always looked in the darkness behind my eyes, I had to make a new picture there showing it the way it was at that moment, and then I had to 'see' where the tent itself was, and Daddy, and the car, and kept drifting in and out of restless dreams trying to keep everything in its place, while outside the black wind hunted and big trucks fled desperately through the night.

FIVE

It was almost dark when we pulled into the small camp about half way between O'Donnell and La Mesa, on a road better suited to camels than cars, Mama said, with the cold norther that had blown in that afternoon when we left Lubbock flattening the flames of the low fires and snapping at the ropes and canvas on the tents and the tarp-covered truck beds clustered on the high bank of a deep dry wash.

That morning I'd walked from the cafe to the school under a sky so bright and blue it made you dizzy to look straight up into it. Yesterday's tractor was working far off to my left, and beyond it, across endless fields of plowed dirt and pale gold stubble, a bouncing old school bus was coming up so fast it had already unloaded by the time I got there.

Three lines had formed up along the front walk. One of primaries, one of intermediates, and one of seniors that was more a group than a line, being made up of only three big boys and five big girls, who were talking quietly to each other with sober faces and doubtful, arguing eyes.

I got in the primary line, behind a cotton-headed boy about my size, who swiveled around to give me a surprised look, then the bell rang and everybody turned to face the flag flying from its pole in the center of what was supposed to be a lawn but was mostly rocks and grass burs. One of the big boys led us in the Pledge of Allegiance, the bell rang again, and we went up the wooden steps, through the double

39

doors, into the smell of O'Cedar floor polish, books and chalk, apples and eggs and old baloney sandwiches.

I didn't see a sign that said 'Office' anywhere, so I followed the cotton-headed boy into a room whose windows looked out over the way I'd come, clear back to the cafe and the house and the tent, and for a minute I wished I could be there instead of here. For while none of the kids stared at me or made remarks to each other behind their hands, like they always did in all the other new schools I'd gone to, I knew they were watching me. That was the way it was. New kids were always watched and measured.

But I'd hardly taken my stand before the judgment seat when the teacher looked up at me, and seeing her full-face, I understood why no one in her room would dare do anything but sit still and at least pretend to be busy with school work. I didn't know the term 'presence,' then, but I recognized the quality when I saw it, and that teacher had enough to cow an entire county.

She was beautiful, too, with silvery gray hair that was marcelled up and over her head down into a bun on the nape of her neck. Her gold rimmed glasses were fastened to her white blouse with a round gold pin from which they rode up to her eyes and back on a gold chain. Her hands were small and white, marked by thin blue veins, and she wore a ruby on her ring finger, dark red and shiny as a gout of pigeon blood.

"I'm Miss Browning," she said, and after a pause, "Do you belong in the second or the third?"

"I belong in the third, but sometimes they put me in the second and sometimes they put me in the fourth."

"I see. Would you like to tell me your name? Remember that that is the polite thing to do when someone introduces himself to you."

I wasn't such a greenhorn I didn't know that, but I was too timid to act on it in front of a teacher until told to. "Yes'm," I said. "I'm Mavis Marie Maddox."

"How old are you, Mavis?

"I'll be eight next month."

"Then why are you not put in the low third all of the time?"

Because too few principals ever simply asked me where I belonged. Some put me where they thought I ought to go because of my size; some wherever they had the most room; some by how well I could read, and since I could read anything they put in front of me, I often ended up in a higher grade than I should have. However they did it, it was always a torment, and I didn't know how to explain it without making everyone in the room laugh, so I just stood there till she said, "Do you have a report card I could see?"

"No'm."

"Why not?"

I looked at her desk, at the clean, polished surface with the neat, squared stack of papers, the green glass jar of pencils, the ruler, the brown reader with the raised orange print on the cover, the pen staff in its holder. "Because we don't stay anywhere long enough for me to get one."

"Don't look at the desk, Mavis. Look at me. Remember it is a mark of character to look everyone in the eye."

I looked at her, then, wishing I knew how to tell good lies about lost or stolen report cards, that I had a regular address, that I had something worthy to offer the cool, quiet sureness of her perfection. But all I had was my usual, "Yes'm."

"And how long will you be with us?"

"Today," I whispered.

"It is highly commendable that you attend school every day you can. I congratulate you and your parents. Now I will have you read for me."

She opened the reader to page 37 and handed it to me and once I began to read I forgot everything but the words, the look and sound of them, the pictures they made, the story they were telling, and I would've read on to the end of the book if she hadn't stopped me after a couple of pages by saying, "That will do, thank you. Annie Mattie, Mavis will sit with you today and assist you with the pre-primers."

Annie Mattie Mallet had squinty brown eyes and skinny brown pigtails and almost buck teeth. But she was Miss Browning's star pupil and my best friend for the day, because, she said, our initials were nearly the same, M. M. M. and A. M. M., we were both top readers, and neither of us had any other friends, anyhow, I because I was new, she because the other girls were jealous of her and called her teacher's pet, though never in Miss Browning's hearing. She said that didn't bother her one bit, because she was going to be a teacher-principal herself when she grew up, and a little thing like spite wasn't going to hold her back.

"I won't be exactly like Miss Browning," she told me at recess. "I don't have the looks. Pa's done said I'm the homely type and might as well learn to live with it. But I aim to be as much like her as I can in every other way, even if Ma does say Still Waters Run Deep and There's More to Miss Browning Than Meets the Eye, else why would such a high-toned lady like her be teaching out here in the country instead of a big school in town? But I think our school's nice enough for anybody, don't you? And if Pa makes a good crop next year, he's going to let me have enough of my chopping and picking money to buy me a blouse just like the ones Miss Browning wears, only out of cotton, not silk, silk's too dear."

I helped her collect the attendance slips from the other teachers and fill Miss Browning's private water pitcher that stayed on the table behind her desk where she kept her principal things. Then while our class had reading, we went down to the first grade room to conduct word drill for the pre-primers. On the way, she told me that on Friday mornings one of the senior girls came to our room and held a spelling bee, because that was when Miss Browning had to fill out all her principal reports.

"I wish you could stay for one," she said. "We could be team captains and see who's the best speller."

I wished I could, too, and maybe be a teacher myself some day, if I could be one like Miss Browning. But I knew I couldn't. We might not even stay in Angelo once we got there, because I'd heard Mama tell Francine the night before, "It'll never on God's green earth work out. I know that old man too well. But Will wants a chance at it so bad I won't fight him over it."

I couldn't tell Annie Mattie that, though. That was family business. But I did walk out to the bus with her at the end of the day, and we waved good-by till we couldn't see each other any longer for the dust. Then I started back across the field to the cafe, where I could see, far behind the tractor's own distant dust cloud, a dark line of thunderheads building.

"This is a pitiful looking excuse for a camp," Mama said. "It's got bad Luck written all over it. We should've stayed in that tourist court back yonder like I tried to get you to."

"I told you why I didn't want to turn loose of the money, Fern. I don't want to get into Papa's broke."

"Broke? With what you picked up at Francine's—"

"What I picked up at Francine's won't amount to much if we have car trouble or the roads turn bad and we get stuck somewhere a couple of days."

"It would've been plenty if you'd gone on and charged her what you said you would to start with."

"You know I had to knock some off, her treating us like long lost cousins the way she did. Feeding us like kings, and—"

"We earned every dime and every bite, and you can count on the roads turning bad, because those clouds are going to open up and start pouring any minute."

"Aw, maybe not. These early northers blow theirselves out in a hurry sometimes."

"This one won't."

"Now damn it, Fern, you're the one wanted to stop for

the night. We said we'd fight it on in to Angelo, and I'm ready to do that right now."

"No, we're both tired out and the baby's fussy with this tooth she's cutting. We'll just make the best of it, rain or no rain, but I'm telling you, this is a bad Luck place."

"Hell, we've camped in worse places, and in the rain, too. If it'll just hold off till morning, we'll get away early and try to beat the mud."

"And if it doesn't, we'll go dragging into Angelo wet and miserable looking as a bunch of drowned rats."

"I don't want to get to Papa's looking like tramps anymore than you do, Fern. We'll clean up at a filling station before we hit town if we have to. Now I'll pick us out a nice high spot and while you fix supper I'll put us down a trench. Our tent's good and tight. We'll be okay."

He stopped on a little knoll next to an old truck fitted out with a tarp over high sideboards, and got out and walked around a minute, jangling the change in his pocket the way he always did when he was trying to make up his mind about something. It was so dark I could only see his silhouette, back-lighted by a fire across the way, its flames almost horizontal in the wind that was coming now in gusts strong enough to shake the car.

He called out something, and Mama rolled the window down so she could hear, the wind flowing in cold as if it were blowing off an ice storm. "This ought to do," he yelled. "We're up some here, and there's no trees around to worry about."

Mama handed Martha May over the seat to me, but before she could get out to help start unloading, a man and a lady came running over from the truck, the lady knotting a headscarf under her chin, the man holding his hat, their faces turning dead white in a sudden streak of lightning that seemed to hit right behind Daddy, exploding around him like a thousand flash bulbs going off at once.

Mama's hands went up and out in a kind of prayer, Daddy and the others ducked, then they were all at the car, lightning still trapped in Daddy's eyes, Mama saying, "Oh my God."

"I'm Amos Taylor," the man said, "and this here's my wife Nell. I'd be proud to hep you get your tent up."

Mrs. Taylor, hugging herself and dancing against the cold, invited us to their place while the tent was being set up, but Mama said no, she appreciated the offer, but we'd just wait in the car, it wouldn't be long. I was glad. I'd been in trucks like theirs before and they were always dark and crowded and full of messy looking pallets and dirty dishes and the smell of sweat and pee.

Mama cooked supper on the Coleman stove inside the tent because Daddy said the wind was too high to risk a fire and he wished everybody else would put theirs out. Mama said the rain would do it for them pretty soon, and she was right. It started coming down before we finished our coffee, in big, hard drops at first, falling so slow I could count them as they hit, then faster and faster, till the tent was filled with the sound of them.

But we were safe and dry, warmed by the stove and the lantern, full of hot fried pone and hotter coffee, and I went to sleep thinking not of the rain, but of the first part of the day, when I'd helped teach the pre-primers with Annie Mattie Mallet, the best best friend I'd ever had.

I was startled awake by what I thought at first was a bad dream: the sound of voices rising above the wind and the rain, the hurrying slap of wet shoes on wet ground, the cranking of cars, the flash of lights across the tent flap, the urgency of a siren coming fast, the hissing of the lantern inside a vacant-house kind of emptiness I knew immediately meant Martha May and I were alone.

Daddy's hand of sol, half-played, was spread out on the foot of his cot. The supper dishes, washed and dried, were packed in the dishpan and covered with a cup towel. Tomorrow's pot of beans was soaking on the unlit stove. Everything was the way it was supposed to be except for Mama and Daddy being gone, which was like saying everything was the way it was supposed to be except for the one landmark you needed most.

Ordinarily, being left by ourselves wouldn't have bothered me. Mama and Daddy often went visiting after supper unless we had a crowd at our own fire. But this wasn't the kind of night people went visiting, and even if it had been, Mama and Daddy would never have gone off without telling me where they'd be, and they'd never have left the lantern burning.

I learned later from all the talk going around, that everyone had kept a light of some kind on to keep their tents from being run over by the men and vehicles trying to get through to the accident. But at the moment, I only knew we were alone in a way we never had been before, that something terrible was happening outside, and that it was my job to take care of Martha May and the tent.

I went over to her box, tiptoeing because the ground was damp and furry-feeling with loose dirt and little sticks and pebbles. Mama usually swept the ground off good before anything went in the tent, but we had come in so late that evening, and the weather had been so threatening, she'd decided to let it go for once. So as soon as I saw Martha May was still asleep, her quilt tucked in around her, I sat down on the edge of my cot and put my shoes and socks on.

The lantern flared white as a star, then faded down to the soft yellow of a coal oil lamp. I knew that meant it needed pumping or refilling, neither one of which I could do, because I was forbidden to handle it or the stove. And before I could think what I'd do if it did go out, the first drop of the first leak hit my shoulder, icy hot as a bee sting.

I got a pan out of the utensil box and put it under the leak and started checking the ceiling, which was beginning to sag now under the weight of the water gathering on it. I could keep Martha May dry if I had to hold her and dodge the leaks as they formed. But there was nothing I could do about anything else.

It would be bad enough to have to sleep on wet cots,

which we'd done a few times, but my main worry was for the camera, the film, the portrait paper, proof paper—everything that made up what Daddy called our Bread and Butter. If any of it got wet, it was ruined.

The lantern flickered again, and a new leak began to ooze out below the first one. I didn't know what to do except to beg Jesus not to let the lantern go out or the leak break all the way through or Martha May and me be left alone forever the way some children were when their parents couldn't take care of them anymore.

Then car doors were slamming in front of the tent, and men were talking in low, tight voices, a woman crying out, "It was a nice, clean place, I tell you." Then a different voice, not a real one, full of buzzing and crackling like a radio, though I didn't understand how a radio could be playing in a camp, drowned everything else till the woman screamed, "No! No! Please no! Don't make me—" and more car doors slammed and the siren went off and Mama and Daddy came through the flap, the water pouring off them looking like blood in the red light turning in the wet blackness behind them.

SIX

The first thing I saw when I woke up the next morning was the shiny streak of hardened paraffin Mama and Daddy had put over the leaking seam the night before, Mama sopping the water up with a towel, Daddy coming behind her brushing on the hot wax, the two of them moving together like champion double-jumpers.

Daddy hadn't had time to tell me what happened, because as soon as the leak was fixed and the lantern was pumped up, he had to go back out. Mama said she would tell me about it in the morning, but when I got up, all she said was, "There was a drowning accident in the camp last night, so we won't be able to leave today. You'll have to wash in cold water. I don't have a burner free to heat any. And spit in the slop jar when you brush your teeth. You can't go outside, it's still raining."

I dressed and combed my hair at Daddy's shaving mirror, making sure my bangs were straight, promising myself as I did every morning, that as soon as I was grown up and had a job, I'd get the curliest permanent it was possible to get and never ever have another Dutch Boy bob as long as I lived. Then Mama took up the last piece of pone, and Daddy came in, wet and shivering, the skin of his face shrunk down to the bone.

Mama looked a question at him and he shook his head and she said, "Get out of those wet clothes and rub yourself down good with this towel. I'll get your other pants out and—"

"No, there's no use changing. I got to go right back. Just give me a quick cup of coffee and a piece of pone. I got to hurry."

"I was hoping they'd be found by now."

"Nah, I knew we wouldn't be able to do nothing much till daylight."

"Then why didn't you all call it off last night?"

"Couldn't nobody rest knowing that man and his little boys was in that water, maybe still alive, hung up on a snag somewheres."

"Whatever possessed them to camp in that wash in the first place?"

"Just greenhorns. Never been on the road before. Probably never been anywhere before outside their little hick town county seat."

"Even so, it was a dumb thing to do."

"Well, Fern, they won't never do it again, will they?"

Mama started to say something else to him, but turned to me instead and said, "Give Martha May a sip of water and be careful not to spill any, we're about out, and this floor— oh, Will! Look at your shoes. They're ruined."

He glanced down at them as if he didn't know whose shoes they were and said, "I'll be back about dinner unless our Luck turns first."

"Please be careful."

"I won't do nothing silly, Fern. I ain't no punk kid trying to be a hero."

Mama put the beans on to cook and made another pot of coffee in case some of the ladies dropped by, mainly Mrs. Taylor, who had moved in and out of my dreams all night as she had moved in and out of the tent, wringing her hands and saying it was all her fault.

Then she pulled the flap back and fastened it and said, "Let's get some air in this place."

We stood there watching the cars coming and going, the

ladies standing around talking, the crowd of boys and dogs roaming from the camp to the gully and back and clustering around the big wrecker parked as close to the bank as it could get without sliding over the edge. There was one long black car Mama called a 'hearse' parked behind the wrecker, and next to it, the sheriff's car, with a deputy standing outside it listening to the radio I'd heard the night before when I didn't even know cars could have radios in them.

Every now and then the wrecker driver would chase the boys down off the winch, or the deputy would say, "Move back, folks, move back. We got to have room to roll here when Sheriff Todd gives the word." Then everybody would walk off a few paces and wait a minute before easing back.

"Well," Mama said, "I can't stand here gawking all day. I've got work to do."

She draped a cup towel over her head and picked up the slop jar she and I used at night because we were scared of snakes, and said, "I hate to throw this out in the bushes, but I can't stand a nasty smelling tent. If your Daddy'd had time to dig a hole for it, it'd be filled with water, anyhow, so— put Martha May on your cot and let her stretch awhile. I'll be right back."

She scalded the slop jar the way she always did, and put Martha May's dirty diapers in the wash tub to soak, and said, "Rain water'll stain these, I know, and I do despise a dingy looking diaper on a baby, but I'm not paying that bloodsucker any three cents a bucket for well water to wash with. He says he has to charge that much because he has to buy it and haul it from town, but he probably steals it from some old skinflint rancher around here, then charges us highway robbery prices for it. Close the flap, Mavis. It's getting chilly again."

Before long everything looked and felt like home. The beans were simmering, the wash was hung on the line Daddy had strung from the top of the center pole to a nail in the food box. Everything but the floor, muddy from so much tracking in and out, was clean and comfortable, but Mama said it needed a shovel, not a broom, and she wished she had some old newspapers to spread on it, but she didn't, so we'd just have to make the best of it.

Then she got out her writing tablet and started a letter to Aunt Millie to let her know we were moving to Angelo, but somebody at the flap called, "Yoo-hoo! Anybody to home?"

Mama slammed her tablet to and popped her pencil down on it hard and said, "Come on in, Mrs. Taylor."

Mrs. Taylor took off her scarf and held up a penny candy sack and said, "I brought us some tea to chirk us up some."

"That wasn't necessary," Mama said. "I've got coffee made."

"I know you do, Mrs. Maddox. You been the Rock of Gibraltar this whole past night through. But seems like tea's more heartening sometimes, especially this here kind. They was a yarb lady in the last camp we was in, and I got some camomile and comfrey from her, nice and fresh dried, and I mixed that in with this bit of store bought I had left. I'd be proud to have you try hit."

"Why, sure," Mama said. "It sounds good. Let me put some water on to boil. It's rain water, I'm afraid. I'm keeping the little well water I have for the baby. But I caught this in my own bucket, so I know it's clean."

"Law, honey, I don't never buy that high-priced water from them fellas. Rain water or creek water either one'll do for me, long as I can go fetch hit and get out of that truck for awhile. Mama don't like being left alone with just Dorrie for company, but—well, I made up a little story about you awanting to borry some tea. I hope the Lord don't hold hit against me too strong."

"I don't think the Lord ought to hold much of anything against people on the road. Except for the really rotten ones. I know there's some He needs to keep Hell stoked up for, but—"

"Mama'd pitch a fit, though. She don't cotton to fibbing of no kind. Old folks're a blessing, but they can be mighty trying, too, sometimes. 'Course, she can't hep being restless and feeling out of pocket any more'n I can. We was always so busy at Home, ever day of ever season, I used to wonder what hit'd be like to just sit and do nothing for a spell, and now when that's mostly what I do all the time—I nearly forgot your 'lasses taffy, Mavis." She reached in her sweater pocket and pulled out a little package wrapped in a clean rag and handed it to me and I said, "Thank you," and Mama said, "Go ahead and eat it now if you want to. It's awhile yet till dinner."

Then she moved the pot off the burner and poured the dead looking leaves into the boiling water and set a plate on top of it, and Mrs. Taylor said, "I know candy's a fearful extravagance, but Amos got three full days of work last week, and Dorrie, she's got such a sweet tooth, I thought, well, hit won't do no real harm, one little batch of taffy. Dorrie don't get much pleasure these days. Not like at Home, when we had our own place. Amos he always set aside a nice piece of bottom land for cane so we could have all the molasses we wanted."

"My grandpa used to do the same thing," Mama said, "on his place in South Texas. But my uncle's running the farm now, and I don't know if he's doing that or not—oh, our tea." She took the plate off the pan, and a sharp, fruity-smelling steam rose from it, and Mrs. Taylor said, "Hit smells mighty good. I hope you all'll like hit."

Mama set the cups out and poured the tea, holding the leaves back with the blade of a case knife, and said, "I'm sorry I can't offer you any sugar or cream, but we drink our coffee black and I don't stock anything I don't just have to have."

"Don't fret yourself about that. Anyway's fine with me—listen. I believe hit's stopped raining. I don't hear nary a sound, do you?"

"No, I don't. Oh lord, I hope it has stopped, and they can find the—find them, and we can get back on the road. We were only going to be here for the night, but what with the accident, and it taking so long to—well, it's a bad business for everybody."

"Amen, sweet Jesus, hep that pore lady."

"Yes . . . well, there's something about this place. I told Will last night when we pulled in here—-there's some left, Mrs. Taylor. Why don't you finish it?"

"Why, thank you kindly—less one of you all want hit. Goodness, I don't know what I done with my manners."

"No, you take it. We've had plenty."

"Then I'll drink to your health and good Luck to us all," and after a couple of sips, "Wherebouts you all heading?"

"To my husband's papa's place in Tom Green County. He has a grocery store-filling station there right outside San Angelo."

"Why, we come through there on our way here."

"How did things look?"

"Well, I don't want to discourage you none, but Amos couldn't find a lick of work there. 'Course if you got somebody to take you in—"

"Oh, we won't be living together with Mr. Maddox. We'll stay in one of his rent houses."

"Well, I say a rented roof's better'n no roof atall."

"I hope you're right." She got Daddy's spare sack of Durham out of her purse and offered it to Mrs. Taylor, but she said, "No, thanky. I'll have me a dip after while," so Mama rolled herself a smoke and scraped the loose flakes back into the sack and said, "Where are you all going?"

Mrs. Taylor let out a long breath and said, "I don't know. Amos, he can't rightly settle hit in his mind. When we lost our place, I was for renting on shares somewhere till times got better. Old Man Harkness down the road from us offered Amos forty acres, but Amos said hit was as drought-struck and wore out as ours, and he don't hold with share-cropping nohow.

"I was born and bred into hit, never knew nothing else till me and Amos married. Him and his people always owned their land, and that's a mighty fine thing. But like I told him, even if hit would be a come down, at least I could keep my cow and my chickens and put us in a garden. He wouldn't hear of hit, though. Too proud. So we sold off everything we had, give hit away's more like hit, and bought the truck and—he's astudying California, but my, that's a fur piece off."

"Yes, Will has a sister out there."

"Doing all right?"

"As far as we know. We don't hear from her very often, moving around the way we do."

"Well, I don't know how we'd fare out there, but the Lord laid His hand on us so heavy at Home, I don't reckon we could be much worse off. We lost Papa, and Mama come down with the dropsy, and my pullets got sorehead, and we either couldn't get any rain atall or else we'd get a gully-washer like this here one that'd scour the land like a plague of locusts. But when we lost our oldest boy, when that blood poisoning took Amos Junior—" she began to wring her hands again, so hard I thought she'd twist them off, and said, "Oh, Mrs. Maddox, I feel so bad for that pore lady. I know what hit's like to—"

"Please, Mrs. Taylor. You know everybody's doing everything they can. The sheriff here's a decent man. He and his wife have taken her in till some of her people get here, and—"

"But hit was us she come to, all wet and wild looking, and we seen them when they first drove in the camp, seen them heading straight for that wash, only we never had no idea they was agoing to camp in hit. Amos would've warned them. He would've—"

"Now Mrs. Taylor, we went through all that last night. There wasn't any way you all could know anybody would do anything so dangerous. And they might not've taken your advice if you'd had a chance to give it to them."

"Yes, but—"

"Mrs. Taylor, if you let every bad thing you see on the road worry you, you'll go crazy. You have to learn to do the best you can and let the rest of it go. I've been at this business a lot longer than you have, and I know what I'm talking about."

"I know you do, honey, I know you do. I just ain't myself these days. All this traipsing around from pillar to post has got my brain so addled and my spunk so wore down, I ain't got no more grit than some puny little gal ahaving her first youngun. But still, that's a hard way to die, being swept—"

"Ma! Ma! They found 'em, Ma!"

"Mama! They been found."

"They found 'em, everybody, they found 'em."

Boys' voices, loud, and dogs barking, and a lady saying, "Quiet down, you boys, and hush them dogs. We ain't a bunch of heathens around here."

We stood outside the tent and watched as the men headed toward the hearse. They were muddy and panting, slipping now and then with their tarp covered burdens, other men moving up to help them get their footing back, to keep the stretchers from being dropped. The sheriff was leading them, motioning people out of the way, saying something to his deputy we couldn't hear.

Daddy was carrying the front end of one of the stretchers that looked like it had only half a load on it. His cap drooped down around his ears, his clothes, sopping wet and wrinkled, clung to his body like some new and terrible skin, and the sole of one ragged shoe flapped and dragged as he walked. Then the crowd moved in around the hearse and I couldn't see him anymore.

The sheriff's car started forward, its red light turning slowly, the long black hearse following along behind it, the people falling back before it, silent, the men holding their sodden hats and caps over their hearts till both vehicles went down the dip and over the hump and onto the highway.

Then the crowd began to break up, to move apart into small groups, the men who had carried the stretchers standing off to one side, explaining it all over again, to each other, to themselves, in tight, narrow gestures and hoarse, tired voices, and Mrs. Taylor said, "Why, looky there. The sun's afixing to come out. Hit's agoing to fair off after all."

SEVEN

While Mama and Daddy loaded the car in that still, sweet quiet of early morning when the light seems to come from the ground rather than the sky, I stood by holding Martha May, watching the tent flap across from us open. A boy and his dog slipped out soft as shadows and trotted off toward the wash, where only scattered, shallow pools were left in the fine sandy bottom that had glistened like gold dust in the light of Daddy's lantern the night before. They might find our footprints, mine and Daddy's and the Mannery men's, but that would be all, for there was no longer any sign anywhere that a man and his two little boys had drowned there.

Since everybody had stayed up late the night before, it wasn't till the loading was done and the rim of the low rise to the east began to burn like the advancing line of a prairie fire, that waking up noises began to cough and cuss and rattle and bang through the camp.

The Mannerys climbed out of their car and started toward us, the men stretching and scratching, the ladies yawning and carrying the babies, hugging them against the morning chill. Mama and Daddy had met them the evening before after supper, when everybody was walking around talking about the drowning and taking up a purse, which was really a cigar box and not a purse at all, for the lady who had lost her husband and children.

Daddy carried the purse, looking like himself again in clean dry clothes and the new shoes he'd bought in town earlier, to the tune of two dollars and twenty-nine cents, Mama said, which proved we were in a nest of hijackers, and as far as greenhorns were concerned, there ought to be signs put up warning them to stay out of West Texas, because if ignorance and dust storms and flash floods didn't do them in, the high prices would.

The Mannerys wouldn't even set up their camp till they put two bits in the purse and heard the whole story, and then they asked Daddy to show them where it happened, and he said he'd be glad to, he'd been meaning to take me, anyhow.

Mama and the Mannery ladies didn't want to go, and Mama didn't think I should, either. But Daddy said it was something he wanted impressed on my mind. He said if I grew up and married some old boy so green he couldn't find his butt with both hands when the light went out, at least I'd know what to do.

Mama said she hoped by the time I was ready to get married people wouldn't be on the road anymore, but Daddy said nobody could see the future and I was to go. So I went. But there wasn't much to see. Daddy swung the lantern around and pointed out where they'd found each body and where the car had gone to ground, and said nobody yet had figured out why the lady hadn't been trapped with the others, and if she knew herself, she wasn't saying. The Mannerys nodded and uh-huhed and ah-hahed and shook their heads over something already no more than a bad dream to me. Then we went back to the tent and they visited with Mama and Daddy while I lay on my cot and listened till I went to sleep.

They were brothers married to sisters, all of them from outside Monahans in Ward County, which they said was dying on the vine. They were going to Fort Worth to look for work after they went to see the sisters' grandma in Lubbock, who they hadn't seen since they were little girls and would never have another chance at, because once they got settled in Fort Worth they wouldn't ever come back to West Texas for nothing or nobody.

The tall skinny Mr. Mannery was married to the brown-haired sister who was plump and wore glasses and started to puddle up every time anybody said anything that reminded her of home. They had a baby girl younger than Martha May and a little boy just learning to walk who cried, "My ninny! My ninny!" every time the baby nursed.

The younger Mr. Mannery was so bashful he blushed every time anybody looked at him and hardly ever said a word. He was married to the towheaded sister who laughed a lot and talked to beat sixty and could whistle through her teeth. She was a tomboy, she said, always helping their Daddy with the goats and sheep while Lureen helped their mama in the house.

"I wasn't going to stay tied to Mama's apron strings like Lureen's done," she said. "When Cleatus started talking about pulling out for Fort Worth, and Lonny said how about him and me getting hitched and going with them, I said okay if he was dead sure we'd go. Mama pitched a hissy, all of us leaving at once, but shoot fire, why marry if it don't take you someplace? So we done it, and I hope we get so danged rich we can live right smack dab in the middle of town where I won't never see another goat or sheep for the rest of my natural born days and my feet don't never set down on nothing but pavement."

When they started knocking out the tent pegs, Mr. Taylor came to help, and Mrs. Taylor called to Mama not to get away till she fetched something she'd fixed for us, and then more people came till there was such a crowd around Daddy yelled, "Timber!" when he and the Mannery men swung the tent up on top of the car.

When it was tied down to suit him, he said, "Well boys, that ought to do her. She's still damp, but I reckon the wind'll dry her on out pretty fast." Then he nodded to me to get in and I handed Martha May to Mama while Mrs. Taylor put a greasy looking sack in her other hand and said, "Hit's sweet taters. The sheriff he give Amos a whole peck of them for doing some odd jobs around his place yesterday evening, and I thought of you all atravelling today and I just baked up a mess big enough for both of us."

Mama said, "Thank you kindly, Mrs. Taylor, we'll sure enjoy them." She started laughing. "Will and I thought we were losing our minds last night, smelling sweet potatoes baking out here."

"Smelled good, didn't they, adripping sugar in the ashes. Made me think of evenings at Home, sitting around the fireplace. They ought to be nice ones. They come in on the train from some kin of the sheriff's in East Texas. I just dearly wish I had some real cornbread and cold buttermilk to offer you to go with them."

"They'll taste fine just as they are. You all have been good neighbors, Mrs. Taylor. Maybe we'll meet again sometime."

Mrs. Taylor smiled and shook her head. "I don't reckon hit's likely. Still, these days, no telling what might happen."

Mama got in and laid the sack on the floor next to the water jug. Daddy shook hands with the men and took a last look around to make sure we hadn't left anything. The oldest Mrs. Mannery began to cry, and Mama said, "Now you don't want to do that. Think how rich you're going to be." Then Daddy got in and pulled the slip knot tight and we all waved and wished each other good Luck and the towheaded Mrs. Mannery yelled, "Look us up if you ever come to old F. T. Worth," and we drove off slow, Mama and Daddy nodding and waving till we went down the dip and over the hump and onto the highway.

"Thank the Lord that's over," Mama said. "I was never so glad to leave a place in my life."

Daddy grunted. "That's a bunch of fine people back there, Fern."

"Yes, they are, poor devils, for all the good it'll do them."

It was mid-afternoon when we rounded the last bend of

what Daddy said was the home stretch, and saw all the cars and trucks parked in among the trees that marked the river, and Mama said, *"Now* what? I hope to God we haven't run into another bad accident."

"Naw," Daddy said. "I don't think it's anything like that. The ford's probably flooded is all. I had a hunch it might be."

"You never said anything."

"Well, I figured we had a fifty-fifty chance the water'd all be run off by the time we got here, and I didn't see no point in borrowing trouble."

"I wonder how bad it is."

He stopped the car and nodded toward a man stepping out from beside a Model A across from us and said, "We're fixing to find out right now."

The man walked up to Daddy's window and said, "Howdy, folks."

"Howdy. Ford flooded?"

"A mile wide and belly deep."

"About what I figured. Where you want me to park her?"

"Right yonder behind that old Hupmobile. We're taking first one side, then the other, turn and turn about."

"Sounds fair to me." He backed up and pulled in behind the Hupmobile and cut the engine and we heard a lot of yelling and laughing and high, yipping whistling coming from off beyond the trees, and the man said, "There goes another one."

Daddy loosed the slipknot and got out and offered his hand. "Will Maddox."

"Lefty Harris, Will."

They shook hands and Daddy introduced us and looked at the man again close, and said, "Lefty Harris. Lefty Harris. Why, sure, I seen you whip Spider Valdez in Nogales in— '22-'23? You still fighting?"

Lefty laughed. "Not in the ring no more. A big old cornfed boy up in Nebraska stomped the liver and lights out of me a couple of years ago, so I retired from that foolishness." He looked back at me and winked and said, "I just bum around the country now, flirting with all the pretty girls."

I knew he was teasing me. I wasn't old enough to be winked at, or pretty enough, either. But it was a nice kind of teasing, and I was just wishing I wasn't too bashful to wink back at him when a car went by us fast, throwing up a fog of fine, white grit, the driver honking and gunning his motor.

"Now looky there at that durn fool," Lefty said. "He thinks he's going to go right on ahead of everybody, just like that Greyhound peckerwood we got cooling his heels down aways."

"Must be the one that passed us outside of Big Spring," Daddy said. "He was pushing that bus like a bat out of hell. I told Fern I guessed he was going to make his schedule if he busted both axles and killed somebody in the process."

"Well, he's older and wiser now," Lefty said. Then the car honked again, everybody staring at it, and he let out a sigh and said, "I reckon I better mosey over there and tell that old boy how the cow ate the cabbage 'fore he wears that horn of his plumb out."

"Need some help?"

Lefty smiled and pulled a big wrench out of his back pocket and said, "Naw. Much obliged, though." Then he touched his cap to Mama and walked off swinging the wrench slow and careless, and Mama said, "I wish you'd get back in the car, Will. There's liable to be trouble."

"What's the matter with you? You act like I'm some greenhorn don't know how to handle hisself."

"No, Will, I didn't mean that. I just don't want you getting mixed up in a fight and getting hurt, that's all."

"There won't be no fight if that guy knows what's good for him. Lefty'll lay that monkey wrench upside his head so fast he won't know what hit him."

But Lefty didn't have to talk to the man more than a minute before he backed up and parked behind the Model A, quiet as a snake with its fangs pulled, Daddy said, and then Lefty called out, "My relief's coming, Will. I'm going to take a little pasear down to the crossing. Want to come along?"

"Sure thing," Daddy said. "Be right with you."

"Don't be gone too long," Mama said. "I don't want us to lose our place if the line starts moving."

"I won't be gone that long, Fern, and if I am, somebody around here'll take the wheel for you. These marshals ain't going to put up with no line breaking."

"But you know how you get to talking."

"All I'm going to do is go down there and look the situation over and see how I'm going to have to shift the load. You all get out and stretch your legs and get acquainted. I'll be back directly."

But Mama kept us in the car, in the heat and dust of what could've passed for a summer afternoon instead of an autumn one, except for the deep blueness of the sky and the thin, circling currents of chilled air flowing through the hot layers, smelling of frost and chrysanthemums and cold rooms in tourist courts late at night. There wasn't much to look at: a few kids roaming among the cars, a few ladies sitting on quilts in the shade, fanning flies off sleeping babies, one old man hunched on his running board, elbows on his knees, head in his hands.

Then Lefty's relief signalled for the cars opposite us to move on up and fill in behind the cars moving off ahead of them. He told our line we'd be next, making Mama nervous because Daddy still wasn't back, assigned newcomers to their places, waving at those who turned around and went back where they came from, and tended to all the other things a marshal had to tend to, the way I'd seen Daddy do when he marshalled.

I'd grown tired of watching, though, past being hungry, beginning to go to sleep, when Mama said, "Well at last. Here comes your daddy."

He was barefooted, his new shoes slung around his

neck, his pantslegs rolled up like a boy going wading, grinning what I later learned was the kind called 'shit-eating,' which meant you had enough grace to feel ashamed of what you'd done, but not so much you hadn't enjoyed the hell out of it just the same.

The marshall signalled for our line to move and Daddy hopped in and started the car. Mama said, "I'm glad you finally found your way back, Will. I thought you'd got lost."

We went forward about two car lengths and stopped again and he said, "Well, I started giving the boys a hand, and—"

"I can see that by your clothes. You're wet to your waist."

"They'll dry out fast in this sun."

"Yes, and look like a wrinkled-up tow sack. I don't know why you think you've always got to be the one to pitch in and lend a hand."

"Because I'm going to have to have help when our turn comes, that's why. I can't fly us across the damn river."

"No, but—"

"There's been plenty of times somebody pulled us out of a hole, don't forget."

"All right, Will."

"If everybody tried for a free ride, people like us couldn't make it on the road these days, and I ain't putting myself in the position of asking for something I ain't willing to give to the next fella."

He got out and sat down on the running board and began putting on his shoes and socks and Mama said, "What are we going to do about supper? If we aren't going to get into Angelo till no telling when—"

"Well, Lefty and some of the other boys're staying in a campground up aways on the other side. They're just over here helping out because it's too steep coming down from the high bank for them to cross. They'd drown out before they got started good. I guess we could pull in there and eat if you want to."

"I don't remember any camp around here."

"No, it's a new one. Been started up since we was through here last."

"Well, if we're going to be on the road half the night, we need a good hot meal. I wasn't planning on stopping in a regular camp, though."

"Lefty says it's a good one, a real crackerjack. But you can bet I told him, I said. 'Friend, I been in about every camp there is between the Mississippi River and the Great Divide, so when you tell me a camp's a good one, I expect something more than a trampled down place behind some signboard or a flat stretch under a mesquite tree.'

"'See for yourself,' he said. 'It don't cost nothing to look. Spend the night and you can go frogging with me and the boys—' now don't get riled up, Fern. I told him we couldn't stay past supper."

"I guess we could stay long enough for me to get my iron out and press your pants. I don't want you getting into Angelo looking seedy."

"Then let's go ahead and start shifting things around. The film and the paper'll have to go up on the back seat with the camera—and the chemicals and the proofframes and the enlarger. I don't want nothing in the trunk or on the floorboards that water would damage."

"You said it wasn't deep enough to worry about."

"Not for people, no. But my equipment—"

"Well then, I want Mavis up here with us."

"She wouldn't be in no danger in the back. You think I'd put one of our kids in any kind of a position where I couldn't take care of them?"

"No, Will, I don't. But I want her up here anyhow."

"All right. You heard your mama, Mavis. When we're ready to go, you'll have to scoot in up here. But for now, everybody out so we can get the old buggy ready for another baptizing."

EIGHT

By the time we were third in line to cross, the crowd had thinned out, some of the people behind us having decided to turn around and go back home; some to move off the road and set up camp; some to just tough it out in their cars till morning, in hopes the water would have slacked off enough by then to let them get across under their own steam.

Lefty said it was about time to shut it down for the day, anyhow. It was getting late and the men were tired and most people that needed to get across had made their bid. He sent word to the parking marshal that shop was closed to anybody not already in line; to the other marshals on both sides to keep fires burning in the middle of the road all night so no one coming through in the dark would run into danger; and said if that didn't suit everybody's coporosity, they could take their chance and go hang.

Then he motioned the first car to move up to the edge of the water. He told them they'd be okay because they were in an old car built high off the ground, and it was the newer, low-slung ones you had to watch, especially the ones with inexperienced drivers, which was meant to buck the driver up and help him show a little false courage. But it didn't work. He was so scared he put a grip on the steering wheel that made his elbows stick out like wings, while his wife covered her face with her hands, and the crowd of kids in the back stared out at us with shocked eyes and open mouths.

"Poor greenhorn," Daddy said. "He'd take a team through standing up and popping the lines, but that car's got him buffaloed. Probably the first one he ever drove."

He eased it into the water, Lefty yelling, "Give her the gas! Give her the gas!" She coughed and hesitated and coughed again, and somebody yelled, "Gun her, damn it!" She caught and picked up speed and went chugging across and up the bank and the watchers clapped, but nobody yelled or whistled, and the guides waded back slow and heavy.

Lefty waved the next car forward. There was a young, pretty lady driving, and an old one holding a baby about Martha May's age sitting next to her. A dog and two kids, a girl bigger than I was and a little boy about four, were squeezed into the back between boxes and paper sacks and piles of clothes and bedding that had been pitched in any old way.

Lefty leaned toward the driver's window and said, "Listen, goodlooking, why don't you scoot over and let a man handle this old buggy for you?"

The lady tossed her head and said, "Listen yourownself, buster. I've handled her all the way from California, so I reckon I can manage a little farther."

Everybody laughed and said, "You tell him, sister," and "Go to it, babe," and he laughed, too, and said, "Okay, sugar. Suit yourself. Just keep her heading straight, and gun her like hell if she starts to stall."

She hit the water fast and went racing across, bucking and backfiring, the kids' heads snapping and rolling, and when she went up the high bank spitting smoke like a runaway freight, everybody whistled and cheered the way they had earlier in the day.

Lefty came to Daddy's window, grinning and shaking his head, and Daddy said, "I'm loaded to the gills. When I pull the choke and open her up, be ready to jump."

Lefty nodded. "You set?"

"Let her rip."

And we went flying straight down into the water—bumper, radiator, hood, windshield, front seat, back seat, all, all. I could feel the top load straining forward, see Daddy's hands tighten, Mama lifting Martha May, the sun ripples flashing on the climbing brown water. Then we levelled out and went faster and faster, white spray churning just beneath the windows, big drops of it flicking in like liquid fire. I felt a surge of power, a lurching sway and counter sway, and we were out on the other side, Daddy waving his thanks to the men behind us, Mama smoothing moisture from Martha May's hair.

Daddy patted the wheel and said, "Well, the old hoopy came through like a trooper," and Mama said, "We should've rolled the windows up, though. Water flew in everywhere."

"Now Fern, you never have seen me roll the windows up when we was taking a ford at high water. You do that, and if anything happens, you'd be penned in and—are you listening to this, Mavis?"

"Yessir."

"All right. Now, you keep your windows down, so if your car falls off in a hole, you can get out easy. The incoming current'll float you right out on the down current side and you can bob to the top like a cork. Understand?"

"Yessir." But I hoped with all my heart I'd never have to be in another car pointing its nose into water. Floating and bobbing might sound easy, but so did flying. Yet when I flew in my dreams, it was hard, scary work. I had to kick and thrash constantly with my legs and pull at the air with my hands till my arms ached. And even then, I'd sink so low sometimes, I'd have to jerk my toes up by main force to get them out of the reach of whatever was chasing me.

We could see the Stirrup City side marshal down the road, his pile of firewood already gathered, turning a car back toward town, and Daddy said, "Keep your eyes peeled for that camp. It's right around this bend somewheres."

"There," Mama said, "that road yonder. Oh Will, it does look nice."

Daddy turned in off the main road, keeping the car in low, saying, "Yessir, old Lefty knew what he was talking about, all right. Look at the blank blank," and Mama said, "Yes, and see how the such and such—"

I was still too dizzy from the water, too tired, too hungry, too desperate to pee to more than half notice the things they were pointing out to each other. Except for being laid out among a lot of big trees, it looked pretty much like any other good-sized campground to me.

I didn't realize then it stood as ideal to them, a symbol of a way of life they were reluctant to put behind them, that for a little while they could believe all camps were like this one, The Way Camps Used to Be, and that they were truly facing, for the first time, the fact that this would be their last turning off the highway into another familiar room in their moving house of many mansions.

I didn't think in any kind of grand finalities, then. I thought only in the small, day-to-day ones that had trained me all my life to accept the goodbye inherent in every place. So even if I had been able to understand that they were celebrating a quiet and aching benediction over the end of their youth, I would've been unable to believe in it. San Angelo, that vague daydream marking the end of the road, seemed as unreal to me as any other daydream, and saying goodbye was too integral a part of my life for me to believe I would ever reach a place where I would never have to say it again.

"How about right down here?" Daddy said. "I don't see but one car. We can have plenty of room to stretch out in."

"That's fine. Anywhere'll do. Let's just get stopped and get some supper to cooking."

Daddy pulled into the clearing and said, "That's the car that crossed just ahead of us. The gal that wouldn't let Lefty help her."

"She did all right on her own."

"She might not have if she'd stalled or hit a sink hole."

"Well, she didn't, Will, and it's none of our concern, anyhow. Now are we going to light or not?"

He got out and called, "You folks mind having company?" which was the polite thing to do unless a camp was so crowded you didn't have any choice.

The lady turned and looked at us like we were old friends instead of strangers and said, "Heck no. Pile out and make yourselves at home."

Daddy introduced us and she said she was Johnnie Wright and the older lady was her mama, Mrs. Best, and the kids were Ethel Ruth, Eddie, and Ernie, and the dog was called Fritzi and didn't bite, and she was glad to have a family for neighbors instead of that bunch of single hooligans she'd been afraid she'd get stuck with.

"Oh, they don't mean any harm," Mama said. "They're just young and full of beans."

"I don't know. I been a little anxious they might come around tonight and—bother me."

"No, no. They're not that kind. And even if they were, the other men would put a stop to it. A real camp like this is a respectable place, Johnnie. People wouldn't tolerate anything like that."

"Still, I'd rather have y'all next door for the night."

"We won't be staying that long. We're on our way to Angelo and just stopped off to eat and get cleaned up a bit."

"Oh, shoot! I was counting on us having a nice visit."

"Spending the night sounds like a pretty good idea to me," Daddy said. "We could take our time getting re-fitted, get a good night's sleep—"

"Oh, do, girl. We can potluck. I was just fixing to send Ethel Ruth off to rustle up some wood so I could get my fire going. What do you say?"

"Well, if Will wants to."

"Let's do it," Daddy said. "You gals can get on with

your rat killing soon as we get the tent down. I want to start re-packing the load first, then—"

"No," Mama said. "Get my chuck box out first, and go down and get me a bucket of well water, I don't care what it costs. I'm not going to drink any muddy tasting river water coffee tonight."

"I'll go get a bucket," Johnnie said.

"No, I want to use some of it to rinse those pants of Will's out in before I press them, and I couldn't use your supply for that. Besides, the coffee's my treat. I'll furnish the makings."

"Well, if you put it like that. The truth is, girl, I'm out of coffee. But I got plenty of other stuff. I wouldn't have said anything about a potluck if I couldn't ante my share."

"You haven't been on the road long, have you?"

"No. Only out to California and back to here."

"Well, I have. A mighty long time. And I can spot a four-flusher or a free loader a mile away. So you quit worrying about me mistaking you for one of them and let's get to cooking. I don't know about your bunch, but mine's starving to death."

Johnnie threw her arms around Mama and laughed a little and cried a little and said, "Oh girl, I haven't had a friend in so long." Then she wiped her eyes and said to Ethel Ruth, "Hightail it out there and get me some wood," and to me, "Don't you want to go along, honey?"

I really didn't. Ethel Ruth standing on the ground was a whole lot bigger than Ethel Ruth sitting in a car. She had a mean, bossy face, too, like the girls who got you off to yourself somewhere and twisted your arm till you begged, or bent your little finger till you went to your knees, then threatened to make you eat a cow chip if you told. But it would've been bad manners to say no, so I said, "Yes, ma'am," knowing I had to find something to squat behind soon anyhow, or disgrace myself one.

We went a little way into the trees, and while I peed,

Ethel Ruth kicked at a log crumbly with age and ants and said, "This ought to be a good place to dig for worms."

I peed as hard and fast as I could. Even if she wasn't the kind who liked to hurt you, she might be the kind that liked to stuff nasty things down your dress or rub them in your hair. As soon as I finished, I jumped up and pulled my bloomers up and got ready to run.

"Well, will you or won't you?" she said.

"What?"

"Are you deaf? Help me dig worms later on?"

I could see the top of Johnnie's car through the trees, catch glimpses of her and Mama moving around, and I knew I could make it easy if I had a head start, which I intended to have if Ethel Ruth made one step in my direction when I finished asking, "Why do you want to dig worms?"

"So my grandma can go fishing this evening, why do you think?"

"How come your grandma doesn't dig her own worms?"

"Because she's old and it don't hurt me. I eat the same as everybody else when she catches something."

"Oh."

"Didn't you ever dig worms for anybody?"

"No. My daddy digs his own."

"Well I don't have a daddy."

"Is he in Heaven?" Because all the friends I'd ever had whose mama or daddy was in Heaven liked to talk about how they were with God and Jesus, looking down on their loved ones, and I thought it might make Ethel Ruth happy to talk about hers.

But she said, "Heck, no! My mama says when he dies he'll land in Hell with his back broke."

"Only bad people go there when they die."

"Then that's where he's at. *If* he's dead. 'Cause he took us out to California and run off and left us stranded, and we waited and waited, and then Mama lost her job and we had to sell our tent and near 'bout everything else we owned to get back home on. Start picking up some wood, will you?"

"But if you don't have a tent, where do you stay at night?"

"Where we stay in the daytime, dumbbell, in the car. And it's plenty crowded and uncomfortable, too, and every time we stop along the road to eat or get some sleep or something, some Law comes by and asks us all kinds of questions and says bad things to my mama."

"My daddy says the Law hasn't got any right to bother you if you're not doing anything wrong. He says we're American citizens, and—"

"It's different when you're just a couple of women and a bunch of kids. *My mama* says that, and she ought to know." She piled some more sticks on the bundle in her left arm and said, "But we're going to move to a big city now, Dallas, maybe, and Mama's going to get a good job and we're going to live in a downtown apartment and go to the picture show every Saturday."

"We're going to Angelo and live in a house."

"You'll be sorry."

"Why?"

"Do you know what a mortgage is?"

"No, what?"

"*I* don't know. Why do you think I asked you? But houses have them and they kill people."

"How do you know?"

"Because one killed my grandpa, that's how."

"What did it do to him?"

"It made him get sicker and sicker till he died, that's what, and that's why we moved. So none of the rest of us would get it. Mama and Grandma kept saying he would've lived if it hadn't been for the mortgage, and Daddy said he sure didn't want it, let somebody else have it, we was heading for California. And that's what we did. Only we didn't like it out there, even if we couldn't catch the mortgage. They call you Okie out there and treat you like dirt."

"What's an Okie?"

"Don't you know anything?"

"I don't know what an Okie is because we've never been to California. But my daddy says the people out there are all crazy, and he knows, because his sister lives out there and writes him stuff he says is radical."

"What's radical?"

"I don't know that, either, but it's plenty bad."

"Not as bad as Okie. That's worse than son-of-a-bitch, my daddy said—when I had a daddy."

"Girls aren't supposed to say words like that."

"*I'm* not saying it. I'm just telling you what my daddy said."

"We were called transients once."

"What's that?"

"Like Okie, I guess, because my daddy was really mad—" shaking with shame and rage—" and he said he wouldn't ever ask for another make-work government job if we all starved to death and they could take their county pork barrel and—well, do something not very nice with it. I wanted to ask Mama what a pork barrel was, but she was so mad, too—" her milk dried up for a day and a half and Martha May had to suck a sugar tit soaked in canned cream and got the colic—"I was afraid to ask her."

"Huh. A pork barrel's nothing but a barrel packed with salted pork. My grandma used to fill up two or three of them every hog killing."

"This was a county one, though. Maybe that's what made it bad."

She shrugged. "All I know is, nothing's as bad as California." Then she put a foot down on one end of a dry limb and grabbed the other end with her free hand and snapped it in two and laughed and said, "But I knocked the pee-wadding hell out of some of them smart alec California kids. They'll think twice before they wise off to the next Okie they meet, I bet. Here, pick that up and let's get back to camp. I'm so hungry my backbone's eating up my belly button."

Both fires were going when we got back, and when I laid my wood down close to ours, Mama said, "Not there. Over yonder. I don't need it now. I swear, sending you off to do something's as bad as sending your daddy. He's been gone after water long enough to haul it in from Angelo. What took you girls so long to pick up half a dozen sticks? Johnnie and I gathered up enough right here to—" somebody came toward us blowing their horn real loud and she jumped and said, "What the devil?" and it was our car, Daddy tooting the horn, a blond lady riding on Mama's fender, a man standing on Daddy's running board, and she said, "Lord have mercy, it's Jules and Evelyn Sinclair."

NINE

Daddy said it was a potluck to end all potlucks, and Evelyn's jar of homemade pickles she'd got for telling a lady's fortune put the finishing touch to it. Evelyn stood up and smiled and bowed just like the ladies in tent shows, and everybody laughed and clapped except Jules, who always seemed to be looking the other way when she did something funny.

Until the following year, when I saw a book in the Beaumont library by Jules Verne, I thought his name was 'Jewels,' and while I'd known ladies named 'Jewel,' I'd never heard it used as a man's name before, or in the plural. But it suited him. He reminded me of a lady's onyx dinner ring I'd seen in a store window once, long and slim, with glass-black hair and eyes, and dark olive skin. He was a quiet person, too, a slow and light eater, the opposite of Evelyn in every way.

She was short and plump, with ruddy skin and bright blond hair cut in a wind blown bob, and wore high heels and silk stockings even there in camp, while all the ladies I ever knew, if they had such finery at all, saved it for church or town. Her dress was for town, too, and her face was fixed like she was going to a party.

She wasn't a bit stuck up, though. She ate as much as Daddy, packing it in a mile a minute, saying funny things the whole time, and bragged so much on Mama and Johnnie for serving such a feast, they blushed and said it was nothing, just potluck, which made everybody laugh again, and when we were all finished, Daddy said, "Well folks, there ain't but two things a man can do after a supper like that—sleep it off or walk it off, and I think I'm going into town and walk mine off taking a look around. How about you, Jules?"

"No thanks, Will. I saw all of Stirrup City I wanted to coming through this morning. I'm going on back to the tent and catch a little siesta before we go frogging."

"I'll drop you off."

"No, I need the walk."

"I'd better get back, too," Evelyn said. "I have some things to rinse out—oh, gee. I can't leave you girls with all these dishes. I feel bad enough letting you all do the cooking."

"That's okay," Mama said. "We'll tend to them."

"Sure," Johnnie said. "You'd ruin your pretty dress."

"Well, if y'all really don't mind."

"Go on," Mama said. "We'll see you after while."

"Yes, as soon as the guys take off. And I do want a ride to the tent, Will. I can't walk that far in these heels."

They started for the car and Mama said, "Can't you wait till I get your other pants pressed, Will?"

"Aw, these look all right. I'm not going to meet the mayor, I'm just going to prowl around a little and see what's going on before the stores close."

Johnnie said, "If you hear of anybody wanting any help, I wish you'd let me know. I can cook, clean, wash, iron—anything that's legal."

"I'll give her a whirl," Daddy said, and got in the car where Evelyn was waiting. I didn't like to see him driving off with somebody else in Mama's place, but she didn't even look at them. She just wiped the sweat off her face with the corner of her apron and said, "Well, Johnnie, you were a smart girl to put the water on ahead of time. It's already good and hot. We'll just wash and dry everything right here and separate them out when we're done. Hand me my dish-pan, Mavis, and you girls get out of the way."

"Why don't you all let me do up them dishes?" Mrs. Best said. "I ain't hardly turned a hand this whole blessed day."

"No, ma'am," Mama said. "You watched the babies and made all those biscuits. You sit down and rest."

"That's right," Johnnie said. "You rest, Mama, or go fishing awhile if you want to. Ethel Ruth'll dig you some worms."

"No, I'll just set a spell, then, if you all say so." But she was disappointed, because ladies liked to brag about how many beds they'd made, meals they'd cooked, dishes they'd washed, floors they'd scrubbed. That was their way of proving their worth, for as Martha May's husband once said, 'Everybody's got to have something to be proud of, even if it's no more than being the town's worst drunk,' and most women of that time had nothing to offer but their labor in the service of others.

"It was a good supper, wasn't it?" Johnnie said.

"Yes, potlucks are fun once in awhile, and we didn't have any dinner to speak of, Will was so anxious to make up time after we hit Big Spring and the road improved—not that it did us any good, getting caught at the ford like we did. Of course, we could've pushed on to Angelo, but—"

"I'm glad you didn't. I feel better knowing you all'll be here through the night, no matter what you say."

"I'm glad, too, to tell you the truth, though not because I think anyone would've bothered you. It's just that this is such a nice camp, and what with Jules and Evelyn turning up—we haven't seen them since Mavis was, oh, I guess about three. Lord, it doesn't seem possible it's been that long."

"From listening to you all talk, you must've had some pretty high old times travelling together."

"Well, we didn't really travel together. Oh, Will and Jules sorta teamed up awhile when they were bachelors, but their work's so different. Jules is a sign painter, a good one, too. He can do anything with a brush, work on glass, do that goldleaf lettering, anything. But where we might spend three or four days in a town, he might spend only one. Or he might get a big job that'd take a week, and we'd have to move on before he finished.

"But we did travel the same general routes for a long time, so we were always running into each other, hitting the same campgrounds or wintering in the same towns. Everything was so different back then. Why, it wasn't anything for Evelyn to pay fifty dollars for a pair of shoes."

"She still dresses pretty highfalutin'."

"Yes, Evelyn had rather have something nice to wear than something to eat."

"Well, she's no piker when it comes to vittles, either, if today was any example."

Mama laughed. "That's Evelyn, all right. She can eat or drink the average man under the table without batting an eye."

"Him, though, Jules. He didn't eat enough to say grace over."

"Oh, Jules has had a bad stomach ever since we've known him. He has to be very particular about what he eats or drinks."

"Then I'm glad we had that buttermilk for him."

"Yes, everybody enjoyed it, especially with Mrs. Taylor's sweet potatoes."

"Still, nothing takes the place of a good cup of coffee." She popped her cuptowel. "My, this towel's wet. I don't think it'd dry another thing, not even a spoon."

"Get you another one, right there in that box, and Mavis, if you and Ethel Ruth have any playing to do, you'd better get at it. It'll be dark in another fifteen, twenty minutes."

"Dig my valise out first," Johnnie said to Ethel Ruth, "and see if you can find my kid curlers. I got to roll my hair up in case Will does find me some work."

We went over to their car and Ethel Ruth rummaged around on the floor in the back till she uncovered the valise. She dragged it out and set it on the running board and said, "I hope your daddy don't find a job for my mama. I hate this place, and we'll be stuck here forever if she gets work. I want us to move to Dallas like she promised and go to the picture show and the dime store and see all the lights."

Before I could say Daddy was only trying to do them a favor, we saw his car coming and went over to where everyone else was waiting, their faces solemn and listening.

He got out and slammed the door and winked at Mama and grinned at Johnnie and said, "You ready to start work in the morning?"

She opened her mouth, but no words came out, and then she swallowed hard and said, "You wouldn't kid me, would you?"

"No, I wouldn't joke about nothing that important. You got you a job, with a old friend of mine, old Hi Walters. He's got him a little homemade fried pie business going, peddling them around to filling stations and cafes, and the lady that was doing his cooking just quit on him not ten minutes before we run into each other. She's moving into Angelo to live with her daughter, and he was out looking for somebody to take her place.

"I told him, I said, 'Hell, Hi, I know a girl'd make you a good hand,' and he said, 'Send her in,' and that's all there was to it."

She grabbed her head with both hands like she was holding it on and said, "Oh, lord. Oh, lord. You don't know what this means to me."

"Now, it's hard work," Daddy said, "and you got to be there at four o'clock in the morning to have a fresh batch ready for him to hit the road with before breakfast time."

"Hard work don't bother me, and I'll be there at four with bells on, you can count on that. Gee, Will, I just don't know how to thank you." And she began that same laughing and crying both at once, hugging Mrs. Best and starting to hug Mama, but Mama stepped back, patting her on the arm instead, and said, "I'm really glad for you, girl."

"I know you are, Fern. You and Will—I just felt like you all would bring me good Luck. Oh, my. I have got to do something with this hair and get me a bath and—Ethel Ruth, go look through my valise again and see if you can find me a pair of stockings not full of runs and snags, and—"

"Slow down," Mama said. "You're working yourself into a tizzy."

"Yes, I guess I am acting like a crazy woman, but now I got a job and things are going to be okay. I don't mind telling you, I'm down to half a sack of cornmeal, about a quarter of a tank of gas, and twenty-seven cents. I just been frantic all day, wondering what I was going to do. But it's okay now, we'll make it, thanks to Will and the good Lord, and I'm going to be back after while for our hen party and put my feet up and let the world go by."

As soon as Daddy left to go frogging, Mama pressed his other pants and gave Martha May her sponge bath and sat down to nurse her, saying, "I don't want to be heating water half the night, Mavis, so you go on and wash up while there's still some left that's warm. Get your feet and ankles good and put your shoes and socks back on, if you want to sit up a little longer. Your sweater, too, it's getting chilly."

By the time I finished washing up, Martha May was asleep. Mama put her in her box, frowning a little at the squeeze it was getting to be to fit her into it, and we went outside where Johnnie and her family were waiting for us.

"I know I look like a haint," Johnnie said, and she did look scary with her hair twisted up in kid curlers and her face covered so thick in vaseline her eyebrows looked pasted on. "But I got to put my best foot forward in the morning. I don't want Will's friend to think—well, you know how it is when you're on the road all the time. No matter how you try, it's hard to keep yourself looking nice."

"You're going to look fine and you're going to do fine. But what about stockings? Did you find a pair you can use?"

"Yeah. Mama had to darn them in a couple of places, but they don't look too bad."

"Well, I could let you have my extra pair."

"Lord no, girl. You and Will done enough for us already. They'll do. And I'm going to rub some of this vaseline on my shoes, polish them up a bit, and listen. I found a really keen place when I was down at the river bathing. A big rock ledge that hangs out over the water, all quiet and green. Let's walk down there and see if we can catch the moonrise."

"I don't know, Johnnie. The baby's asleep, and we couldn't leave without Evelyn. She should be along any minute now, though, with a nip around, I hope. She generally does have a bottle stashed away for special occasions."

"That *would* put the icing on the cake," Johnnie said. "I got some goodies, too, ten ready rolls here in my pocket *I* been saving for a special occasion. Oh, my lordy, lordy. A shot of bourbon, a good cigarette. What *are* the poor folks doing tonight?"

Eddie was already asleep in Mrs. Best's lap, Ernie leaning against her droopy-eyed, Ethel Ruth off to one side, giving me 'I told you so' looks that meant she was plenty mad, so I sat down on the ground next to Mama's stool, even if it was our quilt they were sitting on. Then Evelyn walked up waving a paper sack, saying, "Here comes the party. Any players?"

She wasn't wearing her high heels and her pretty dress. She had on a man's shirt and a pair of man's britches that flared out at the thighs and fitted into laced up boots, and for an instant I saw high sunshine and white water behind her and Mama said, "Ye gods, Evelyn, you mean you've still got that outfit little old Chunky Peters gave you when we were in Colorado?"

"Heck yes, girl. I always wear it when I've absolutely, positively got to do any walking. Shoot, I'd have broke my neck getting over here in heels, and you know how tight Jules is about letting me drive." She took the bottle out of the sack and opened it and poured drinks into the mix of cups and glasses Mama had setting on a box and raised hers up and said, "Here's to old Chunky Peters. He was a sweet guy."

Mama and Johnnie and Mrs. Best raised theirs, too, and after Mama took a sip, she said, "He was sweet on you for sure."

Evelyn smiled, her eyes flashing like my best piece of blue glass, and said, "It didn't mean anything. Everybody was sweet on somebody back then. It was a sweet time. That's when you should've been on the road, Johnnie, when times were good and everybody drove new automobiles and wore smart clothes. Why, Will kept you and Mavis dressed like a couple of china dolls, Fern, and everybody called you 'Sugar,' remember?"

"Well," Mama shrugged. "That was a long time ago." But I could tell she was pleased to be reminded of that time, to see herself dressed up pretty riding in a fancy car, and I wished I could remember those days, too.

"We were all working near an engineering camp up around Raton Pass," Evelyn said to Johnnie. "That's where I first met Fern and Will. Me and Jules hadn't been married long—"

"You were still wet behind the ears," Mama said.

"Well, I wasn't but sixteen. And thought the world was my oyster. Anyhow, they were cutting roads and building bridges and stringing telephone lines—the Corps of Engineers, Uncle Sam's boys. They had a big camp laid out just like a town, except it was all tents, rows and rows of them. 'Course we lived in tents, too, but we had our own camp separate from theirs, with all kinds of people doing business. Will was making pictures and we had a couple of barbers and a saloon and a shoe man and some women who took in washing and some who—"

"It was a mixed up kind of life," Mama said. "We worked more at night than we did in the daytime."

"In between the parties," Evelyn said. "Talk about a hot time in the old town tonight."

"It wasn't all parties," Mama said. "Will had sittings for the soldiers at night, and that's when I did his retouching. We swapped out work among ourselves some during the day, and the sightseers gave us a little business. Then Will had to make those long hard drives into town for supplies."

"I know everybody worked hard," Evelyn said. "I told my share of fortunes, don't forget. That may not sound like work, but I wore out three or four packs of cards while we were there."

"I didn't know you read the cards," Johnnie said. "Will you read them for me?"

"Later, I guess, if Fern's got a pack. But I was telling you about the parties. The last one was the best. When they finished off that big bridge and we took the Victrola out there that night and danced and Jules couldn't drink because his stomach was acting up—remember, Fern?" She laughed. "Old Chunky, he was an army doctor, and he said he'd give Jules a whiskey enema so he could get tight without hurting his gut, and it made Jules so mad he drank nearly a pint without stopping, and—"

"And damn near died," Mama said. "He hemorrhaged on and off for two days, Evelyn."

Evelyn cut her eyes at Mama in a funny way and said, "Yeah, we had a *couple* of bloody messes there, didn't we?" and Mama looked back at her scared and mad and daring her all at the same time till she turned away and said, "Oh, well. Jules is stronger than people think, and I'll tell you this, Heaven to me is going to be dancing on a mountain bridge in the moonlight."

"Oh, gosh," Johnnie said. "If we don't hurry, we're going to miss our own moonrise."

"What moonrise?"

"Well, there's this big pretty rock ledge I found when I went down to the river to bathe, and I thought we'd walk down there and watch the moon come up. It ought to be at true full tonight."

"I'm game if Fern is. I need to stand up and move around some, anyhow. My fanny's asleep."

Mama looked toward the tent. "Well, I—"

"Don't fret about the baby," Mrs. Best said. "My two's already down for the count, so I'll just sit right here and look after the three of them. You all go on and enjoy yourselves."

"Well—thank you kindly, Mrs. Best. I believe I will, then. Mavis, do you girls want to come along?"

We went out into the darkness, down the dull, chalky smear of the road, past low fires and quiet 'howdies,' Mama and Johnnie and Evelyn in the lead, not talking much, Ethel Ruth and I following, not talking at all. She was too sulled up about not getting to go on to Dallas, and anyhow, when one kid was leaving and one was staying, a kind of distance formed between them that made all the things they might have told each other close down into themselves like the little collapsible cup I'd once had.

Johnnie led us down a bumpy, pitch-black path out onto a heavy ledge of limestone that hung over the sound of moving water. Dimly lighted by some source within itself and giving off the last, faintest breath of warmth from the day's sun, it bore us on its back like some great, sleeping animal, a snow beast that might at any moment wake up and glide silently away with us.

We sat facing the opposite bank, hugging our knees to our chests, looking across the water. We could see a lantern far off to our left, appearing and disappearing in the darkness; could hear men's voices, a whistle, a laughing curse, a loud splash; smell mud and woodsmoke and the Christmas scent of cedar.

Then the weight of the sky in front of us thinned and the taller trees moved forward, standing out separately against what might have been the sky glow of a boom town, taking on shapes and densities different from their daytime selves as the first burning arc of the moon rose above them.

We watched it climb, slow and heavy, and Mama said, "Grandpa would've called that a Comanche moon. They'd have been penning the horses and forting up the houses under a moon like that when he was a boy."

"Well, at least those hard times are long behind us," Johnnie said. "Now it's just a plain old harvest moon."

I didn't like the way it shifted the trees about and made the talking water shine with secrets I was afraid to hear, but when Evelyn began to whisper-sing

Shine on, shine on, harvest moon up in the sky,

with Mama and Johnnie joining in for the rest of the song with that same hushed sweetness, the whole night turned so beautiful I hated to see Mama bring it to an end by standing up and brushing off her skirt.

"I'm sorry to be the one to put a damper on things," she said, "but I need to be getting on back."

"Yes," Johnnie said, "me, too. Morning's going to come mighty early for me."

"They're all alike anyhow these days," Evelyn said. "What's the rush?"

But she stood up and knocked the grit off her clothes like the rest of us, then we walked back to the tent through patches of moonlight and shadow, past dead fires and silent camps, beneath the big trees beginning to tremble under a new wind, and as we moved into the light of our own low fire where the little huddle of sleeping figures waited, she said, "Why can't things be like they used to?"

TEN

We pulled out of the camp in a stiff norther, under a sky heavy with clouds, onto an empty road that stretched out forever between miles of bobwire fencing off dead grass and bare outcrops of crumbling rock, and Mama said, "Lord! When I think of spending the rest of my life in this kind of country!"

Daddy just grunted. He hadn't come in till Johnnie was leaving for work and one of our tent pegs had pulled loose and things were in such an uproar he never got to bed. Then he cut himself shaving and had to put a little corner of cigarette paper on it to stop the bleeding, which Mama said she would soak off for him later and it didn't look that bad and he should've come in at a decent hour anyhow.

"I thought I was coming in at a decent hour for a frog gigging night," he said. "I didn't know I was going to have two tore up camps full of scared women and squalling kids to deal with."

"We weren't scared. We were just worried. And the only kid crying was Martha May, and she wouldn't have been if I could've patted her back to sleep instead of being outside trying to keep the damn tent from blowing away."

"Well it looked like a shambles to me." He started laughing. "There I was, hoofing it along, thinking I was going to get to grab a couple hours sleep in a warm bed, when I saw light flaring up in the trees. It scared the hell out of me. I thought it was a fire. 'Course I hadn't run a dozen steps before I could see it was Johnnie's headlights swinging around, and then I saw you hanging onto the tent and heard Martha May squawking and there was Mavis holding her hair down with one hand and pulling on the rope with the other, Johnnie's crew wrapped up in quilts like a bunch of Indians. Why didn't you just light the lantern and guide her out onto the road?"

"I couldn't turn loose of the tent long enough."

"You ought to known one pulled peg wasn't going to wreck the whole tent."

"With that norther coming in like a cyclone?"

"Yeah, it did hit hard. We was all sitting around Lefty's fire drinking coffee and I bet the temperature dropped fifteen, twenty degrees in five minutes."

"I feel awfully worried about Johnnie and her bunch. I'm glad you strung that line for them and helped Mrs. Best lay quilts over it for a lean-to. That'll at least cut the wind some. But Johnnie has to have the car to get to work in, so I don't know what they'll do if it starts raining again."

"Oh, that ain't likely."

"It's not likely for one norther to blow in on the heels of another one, either, but it did."

"They'll be all right. They'll find a place in town once Johnnie gets a payday. Hi'll give her his day-old pies. Mrs. Best can fish. I left them that big mess of frog legs and slipped the old lady two bucks when no one was looking. They'll manage."

"All the same, it hurt me to leave them like that and it threatening rain. Eddie's not as old as Martha May."

"I'm telling you, Fern, they'll do all right. Hi might grubstake Johnnie and take it out of her pay a little at a time. He knows I wouldn't send him anybody that wasn't on the up and up. He might even take them in hisself. He ain't so old he can't appreciate a goodlooking gal bouncing around the place."

"I thought you said he was a confirmed bachelor."

"I said he might take them in, Fern. I didn't say he'd offer to marry the girl."

"Johnnie wouldn't go for anything like that."

"Oh, I expect she's hustled some before, and would again if she had to."

"Will!"

I couldn't understand why Mama got so upset about the word 'hustle.' I thought it meant to work hard or hurry up, the way people were always saying, 'Let's get a hustle on' or 'Hustle it up, boys,' and I didn't see how a word could be all right sometimes but not others, or what hustling had to do with getting married.

"I don't mean Johnnie's not a good old girl," Daddy said. "She's keeping her family together, her mama and her kids, and she'll see they stay together the best way she can, here or in Dallas or wherever they end up. I don't hold nothing against a woman like that doing whatever she has to. After all—"

"Yes, Will, I know. Everybody's got to eat."

"Well, they do. Stirrup City's coming up any minute now. Keep your eyes peeled for a clock, Mavis. I'd like to see how we're doing for time."

We passed cars and wagons, little scattered houses, a Baptist church, a row of shotguns with two Mexican ladies standing on the steps of one, talking, and a yellow dog curled up close to the other, trying to hide from the wind. I looked for a filling station, a big company-owned one. They were the most likely place for a clock, unless there was a courthouse with one, or a bank.

"Yonder's Hi's place," Daddy said. "Right down that side street there. Wonder how him and Johnnie got along this morning?"

"Well, she'll work hard for him, I know that, and in a respectable way, too, I don't care what you say."

We were out of town then, the last tumbledown little shacks straggling away behind us, and Daddy said, "Did you spot a clock, Mavis?"

89

"Yessir, but it wasn't working."

"Well I can't tell a thing with it being so cloudy—ah, there goes a school bus. It can't be too late."

It went by us fast, trailing smoke and dust, and Mama said, "I'll certainly be glad to get Mavis back in school. This'll make three whole days in a row she's missed."

I'd be glad to get back, too. I didn't want to grow up ignorant like some of the people we met, bringing letters to Mama to read for them. Or the ones who came to her to write for them, taking a postcard or a sheet of paper and an envelope out of a carefully folded bandana or from between the pages of their Bible. She could write faster than they could think out the words they wanted her to put down, but she never hurried them, and when they offered her something for her trouble, a little present of some kind or a few pennies, she would always say, 'No, I'm glad to do it.'

"She's smart," Daddy said. "She'll catch up."

"We've just never let her miss that much before."

"Well, things kinda got out of whack there for awhile, but we're going to be settled now and she won't have to miss no more.

"I'm going to keep my own business going on the side, nights and by special appointment, and I'm going to take that little store of Papa's and—you won't be living in one of his shotguns long. One of these days you'll have a big home in the best part of Angelo. You'll be dressed fit to kill and driving your own snazzy little roadster, and when you go downtown, people'll say, 'That's Mrs. Will Maddox,' and they'll say it with respect, too."

"Oh, Will. I don't even know how to drive."

"You can learn."

"It's so farfetched."

"You learning to drive?"

"No, all the rest of it. Expecting so much. It's silly."

"No. It ain't. This is still a free country, Depression or no Depression, and a man can still do whatever he's big

90

enough to, if he works hard and takes advantage of his chances, which I aim to do with this one."

"Well, I wasn't sure what you'd end up doing. When you stayed gone so long last night, I was about half-scared you'd changed your mind and decided to go on to California with Jules and Evelyn."

"I don't know what put that idea in your head."

"Oh, Evelyn. After we got the kids in bed and Mrs. Best turned in, we had a nightcap and finished Johnnie's Luckies and Evelyn told our fortunes, and then—"

"You know I don't like you fooling around with that mumbo-jumbo."

"We were just having a little fun. She told Johnnie a bunch of stuff that got her all pepped up, and told me I was going on a trip, and I said, 'Why yes, Evelyn, you know we're going to Angelo,' but she said no, it would be a long trip, one I'd make without you, and—I don't believe a word of that nonsense, Will, but anyhow, after Johnnie left, she started putting the sell on me about California, so I figured Jules was doing the same to you. They think there's a lot of money out there."

"Jules always thinks there's a lot of money somewhere, but I notice he don't never end up with any of it."

"This has something to do with the government, Evelyn said. A program of some kind for artists and photographers and writers and people like that. She said—"

"You know how I feel about the government."

"This is the federal government, Will."

"It's all the same politicking mess. How green does Evelyn think I am? I seen some of that program when we was in Dakota.

"Pictures of men watching their farms blowing away, some poor woman standing at the side of the road wondering how she was going to feed her kids—they ought to be shot, shaming people like that.

"When I take somebody's picture, they got something

to be proud of, something they can put on their mantel, show their friends, not something they want to hide.

"No, damnit, I don't want no part of no scheme that calls for a man to do things that'd make a billy goat's flesh crawl, and I ain't chasing after some rainbow Jules and Evelyn dreamed up. I don't want a hand-out, Fern, I want a chance. I want to turn that store of Papa's into a money-maker and get my business going on the side and—"

"If only times weren't so hard."

"People have got to buy groceries, and they're going to buy gas—why, just look how the traffic's picking up. Somebody in Angelo's doing some business."

She said, "I hope you're right," and handed Martha May over to me so they could both have a stretch and then said, "I've been thinking about those little shotguns of your papa's. If we could have that last one, the one on the corner, it has a pretty good-sized yard as I remember. Maybe later we could fence it off and have a garden and a few chickens, a cow."

"I don't see why not. Papa might have it rented right now, but we'd be in line for it when it did come vacant. How'd you like that, Mavis, a pretty little Jersey cow?"

I was scared of cows. My heart was set on a pinto pony. But I knew he wanted me to want a cow, so I said, "I'd like it fine, Daddy."

"Okay, it's a deal. I'll take you with me when I go to buy her and you can name her. You're good at naming things. You take after your mama there. Carlsbad and Sanatorium coming up. It won't be long now till we'll be Home."

I stood Martha May up in my lap so she could see out the window. But there wasn't a whole lot to look at. A school, the empty swings clanking back and forth in the wind, two big girls running down the sidewalk holding onto their hair, a seven-passenger Buick bus loading fares in front of the City Cafe, an old colored man standing on the corner grabbing at his hat as a sudden strong gust caught up the flying grit and loose straws and scraps of paper and spun them into a dust devil that nearly knocked him over as it went careening on down the street toward the railroad tracks.

"Oh God, oh God," Mama said. "West Texas."

ELEVEN

"Mavis?"

West Texas at its worst wouldn't have deterred Naomi. Neither rocks, stickers, cactus nor the Concho River in full flood could've kept her from her appointed rounds. "Come on in," I said. "I'm not asleep."

"I know. I peeked first to make sure."

"Is something wrong?"

"No, but it's getting close to noon, and I wondered if you felt like eating something now."

"Didn't the phone ring while ago?"

"You must have ears like a bat. Yes, Mary Fern called."

"Is she all right?"

"Oh yes. She's just concerned about you."

"I'm concerned about her. This past year hasn't been easy for her, either. I know she's a grown woman and this isn't the first hard blow she's had to deal with. But she was just beginning to get over her divorce and all the hell it caused when this thing hit Paul, and close as she was to her daddy—I hope you told her I'm okay."

"Yes."

"Well, what is it? You've got that juggling-a-hot-potato look."

"Billy called, too."

"About that damn condo, right? I don't know why he

thinks that just because he's my brother—where are my cigarettes?"

"Right there on your table, gripey-gut. If you'd just go look at it, Mavis. It's a beautiful place, facing the lake, not ten minutes from everything. Why don't we talk about it over a sandwich?"

"I don't want to talk about it, and I'm not hungry."

"I made fresh tea."

"Well, that sounds good. If you picked some mint, and if you won't start in again on that condo."

We went in the kitchen and it was still all in one piece, the dishes done, the floor swept, our glasses filled with ice. "Condos are good investments right now," she said. "Live in it a few months—thirty days for that matter, and if you're not satisfied, flip it and make some money on it. Billy explained the whole thing to you after the funeral yesterday."

"When my mind was really at its best."

"Paul was sick a long time, Mavis. You're bound to have given some thought to what you'd do when he was gone."

Yes, in the long stretches of the night when I was so tired, God forgive me, I wished he'd go on and die and end the suffering for us both, when I dreamed of the springs at Balmorrhea and the late snowfall in Pampa the night Martha May was born and the clean, sweet winds on the prairies, and I wanted to get in the car and drive forever, in the world the way it used to be.

"Of course I've given some thought to the future, Naomi, and I may make some changes. But buying a condo?"

"You sounded interested when Billy was explaining the options you'd have with one."

"For heaven's sake! Billy's always explaining some new iron he's got in the fire that's going to make us all millionaires. Just because I nodded and said uh-huh and unh-unh doesn't mean I was listening. When did he call? I didn't hear the phone but once."

"When you were in the shower, I guess."

"Why didn't you tell me then?"

"Because I wanted you to go on and get some rest. Did you?"

"Yes—listen, I'd better call him back right now and nip this in the bud."

"Wait a minute, now. Wait a minute. Think about a smaller place, Mavis. One that's well-planned, without any maintenance worries, one that would give you a chance to turn a nice profit in case—"

"You might as well hush, Naomi. I'm not going to be rushed into anything. And if I should decide to sell, what makes you think I'd move to Austin?"

"Why, you love Austin."

"To visit, yes, but—"

"But think if you lived there! Think how great it'd be, you and Billy and I all in the same town, Mary Fern and the boys in Round Rock, twenty minutes away."

"I don't drive as fast as you do."

"Oh, you know what I mean."

She sat there all eager and excited, full of the pleasure of good investments and good intentions and the opportunity to manipulate my life, the carat and a half ring of near perfect blue white diamonds that had once glittered from Aunt Hallie's brooch scattering brilliants across the table cloth. I coveted it again, not for the ring it was now, or for its monetary value, but for the brooch it had been, its sentimental value, and looked away from it quickly, not wanting to stir up the old hurt of our most bitter fight.

"Good lord, Mavis," she'd said. "It was only a brooch, not a holy icon."

"But it was an heirloom. It belonged to your grandmother."

"I've got rid of lots of things that belonged to Grandmother."

"Yes, but your mother would've worn that brooch if

she'd lived, and you took her place to Aunt Hallie. How could you have it torn up and made into a ring?"

"Brooches look tacky these days. Nobody wears them."

"Not many people have one that beautiful to wear, or one that belonged to—"

She snatched it off and shoved it at me and said, "Here. Take the damned thing if it means so much to you."

I pushed it aside and said, "It didn't come down to me from a member of my family. If it had—"

"If it had, you'd have built a shrine for it." She threw it at me. "Take it. I hate it."

I threw it back, hard, and said, "No, Naomi, you take it, and you wear it, and I hope it burns a hole in your ungrateful hide."

I wondered now that brooches were in again if she'd ever wished she'd held onto it.

"You wouldn't have to sell this place," she said. "You could rent it, or just close it up."

"I buried my husband yesterday morning, Naomi, a little over twenty-four hours ago, and you're hounding me to make a decision I'll have to live with the rest of my life."

"You said you'd already been thinking about some of the adjustments you knew you'd have to make."

"Yes, but—"

"Billy and I aren't the only ones who want you to shuck this place and buy that condo. Mary Fern thinks it's a good idea, too."

"You just don't give up, do you? I ought not to be surprised, though. You don't care how long something's been around. When you're through with it, you're through with it."

"I don't let things that've outworn their usefulness dominate my life, no. And if you spent less time dwelling on what's past and done, and more time thinking about making the most of what's ahead the way I do—"

"Yes, yes, Naomi, I know. You live right in the middle

of the here and now—except when you're in Grandma's chicken pen."

"Well, at least I don't think the real world ended in 1945."

"Naomi, it's true I don't like change, and I am attached to this house. But the main thing is, I have to think about money. I realize that's never been a problem for you, but—"

"Oh God, now you're back to being a poor relation."

"No, I'm back to worrying about how I'd repay Billy for the down payment on a new place if I couldn't sell this one. How I'd make the monthly payments. What taxes and insurance run in Austin. This house is paid for. It's homesteaded. They can't kick me out of here if I never pay any more taxes."

"Billy wouldn't let you get kicked out of anywhere, and you know it. And as far as a down payment goes, he never has pressed you for money, has he?"

"No, but he's never had to, either. We've always paid back every cent we ever borrowed from him."

"I know that, and he certainly knows it, so why are you reluctant to let him help you now? Sometimes I think you resent the boy's success, Mavis, I really do."

"He's not a boy, Naomi, he's fifty-five years old, and no, I don't resent the money he's made. I know better than anybody what he did for Mama and Daddy, at a time when he had very little to do with—what he's done for all of us. The bail he raised and the fines he paid for that sorry ass Martha May was married to, the loan that let Paul get his doctorate sooner than he could have otherwise, the money that helped Mary Fern go to The University comfortably instead of on a shoe string. His generosity has made all the difference in the world to all of us, and I don't forget things like that, whatever you might think. But—"

"But he just didn't turn out to be what you wanted him to, did he? Didn't get an education, doesn't associate with the right people—"

"Oh my God. Listen to the world's worst snob trying to

make me feel guilty because I *regret,* Naomi, not resent, that he's had to make it dealing with—"

"What you really think of as the lower orders?"

"Not if you're talking about the regular workmen, I don't. Honest sweat's never bothered me, and you know it. It's the hungry politicans and the greedy developers in collusion to wipe out the known world that I despise. They're such four-flushers, they're so arrogant, so ignorant—"

"They're bringing a lot of prosperity to the state."

"Of a kind that's robbing us of whatever virtues we once had."

"Well, regardless, it hurts Billy to know you look down on the people he does business with. And somebody's got to provide places for all the new people coming in."

"Oh hell, Naomi, I'm not going to sit here and argue with you. It's 12:30. I want to call before he goes off to lunch with some of his fellow nabobs."

"Will you listen to me first? With an open mind?"

"Make it fast."

"What we all want you to consider—"

"Oh, that's right. I'd forgotten Mary Fern's a part of this conspiracy."

"It's not a conspiracy, Mavis. What a thing to say about your own daughter."

"And what an attitude for her to take toward her own mother. I don't tell her, or you or Billy either, how to live your lives, and a hell of a lot of good it'd do me if I did, and I think you all have the nerve of a brass billy goat to start telling me how to live mine. What's the matter with you people? Do you think I'm too dumb to manage without Paul? Or that I've suddenly become senile?"

"We think you're worn out and confused and that the people who love you have an obligation to help you make the right choice about how you're going to spend the rest of your life. We want you to face the fact that this place is falling apart, and—"

"Thank you, Naomi. I hope I can say something that gracious about your home someday."

"It's an old house, Mavis. It was old when you all bought it. You spent a fortune on it then, and it'd take another fortune now to do everything that needs doing. And what would you have if you did put another ton of money into it? The neighborhood's going down—"

"Just because we're all getting older around here and don't have the money and the energy to keep our places the way we once did, doesn't mean—"

"You said yourself the Mexicans are beginning to move in."

"Ah, yes. Once a South Texan, always a South Texan. Gee, I should've explained to the Cantus how dangerous it is for them to be living in a house, because my great-grandma said Mexicans didn't die like flies from TB and pneumonia till the white man started putting up shacks for them. That so long as they lived in their wagons, or *under* them, they did just fine."

"That's not what I meant."

"Like hell it's not. You think I don't remember what a stink it raised when Mama took some paregoric down to the quarters one evening for a baby half dead with teething diarrhea? I thought Grandma and Uncle Dan were going to pitch us out on our ears they were so mad."

"I don't believe that."

"I don't give a damn whether you believe it or not. You may not believe that Ruby Cantu came over here several times a day to help me turn Paul and bathe him. But she did. Her husband took care of my car and ran a hundred errands a week for me, and her kids kept my lawn mowed and wouldn't take a nickel. They brought us fresh yard eggs and home grown vegetables and said a thousand novenas—you call Billy, Naomi. Call Mary Fern, too. Tell them I wouldn't have that condo on a silver platter. Now I'm going to go sit on the back steps a few minutes."

Which she well knew meant in the lexicon of our childhood that I wanted to be left alone. For back steps then were places of refuge as well as places for visiting, and the wise person honored the difference—though where Naomi was concerned my claim to wisdom was about as tenuous as my claim to female privilege that Saturday morning so many years ago when I sat on Grandma's steps waiting for Uncle Dan to take us to town.

TWELVE

There wasn't much to look at while I waited. Nothing I was used to seeing, anyhow. No cars coming and going, no ladies stopped to chat or men huddled over an open hood, nobody toting a jug of coal oil or sack of groceries, no big kids stalking by inside their own importance, no kids my age playing or fussing or skinning down the street with empty pop bottles to sell—nothing at all that belonged to the kind of places I belonged to.

Not like the one at Grandpa Maddox's, where even if we did have the worst hard times we'd ever had, we at least fit in among the other roomers, the people living in the shotguns, the whole neighborhood of little unpainted West Texas houses clustered around the small grocery store-filling station that was supposed to make our fortune.

And certainly not like anywhere on the road, though I had tried for awhile to pretend the bare dirt backyard was a campground and the smell of wood smoke coming from the chimney was coming from a camp fire. But that only made me more lonesome for Daddy than I already was, and more sure than ever we would never fit in here at Grandma's, where the people and the rules were so different from those I knew and felt at home with.

We'd been ready a long time, Mama and Martha May and I, because while it was all right for us to have to wait, it wouldn't have been for Uncle Dan, who was never to be kept waiting, for anything. His meals, his clean clothes, his paper, his mail; his hot water to shave in, his fresh water in the wash basin on the back porch each noon and evening; his turn at the privy, his weekly trip to town. Whatever he wanted, it was our job to see he got it without delay, because he was the Old Bachelor Boss of everybody on the Home Place, including Grandma and Grandpa.

Mama had explained how to act around him and the rest of our relatives over and over again the whole, long way from Angelo, a trip we made all by ourselves on the Travel Bureau, which was more like riding one of the seven passenger Buick buses in West Texas than a Greyhound, only not near as nice or fast.

Buses had regular stations at cafes or hotels in the towns they went through, regular routes, regular schedules, and regular drivers who took you all the way to wherever you wanted to go. But the Travel Bureau was a hard-to-find room you went to someplace downtown where a man wrote your name on a blackboard under the name of the town you were heading for. When there was a full load going there, or enough people going someplace on the way there, another man would pack us into his car like a bunch of sardines and drive us to what he called his end of the line.

For unlike the West Texas bus drivers, who thought nothing of making the round trip from Angelo to Del Rio in one day, none of the Travel Bureau drivers would make a run farther than around seventy-five miles, so you had to get out about every three hours and wait in another room till another man put your name on another blackboard and enough other people wanted to go to the next town on your way.

By the time we finally did get to Robb's Prairie, which Mama said she thought for awhile we weren't ever going to do, we'd used up most of the money Aunt Millie had sent us for our fares and meals, and I knew from the bottom of my upset stomach to the top of my aching head that there was something shameful about having to go live with relatives, something wrong in itself, like being an Okie or a transient, even if Mama never did come right out and say so.

I didn't count Aunt Millie or Naomi as relatives. Aunt Millie never made me wish I knew what it was I was doing wrong so I could stop doing it, or what it was I was supposed to be doing so I could go on and do it. And neither did Naomi—not just because we were the same age, either. Our cousins Lottie and Dottie were only a year older than we were and they made me feel bad plenty of times.

Of course, Aunt Millie was living with relatives, too, and so in a way, was Naomi, and that kind of put us all in the same boat. Besides, Aunt Millie was Mama's baby sister, Mama said, the same as Martha May was mine, and that made her more like family than kinfolks.

She was as pretty as she was nice, too. She fixed her face every morning and put a henna rinse on her hair every week when she washed and set it and worked on her nails every night after supper when she and Mama finished cleaning up the kitchen. She wore silk stockings and smart clothes and her half of the dresser was covered with little bottles and jars and boxes of things that smelled good.

"They're just samples," she'd told Mama when we first came. "All the salesmen give them out to the counter girls in their territories so we'll push their lines. And they're a godsend to me, I don't mind admitting. I have to look nice, meeting the public the way I do, and I can't afford to buy stuff like this. It's all I can do to keep myself in decent looking clothes and pay Perry for my rides and stick a dollar or two in the bank every week."

"From what you say about some of those fellas, though—"

"Oh, they're harmless."

"You said the one they call Pinky—"

"That old poot? He's all talk."

"I don't know, Millie. Most people don't give something without expecting something in return."

"And they get it. I do push their lines."

"That's not what I mean, and you know it."

"Listen, Fern, if I don't look up to snuff, Mr. Rathgaber will get someone who does. You can't sell really good toilet water and fine boxed candies and expensive cigars unless you're an advertisement for them yourself, the kind of a girl men don't want to look cheap in front of."

"In other words, you make some poor hick feel like a piker if he doesn't spend more than he can afford."

"Not if I know they haven't got it, I don't. But if they do, yes. That's my job, Fern, and if I don't do it, there's plenty waiting to take my place."

The drugstore didn't open till eight o'clock, but Aunt Millie got up with the rest of us so she could catch her ride with Perry Poage, who was our mailman and had to be at the post office real early to get his mail sorted. He lived down the road with his Mama and his old maid sister and his stamp collection, which Aunt Millie said took the place of a wife or sweetheart, because Perry didn't like ladies. But I thought he must like them some, else why would he live with his mama and his sister and let Aunt Millie ride to work with him even if she did pay?

Aunt Millie straightened stock and dusted shelves and pasted labels on medicine bottles till it was time to open. That paid for her lunch at the soda fountain, where they served cokes and banana splits and fancy sandwiches with pickles and potato chips on the side. Since Perry finished his deliveries long before she got off, she had to catch a ride home in the evenings with anybody coming our way, or Uncle Dan had to go get her, something he didn't like to do after a hard day in the field—riding around on a horse telling the Mexicans what to do, Mama said.

She asked Aunt Millie once why she didn't live in town with Aunt Hallie so she could walk to and from work and not have to depend on Uncle Dan at all. But Aunt Millie said, "Not on your life, girl. I can sneak off from here once in awhile for a little fun, but if I lived with Hallie, I wouldn't know what a good time was."

Aunt Hallie was Grandpa and Grandma's oldest child. She was a widow and lived in a big white house on Travis Avenue where all the houses were big and white and had smooth grass lawns bordered by clipped privet hedges and little houses or garage apartments in the back for the colored ladies who did the washing and ironing and heavy housework.

All the colored ladies had husbands or sons or grandsons who took care of the yard and ran errands when they came in from their Regular Jobs, if they had one, working at the hotel or one of the cafes or filling stations, or doing seasonal work in the fields or at the gin.

Ola Mae's husband, Matthew, who lived with her in the little house behind Aunt Hallie's, was a preacher. During the week he washed dishes at Weber's Diner and kept Aunt Hallie's yard. But on Wednesday nights and all day Sundays, he tended to his flock, which was what he called his congregation. He was a little bitty man, with white woolly hair and happy eyes and a voice so deep and beautiful it made the bones in your chest vibrate.

Naomi and I wanted to go hear him preach, but since Aunt Hallie drove us to the First Baptist Church and picked us up afterwards, we couldn't go on Sunday mornings. And we couldn't go on Sunday or Wednesday nights, because neither of us ever went anywhere at night. But someday, when we were grown up and had our own car, we'd go, because then we could go where we pleased whenever the notion struck us, and we would never be strict on our children the way our parents were on us.

Aunt Hallie wasn't really Naomi's parent. She was her grandma. Naomi called her Grandmother because Aunt Hallie liked that name better and because it distinguished her from Grandma, who was actually our *great*-grandma—and that was only one example of why it had been so hard for me to get all the people I was kin to by blood and marriage sorted out and established according to the places they occupied in that larger family I was both bound to and somehow separate from. For while I had my place, too, it was a small one, seated in that limbo at the edge of things where Mama and Martha May and I rode our uncertain little satellite around their fixed, immovable moon.

Mama said Aunt Hallie was extra strict on Naomi because raising a child at her age was a heavy responsibility. But I figured since she'd been doing it from the time Naomi was three, when her mama and daddy's car got hit by a train as they were coming back from a dance in Beeville late one night, she ought to be used to it. She was just a strict person. Even Uncle Dan toed the line for her. But Naomi loved her, because she was more than a relative to Naomi, just as Naomi and Aunt Millie were more than relatives to me.

Love didn't have anything to do with it, anyhow. You were kin to certain people whether you wanted to be or not, and that was that. You had to respect them and meet your obligations to them and Naomi was just lucky she could love her grandmother, as I was lucky I could, if not exactly love her and Aunt Millie, at least like them better than anybody else after Mama and Daddy and Martha May, whom I did love, in a new and desperate way.

Uncle Lafe was the baby of the family. He was a professor at The University in Austin and married to Ada Morgan, who played the piano and gave teas and was a Beauty. They'd sent me a book called "A Child's Garden of Verses" right after we got to the farm, with a note saying they hoped I'd enjoy it, which I did, more than any other book I'd ever read.

I wished they'd come for a visit before Daddy sent for us, but they hardly ever came back to Robb's Prairie, because they were so busy, Grandma said. Aunt Millie said even when they did come Home they always stayed with Hallie, and that Grandma said it was on account of Lafe and Hallie being so close, but Dan said it was because Ada Morgan thought she was too good to use a privy.

I couldn't understand why it made Uncle Dan mad for Uncle Lafe to always put a five-dollar bill in the letter he wrote Grandma every month. I thought it was nice to be rich enough to send your mama money and your great-niece you'd never even seen a brand new book of her very own.

Aunt Eunice lived on a big farm in Nordheim with Uncle Werner, who was bald and had bad teeth. They had three children: Martin Luther, who went to the agricultural college and was mean as an acre of snakes, and the twins Lottie and Dottie, who Naomi and I dreaded to see coming worse than anybody else in the whole world, kinfolks or not.

We didn't like Aunt Eunice, either, because she was always making snide remarks about Uncle Lafe and Aunt Ada. Every Sunday when they came to Grandma's for dinner, she'd ask if Lafe was still running The University and basking in the presence of La Morgan. Naomi and I didn't know what kind of name 'La' was, but we liked it, in spite of the snotty way Aunt Eunice said it, and sometimes called each other 'La Maddox' and 'La Schneider' when we were by ourselves.

"I feel like telling her to go to blazes," Aunt Millie would say later. "She's just jealous because she's married to that dumb Dutchman and has the ugliest kids in the county. She had as much of a chance as Lafe. Grandpa was running things back then, and there was enough money for all of them to make whatever they wanted to of themselves. Mama, too, honey, you know that."

"Yes, Millie, I do. But it's not our place to say anything to her. Just wait. One of these times she'll slip up and pop off like that in front of Hallie, and when she does—"

My grandma Dequincey, Mama's and Aunt Millie's mama, lived in San Antonio. But outside of somebody occasionally asking if anyone had heard from Effie lately, they never mentioned her. Except for the one time Uncle Dan said if Effie had listened to him she'd been better off, and Grandma said, well, Effie made her bed, she had to lay in it. I wanted to ask Mama what that meant, but she looked so cross and upset I didn't.

That evening when Aunt Millie got home they went in

the bedroom and shut the door and talked a long time while I helped Martha May practice walking and recited some of the poems in my book to her. When they finally came out they were both laughing, making me glad all over again we had Aunt Millie around to cheer us up.

We were going to get to see her later on, because Uncle Dan always stayed till dinner, and Mama said that'd give us plenty of time to make our purchases and do a little visiting, too, and yes, we'd see the whole town, but not for me to get my hopes up, because there wasn't much to it.

THIRTEEN

My hopes had been up, though, till earlier that morning. I was still lying in bed, still half asleep, thinking about our trip to town and the New School Clothes I was going to get, half listening to Mama and Aunt Millie talk while they finished dressing.

"I feel so guilty about not giving this three dollars to Dan," Mama said. "But Mavis has got to have some new clothes. Her shoes are absolutely falling off her feet and her sweater's so thin you could throw straws through it."

"Dan doesn't want that money, Fern. He may be a gripey old goat, but he doesn't begrudge you and the kids being here. My lord, look at the help you are to Grandma. To all of us."

"I don't know, Millie. I get so blue. And I worry about Will. Sometimes my food just sticks in my throat because I think maybe he's going hungry to send us what little he does."

I was going to bury my head under my pillow so I couldn't hear anything else sad about Daddy, but they went on out, so I got up and dressed as slow-pokey as I could, and went to the kitchen taking teeny-weeny baby steps all the way. Everybody else had eaten and left the table by the time I got there, but I felt so bad about Daddy I didn't care if Mama did fuss at me. She only smiled, though, like she knew a secret, and when I turned my plate over, there was a nickel under it, from Uncle Dan, she said, to spend in town for whatever I wanted.

I knotted it in the corner of one of my everyday hand-kerchiefs for safety. It could buy a candy bar, a soda pop, a ticket to the picture show—a little can of milk with two pennies left over, a small loaf of bread, a couple of eggs, a pound of meal—I didn't want it. I didn't want the New Clothes, either, if Daddy had to go hungry to buy them for me. But I didn't know how to tell Mama something like that, so I ate enough breakfast to keep her from asking me any questions, and went out to the back steps to pray Daddy would be all right and wish I didn't have to go to town.

Still, I liked towns, and in all the weeks we'd lived outside Robb's Prairie, I'd never really seen it. Everything was dark and closed up the night we'd come in on the Travel Bureau, and on Sunday mornings when Uncle Dan took me in to Aunt Hallie's to go to Sunday School, he cut off the main road before the businesses began and took a back way to her house, the same as she took a back way to church and the bus took a back way to school. If I stood on the north corner of the playground, I could see all the way down Bonham to where it met Houston at the hotel, but that was as close to downtown as I'd been.

We spent our Saturdays getting ready for Sunday and the week ahead. Martha May and I got our hair washed and took a bath in the wash tub in front of the kitchen stove. Mama and Grandma killed and dressed the hens or skinned the hams, made potato salad and washed and greased the yams, cut up the giblets for gravy, and did everything else they could ahead of time, because so many people came for Sunday dinner they couldn't have got everything done otherwise.

"Lord, the work!" Mama said to Aunt Millie one Saturday night. "I know everybody brings something and helps set out and clean up afterwards, but—Hallie could have everybody at her place once in awhile, and Eunice, too. They ought to stop and think that Grandma might like to go to somebody else's house for a change and not have to worry about fixing anything but a platter of gingerbread or a skillet of creamed corn. I don't see why she puts up with it."

"Now honey, you do, too."

"Yes, because she knows if she doesn't do it nobody else will and she'd never lay eyes on any of them. They don't set foot in this place any other time."

"Well, they do usually call sometime during the week, and besides, what would she do about Grandpa? He won't ride in a car anymore, for hell or high water. The last time Dan tried to take him in for a haircut and beard trim, he fought like an old tiger. So they have to get Dickie to come out here when he can, and even then, Grandpa may let him cut his hair and he may not."

"I'd stay here with him. I'd be glad to. I hate having to face that mob."

"Why, Grandma wouldn't leave him for all the tea in China."

"No, I guess not. But I tell you, Millie, I'm getting to where I dread Sundays."

I understood about the work. You couldn't be in the middle of it from sunup to sundown and not see what it took. Plus, it was my job to entertain Martha May while Mama helped Grandma, and that was getting to be a chore in itself, headstrong as she was turning out to be. But Sunday was still my favorite day of the week.

No one ever slept late at Grandma's, on any day. But at least on Sundays I didn't have to jump right up and start putting my clothes on the minute Mama said, "It's Time, Mavis. Crawl out."

I could wake up slowly, knowing 'Santa Claus, Santa Claus/We're at our grandma's', which I didn't like as well as 'Concho River, Concho River/Don't you sink my daddy's flivver,' but which served its purpose all the same.

I could enjoy looking forward to Sunday School, and to knowing Naomi and I would have the whole long day together, and to the big Sunday paper that had come in from

San Antonio on the last night train and been brought out to our mailbox long before dawn by Vance Miller, a fourth or fifth cousin on Grandma's side of the family, who delivered it to every subscriber on our RFD route.

It would be laying by Uncle Dan's plate, thick and inky smelling, the front section of it crackling with authority as he opened it up and looked at the headlines before re-folding it and putting it aside till later, where it pulsed silently with the power of ten thousand words waiting to take me into a different, larger world when the company had gone and we had the house to ourselves again, thank the Lord, Mama said.

Then there would be the ride into Aunt Hallie's, Uncle Dan in the set of starched khakis Mama did up to perfection for him every week, along with two sets of work shirts and jeans, which didn't have to be starched but did have to be ironed, because everything had to be ironed at Grandma's, except for socks and cuptowels and Mama told Aunt Millie she reckoned they'd be next.

I wore a regular school dress under my sweater, because that was all I had, but Mama always did it up especially nice, dipping the sashes in the starch till they ironed out stiff as pokers and made a bow that would've stopped a bullet. I carried my Sunday handkerchief Grandma had made for me, my New Testament Naomi had given me, and a penny for the collection plate from Aunt Millie.

Aunt Hallie and Naomi were always waiting by the car under the portecochere in their good dark coats, Naomi wearing her brown wool dress with the creme peau de soie collar, Aunt Hallie in her navy blue crepe with the diamond brooch her husband John Burkett had given her as a wedding gift pinned on her bosom. If she had her hat and gloves on, too, that meant she was going with us and we'd have to stay for church. But mostly she just dropped us off for Sunday School and picked us up afterwards and we went straight on out to the farm.

John Burkett and Uncle Lafe had been friends at The

University when they were young men. But while Uncle Lafe had stayed there, Uncle John had come back to Robb's Prairie to marry Aunt Hallie and take over his family's hardware store, which he ran till he died. His mama and daddy still lived in Robb's Prairie and Naomi spent some of her Saturdays with them because she was all they had left of their son.

Aunt Hallie herself never visited them. They had had a big falling out when Uncle John died and she sold her half of the business and put her money in the bank in San Antonio so she could live off the interest. Aunt Millie said she had other income, too, from Uncle John's insurance and rent property the lawyers in San Antonio tended to, but nobody knew for sure, and nobody had the nerve to ask.

At Sunday School, everybody went into the big room first, where Mrs. Dr. Bivens said the opening prayer and read the scripture lesson. Then crippled Mrs. Henderson played the piano, and Scooter, our second cousin once removed as near as we could figure, led the singing. She sounded like an angel, and was so sweet and pretty and full of life, Mama said she should've been named 'Merry Sunshine.' When we were dismissed to our classes, she always ran over and hugged Naomi and me, causing the other girls to commit the sin of envy and us the sin of pride.

She lived with her mama and daddy and her grandpa, mine and Naomi's great-great Uncle Homer Robb, who was Grandma's last surviving brother. He had been a Texas Ranger once, under Captain McNelly, and still worked what was left of the farm where he and Grandma were born.

On the Sundays her family came to dinner, she carried Martha May around till it was time to eat, because she loved babies and said it was perfectly awful being an only child and when she got married she was going to have a whole houseful of children to play with. After dinner, when Mama put Martha May down for her nap she'd sit on the back steps with Naomi and me and Lottie and Dottie, who didn't act ugly around her, because nobody could, and tell us all the gossip at the high school and the story of the latest picture show she'd seen, and then we'd plan what she ought to wear to the Senior Prom in May. Sometimes we favored blue moire taffeta, sometimes white dotted Swiss or pink organdy, sometimes yellow voile.

"You all'll be going to the Prom someday," she'd say, "and I'll be an old married lady with five kids and a grouchy husband, and you'll come by with your dates to show me how pretty you look and we'll remember when we used to talk about what I'd wear to the Prom, and we'll all cry and our mascara will run," and then she'd laugh and hug us and we knew we could never be that quick and shining and beautiful—nor wanted to be, if it meant Scooter had to change the least little bit from what she was that very minute.

There were nine girls in our Sunday School class, and Miss Zenda Calloway was our teacher. She had a soft, slow voice and milky brown eyes and powdery gray hair that kept straggling loose from under her hat no matter how often she tucked it back in and reset her hairpins. During the week, she worked in the bank under Mr. Tipton Junior, and in July of every year she made a trip to Corpus to visit a friend she'd gone to convent with when her daddy was president of the bank instead of Mr. Tipton Senior, who didn't do anything anymore, Aunt Millie said, except sit in his office checking over the books to see how much everybody in town owed him.

Miss Zenda didn't have pets. She treated everybody alike, calling on us in turn to recite our memory verse or to read from her big Bible with the red ribbon in it. She helped anyone who forgot or who couldn't pronounce some of the hard names, and she always had a surprise for us. Once it had been some unleavened bread, and once some dates, both of which Mr. Peavey had had to order special from San Antonio, and once a pair of dice for us to throw when we were studying about the Roman soldiers casting lots for Jesus's clothes.

The dice surprise almost caused a Scandal. Some people thought Miss Zenda ought to be drummed out of the church at the very least. They visited around and got on the party lines and talked and formed a committee to call on the preacher and the deacons. But nothing came of it. Because, Grandma said, Zenda might be an Old Maid and a trifle touched, but she was a good Christian girl and a Calloway, and there were too many people in town who remembered what they'd once owed her papa for them to take part in any ruckus against her, and while she herself didn't hold with gambling—her own sons having lost whole chunks of money to it when they were young, Mama said—if it came from the Bible and taught a lesson, there couldn't be too much harm in it.

But Aunt Hallie said it was because the preacher and the deacons knew which side their bread was buttered on, and they weren't going to take a chance on splitting the church for a few old sourfaced Puritans, not to mention the fact that just because Zenda didn't spend money didn't mean she didn't have a tidy sum tucked away somewhere, and they hoped to get their hands on a sizable portion of it someday.

For whatever reason, the Scandal died a-borning, and if Miss Zenda ever knew she was riding the wings of a storm, she never let on. Only two families transferred their letters, and pretty soon people found something else to talk about, which they always did, Aunt Millie said. But Mama said just because they quit talking about it didn't mean they'd ever forget it, and it would work its way to the surface in a hundred hidden acts down the line that would cause hurt to people who'd never know why they'd had the rug jerked out from under them, because that was the way small towns were, and she wondered if Will was ever going to send for us and get us out of there.

And if that was the only way we could all be together again, safe in a place of our own, that was what I wanted, too, which God very well knew, even if I did sometimes have secret daydreams—

116

"Mavis," Mama called out the back door, "get in here this instant. Uncle Dan's ready to go."

FOURTEEN

We stood in the driveway waiting for Uncle Dan to back the car out of its special shed at the side of the barn, while the wind blew strips of cloud along, covering and uncovering the weak winter sunshine that made me feel a little sick at my stomach the same way weak coffee did. It whipped the liveoaks and flattened the dead grass and lifted long gray drifts of dust across the plowed and harrowed fields I passed every day on my way to and from the hottop where the school bus stopped.

I knew the driver now, and the names of some of the kids, and I wasn't afraid I'd get left behind anymore. But that first day . . .

"Now you stand right by the mail box," Mama said. "The bus'll pick you up there and bring you back there this afternoon."

"Yes'm." I'd never ridden a school bus all by myself before. There'd always been other kids from whatever camp we were in for me to follow along after, and I thought if I didn't miss it that morning, I probably would that afternoon, and what I'd do then I didn't know.

"When you get to school, ask somebody to show you Miss Temple's office. She's the principal. Just tell her you're Fern Dequincey's little girl, and—"

"But, Mama. You're Mrs. Maddox."

"Yes, I am now. But Miss Temple will remember me by my name when I was a girl. Do you have your note from Miss Burns?"

I opened the cover of my tablet to make sure, and there it was, neat and clean in its own envelope, saying what grade I was in and that I was a good pupil and would be missed at Fourth Ward. "Yes'm."

I couldn't understand why Mama was making such a fuss about telling me what to do. I'd been finding my way to principals' offices since I'd started to school, without a note to my name before, and I wondered if her worrying meant this school was different somehow, that I'd do everything wrong or the note wouldn't count and I'd have to go through the whole long process of reading for Miss Temple and telling her how old I was and—

"I don't know whose room you'll be in. I suppose most of the teachers I had are dead and gone. Though I don't know. If Miss Temple's still alive and kicking, some of them may be, too. Anyhow, she'll tell you where to go, and you have cousins there of one degree or another, so it won't be completely strange to you. You'll make friends fast."

Only I didn't. There weren't any cousins in my room, and when I did meet some of them, they were nice to me the same way all the girls were: the important ones whose fathers owned prosperous farms or their own businesses, and whose mothers drove their own cars and got their names in the Beeville paper; the unimportant ones whose fathers clerked or tenant-farmed or straw-bossed at the gin or on the county roads, and whose mothers wore cotton dresses to church and counted themselves lucky to ride there in the family jalopy.

They all spoke to me in the halls or at the water fountain, and the unimportant ones let me sit by them in the lunchroom and sometimes invited me to jump rope or pop the whip. But it was an absentminded kind of niceness, grounded in the good manners drilled into all small town girls in those days, and prompted by reminders from some parents, at least, that shaky as my position was, I still belonged to an old family not yet without some ability to confer favors or exact vengeance.

I had nothing of brilliance or beauty to offer. Outside of reading and spelling, my grades were average. I couldn't sing or dance or play an instrument. I could recite poems, but since I'd never had lessons in elocution, my teacher felt I didn't know how to deliver a piece with the proper dramatic expression. My hair was as straight as ever, my face as plain, my clothes as shabby, some of which could've been said about many of the girls, important and unimportant alike. But the difference was, they shared a body of common experience closed to me.

They were born and raised in the same town their parents and grandparents had been born and raised in. They thought moving meant leaving one nice house for another nicer one a couple of streets over, or going from one tenant farm to another just like it a mile down the road. None of them had ever been farther away from home than San Antonio or Corpus, and most of them never beyond Kenedy or Cuero. They thought only Mexicans and gypsies lived in tents, and had no idea what being on the road was like, or living in an apartment in a big town.

I wasn't exactly unhappy there, being still in love with school then, but I would've been happier if Naomi could've been there with me. She had to go to the Lutheran Academy, though, to please her other grandparents, her daddy's people, because she was all they had left of their son, too—which would make her a wealthy woman someday, Aunt Eunice said, being the only heir of two generations of Burkett, and one of Schneider, money.

Aunt Hallie put her foot down about the Lutheran church, however. She said the Lutheran school might offer advantages the public school didn't, but the Lutheran religion couldn't hold a candle to the Baptist faith, let the Schneiders cuss, cry, beg, plead, and be damned as they chose. She said we were all born and bred Southern Baptists and that was the way we'd die, and they knew Naomi's mama had never changed her beliefs, in spite of all their underhanded attempts to get her to, so there was no reason for them to expect anything different from Naomi.

"My lord," Mama said. "What's keeping your Uncle Dan? We've been standing out here in this wind long enough for him to fetch the car back from the moon."

She had on her high heels and a hat and coat Aunt Millie had loaned her and was wearing rouge and lipstick and looked so nice and dressed up I felt like I was standing next to a stranger who might suddenly turn around and say, "Yes, little girl?" But then she leaned down and straightened the new pink cap Grandma had knitted for Martha May and turned back into herself and I wished it was Daddy driving up so he could see how pretty she was.

But it was only Uncle Dan, and we hurried to get in, Mama and Martha May in front, I in back. Behind Mama, though, not Uncle Dan, because that was my place in our own car, when my daddy was at the wheel, and Mama said, "What do you say to Uncle Dan?"

I felt the nickel, hard and smooth in the corner of my handkerchief, saw Daddy smiling at me plain as day, said, "Thank you," and began to cry and cry, like I was some little old baby.

"What on earth is the matter with you?" Mama said. "Are you sick?"

But if I said, 'I want my daddy,' what good would it do? If I said, 'I don't want a new sweater if Daddy has to go hungry to pay for it and I wouldn't want new shoes either if I could be brave enough to go barefooted and not care when the other kids made fun of me?' If I said, 'I hate Uncle Dan and I don't want his old nickel?'

"You stop that right now," Mama said. "You're going to get Martha May started. My goodness, here we are going to town to get you some new clothes, and you have money to spend. Why, when your Aunt Millie and I were little girls—"

"Leave her be," Uncle Dan said. "Trying to talk to a bellering youngun's like trying to talk to a mule. They don't neither one of them understand a word you say."

I'd never heard him talk to the mules at all, except to cuss them and threaten to poleaxe them, whatever that was, so I didn't see how he could tell whether a mule understood or not. But thinking about it helped me quit crying, and by the time we turned onto the hottop, when I was sure Mama wasn't looking, I wiped my nose and eyes on the sleeve of my sweater, because my handkerchief was too nice to use for something like that.

Grandma had made me three of them, out of some scraps she found in her piece goods box. My Sunday one was edged in lace and they all had little blue forget-me-nots embroidered in one corner, and I wouldn't have blown my nose on one of them for anything in the world.

The school at Robb's Prairie was the first one I'd ever gone to that had hygiene inspection. Every morning right after the Pledge of Allegiance, whichever one of the important girls was acting as monitor for the week would go by every desk, tally book in hand, and check to see whether we had clean fingernails and a clean handkerchief. Anybody who didn't got a black mark against his deportment.

All the boys said it was sissy to have clean fingernails and carry a handkerchief and they wouldn't do it no matter how many bad marks they got. But all the girls took it so seriously, I was desperate enough not to be the only girl in the room, in the whole school so far as I knew, without a handkerchief, that I broke my own strict rule never to ask Mama for something I knew we couldn't afford.

We weren't susceptible to colds, and had never even heard of an allergy. The rare times we did have to blow our noses, we used a torn off piece of old rag we could throw away. But I couldn't take something like that to school, and didn't even have to say so, because before I got half-way through explaining it to Mama, Grandma said she didn't want Hallie throwing a fit about me providing talk for all the busybodies in town, so she sat up late after supper and made me one for the next day, with the promise of two more to come.

I liked to see it there every morning beside my outspread fingers, soft and white and neatly folded with the flower corner up, knowing it was as pretty as anyone's, including Jane Bradshaw's, even if she did wear silk socks and peach colored rayon step-ins and a different dress for every day of the week. My Sunday one, especially when Aunt Millie dabbed a little of her lilac toilet water on it, outshone even Lottie's and Dottie's pink ones that matched their taffeta hair ribbons, and they were still Change of Life Babies, no matter how fancy they dressed, which I knew for a fact, because Naomi heard Aunt Hallie call them that to Grandma once.

Naomi said that when she asked Aunt Hallie what a Change of Life Baby was, Aunt Hallie pretended it was just a saying people had for babies born late in a lady's life when her other children were nearly grown. But there was more to it than that, because Aunt Hallie also said it wasn't something to go around talking about and she didn't ever want to hear that expression cross Naomi's lips again.

"But I don't think telling you is going around talking about it," Naomi said, "even if it did have to cross my lips. You're my best friend, and best friends tell each other everything."

That made me feel bad, because I knew one Secret I could never tell anybody, not even her. But I thought I ought to do as much of my part as I could, so I did tell her how scared I was that Daddy might never come for us and we'd be left behind forever, the way Ethel Ruth and them had been—not because Daddy would ever desert us, but because something bad might happen to him and he couldn't come.

"Oh, you don't have to worry about that," she said. "He'll come. Grandmother says he will."

Mama was always saying it, too— "When your daddy comes," or "When Will sends for us," but—"How does she know?"

"Well, she's very smart. Even in business, Uncle Lafe says, and he ought to know about people being smart if he's a professor."

"Yes, but—how can she be sure?"

"All I know is, she said when everybody's finally all settled down and things are going smooth, he'll come back and drag you all off and we'll never see you again."

"Oh."

"She said it never fails."

"Daddy doesn't drag us anywhere. We want to be with him."

"Oh, she knows that. But she doesn't want you all to leave, because Grandpa's going to Take To His Bed one of these days, she says, and if Fern's a blessing now, think what she'll be then. She can't come out here every day, she said, and Eunice can't, and Effie won't—"

"I thought Aunt Hallie liked us."

"She does."

"Then why does she say bad things about Daddy?"

"She didn't mean anything bad, Mavis. I want you all to stay, too, and I wouldn't ever say anything bad about Uncle Will."

"I guess what it is, is, relatives only like you when you're doing something for them. That's the way it was with my Grandpa Maddox, I know. He quit liking us the minute Daddy said he couldn't keep working for him unless he gave him his share of the partnership money. But he wouldn't give Daddy one extra dime, and went out and got him a new wife, at His Age, Mama said, and asked Daddy how he liked them apples, and Daddy didn't even have any apples.

"Of course, I don't think he liked us very much to start with, because we never did get to live in one of his little shotguns and have a garden and chickens and things. We had to live in his attic and—," but that was skirting close to

the Secret Mama made me swear never to tell and said she
wouldn't admit to on the rack— "and Daddy never had time
to work on his own business on the side, so we came here
and Daddy went back on the road, even if he had already
sold our tent, and—I don't care if I do go to Hell, I hate relatives."

"But we're not relatives, remember. We're blood first
cousins and eternal best friends forever. We took a sacred
pledge on that, Mavis."

I wished I'd never let her talk me into making that
pledge. I'd tried to explain to her that once you moved away
from somebody you couldn't be best friends anymore. You
could still think about them, and remember the good times
you'd had together, but even if you met again, in some town
or campground somewhere and talked about old times, it
wasn't the same. Too Much Water Under the Bridge, Mama
always said.

When Uncle Dan pulled up in front of the post office,
we all got out and smoothed our clothes and he said, "I want
to stop in here a minute, then I got to go to Peavy's and fill a
list for Ma, and go by the bank." And the whole time he was
talking, he was glancing over at Red Reilly's Pool Hall and
Domino Parlor and glancing back real quick, like that wasn't
what he was doing at all. "I don't reckon I'll have my business tended to till dinner time, anyhow, if that suits you."

"That'll be fine," Mama said. "Where do you want us to
meet you?"

"Better make it down at the depot. I always like to jaw
with Clinton awhile, and if I do get held up somewhere, you
and the younguns'll have a place to sit. Less you'd rather
walk over to Hallie's."

"No, we'll be at the depot, at twelve sharp."

He hitched up his pants and took one last look at Red
Reilly's and went in the post office. Mama brushed the dust
off her coat where it had blown against the car when she got
out, and picked up Martha May and said, "Now you stay

right beside me, Mavis. I don't want you darting out in front of somebody and getting run over."

There were lots of cars and wagons and people around, but I'd crossed far busier streets walking to and from school when we lived in big towns like Pampa and Paris and Amarillo and Angelo, and I hadn't got run over yet, but I just said, "Yes'm," and stayed at her side all the way across to Hermann's Drygoods, our wavering reflections in the big glass windows coming to meet us through pleated lengths of plaid gingham and a life-sized paper doll of Buster Brown holding a pair of shiny new shoes.

FIFTEEN

"Something sturdy," Mama said. "She's hard on shoes, and I'll tell you straight out, Irene, they have to do her for Sunday and everyday, too, so an oxford of some kind, but a little on the dressy side, if you have anything like that."

Irene was Jane Bradshaw's mama and an old school friend of my mama's. She wore lots of rouge and lipstick and had her eyebrows arched higher and skinnier than Aunt Millie's. Her hair was marcelled in front and shingled in back and when she leaned forward, you could smell Cashmere Bouquet soap and see the wrinkles in her neck.

"I've got just the thing," she said, "and I have them in her size in both colors." She took some boxes off a shelf and rustled under the tissue paper to bring out one black shoe and one brown one, and they were the exact same kind Jane wore to school.

"I think you'll like these. The leather's good quality, and the patent tongue and trim here where the laces go dresses them up a lot."

"But do they hold up good?"

"Well, I bought Jane a pair to start school in this past September, and I haven't had to have them re-soled or stitched up or anything."

"I don't know. I just wonder if that patent won't crack bad."

"Not if you rub a little lard into it once a week and buff it good."

Mama kept turning the brown one over and over, holding it out of Martha May's reach, then finally said, "Are they expensive?"

Irene laughed, snorting a little, and said, "Lord girl, I couldn't buy them if they were."

I knew that wasn't true. Jane not only had five different school dresses, she took dancing lessons and elocution lessons and had a string of seed pearls to wear with her Sunday dress, not to mention the rayon step-ins and silk socks.

"One seventy-nine," Irene said. "I know that's not cheap, but for a good shoe that'll last till she outgrows them, they're a bargain."

Mama said, "Which color do you like best, Mavis?"

I thought about Daddy, and then about how the patent on Jane's brown shoes flashed in the sun like new pennies when she skipped and said, "The brown. I like the brown ones best."

"Yes, I think I'm partial to the brown ones, too."

"Okay," Irene said, "let's try them on. They're your size, but we want to be sure they feel right."

Mama mashed on them to see where my big toe came to, and had me turn my back to her so she could see how they fit around the ankles, and said, "Do they pinch anywhere? Be sure, now, because we can try another size if they do."

"Walk around a little," Irene said. "That's the best way. But stay on the rug."

I walked over to the long mirror that was propped up against one of the columns, the slick soles slipping on the narrow strip of rug. Nothing hurt and they looked beautiful and if I stood just right, no more than an inch of my black cotton stockings showed.

I hated those stockings like poison. Not just because they were thick and ugly, but because they were a sure sign, if an additional one were needed, that you were not among the girls who counted. Long after those girls had gone to wearing socks, anklets they were called, girls like me were still wearing those long rusty-black or muddy-brown lisle stockings pinned to the legs of our bloomers or held up by garters cut from old inner tubes. They were cheap and wore like iron and did provide some warmth in winter, though except for the coldest days, most of us rolled them down into dark, sausage like coils around our skinny ankles. But that didn't hide their color or the doughnut shape they made. Up or down, they were recognized for what they were, and so were we.

I walked back to Mama and she said, "Well, how do they feel?"

"Fine. They feel fine."

She and Irene stood up and Irene said, "Do you want to wear them or carry them with you, Mavis?"

But I didn't make decisions like that, so I looked at Mama, and she said, "Oh, let her wear them. But go ahead and box the old ones. She can still get some wear out of them around the house."

Irene said, "All righty," and took her sales pad off her belt and fixed the carbon and wrote down the shoes and how much they cost and said, "Now, is there anything else I can show you? We have some good prices on all our winter merchandise."

Mama looked at me and turned away real fast and said, "Yes, she needs a sweater, Irene, and—and a couple of pairs of socks. Not silk. Cotton'll do. A red pair and a blue one."

They would match my dresses. The red gingham I was wearing and the blue print Grandma was letting the hem down on. I would go to Sunday School the next day, not in the shameful stockings, but in socks that matched my dress. In new shoes, in a new sweater.

Irene picked up the socks in my size, and they looked almost as nice as the silk ones, all flat and creased down the middle, with the tops folded over just so. Then we went to the counter where the sweaters were, and a tall, thin old man in a loose, dark suit, with skin the color of the tissue paper in my box, came up to us and said, "Fern? Is that you?" and Mama went as still as the people on the screen in a picture show when the reel sticks.

"Why haven't you been over to see me and Mama?" he said. "We've been waiting for a visit ever since we heard you were Home."

Mama turned to him and said, "Hello, Mr. Papa. How are you?"

He shrugged a sad, sighing kind of smile and said, "Are these your children?"

"Yes, Mr. Papa. This is Mavis Marie, my oldest, and Martha May, the baby. Say hello to Mr. Hermann, girls."

I said hello and Martha May ducked her head into Mama's skirt and he looked at us for what felt like a long time. Then he reached over and touched Martha May's cheek and I was scared he would touch mine, too, or pat me on the head, but he only said, "They're fine looking young ladies. Pretty like their mama."

"Well, they're good girls," Mama said. "How is Mrs. Mama?"

He shrugged that same sad smile and said, "Our old trouble never leaves her any peace. A mother's heart—" and he bowed his head before the awfulness of whatever it was. I could see the customers looking at us and whispering, the clerks moving closer, pretending to straighten the counters, Irene holding the socks and the shoe box up to show she had business there, had a right to be there, her face serious and important, Mama's set to endure.

He cleared his throat and said, "A little visit from you and your babies would be a treat for her, Fern. I think she'd bake you some strudel."

"That would be nice, Mr. Papa, but it's very hard for me to get away."

"Yes, I told Mama that." He felt the knot in his tie and let his hand slide down his lapel and said, "But if you're Home for good?"

"Oh, no. No, I'm only here to help look after Grandpa for awhile."

"And how is the old gentleman?"

"About the same, thank you."

"Ah."

Mama picked Martha May up and said, "I'm sorry I have to rush. Give Mrs. Mama my regards and tell her I'll do my best to get over to see her before we leave."

He patted her arm and said, "Yes, take care of yourself, Fern," and turned away, everybody moving aside for him, Irene's eyes asking Mama something Mama refused to answer, so she let out a deep breath and said, "Well!" and started looking through the sweaters. "An eight or a ten? They're nice ones, Fern, on sale for fifty-nine cents, down from ninety-eight, which makes them a good buy. They're a little heavy for this time of year, but our mornings are going to be chilly for some time yet. If you get a ten, she could probably wear it next year, too."

Mama motioned for her to be quiet and set Martha May down on the edge of the counter and said, "I was hoping he wouldn't be here. I was hoping he'd be at the bank or the post office or someplace where I could get in and out without having to see him."

"You aren't still blaming yourself after all these years, are you?"

"I never did blame myself, Irene."

"Well after all, Fern, Percy did—"

"What Percy did was of his choosing, not mine. But I've always thought a lot of the Hermann Seniors and I hate to know they're so—" She picked up one of the sweaters, her hands trembling, and said, "Try a ten on her, I guess. Which color do you want, Mavis, red or brown?"

"Red."

"Let's slip it on," Irene said, so I took off my old sweater and put on the new one and when Irene turned the sleeves back to make cuffs, it wasn't very much too big at all.

"That'll do," Mama said. "Let her wear it and sack the old one."

"Is there anything else you'd like to look at? Dresses? Underwear? We have—"

"No, this'll be all. We've got to get on over to the drug-store to see Millie."

We went to the main counter and Irene put everything into a sack and wrote some more on her pad and added it up and said, "That'll be two fifty-seven."

Then she wrapped the three dollar bills Mama gave her inside the pages she tore from her pad and put it into a brass tube that made a bell go ping-ping-ping as it went whoosh-ing up to the mezzanine where a lady behind a big cash register rang up the sale and sent the correct change and one page pinging and whooshing back down to us.

Irene handed Mama her change and put the receipt in the sack and handed it to me and said, "We sure appreciate the business, Fern, and it was good seeing you and your kid-does. I keep thinking I'll give you a call some night so we can talk over old times, but seems like when I get home—"

"I know how it is," Mama said. "I'm worn out myself by the time evening comes."

"Well, anyhow, thanks again, girl, and you all come back."

Mama smiled a tight little smile and said, "So long, Irene," and walked off so fast I could hardly keep up with her in my slippery new shoes.

SIXTEEN

The sidewalks were crowded from the walls of the buildings out to the bumpers of the cars nosed up to the curb, where knots of men leaned on doors or fenders, some silent, some talking, some nodding or lifting a hand to passersby, some paring their nails with pocket knives, all of them lean and leathery from hard work and hard times.

I wanted to look in the window of McCrory's, where I'd hoped to spend my nickel, in spite of how I'd felt about it earlier. But there were so many people around us and Mama was hurrying us so, all I could see as we went by was a blurred image of my new red sweater and my straight hair blowing like sticks in the wind.

We crossed a side street to the drugstore through the midst of a Mexican family and some high school boys in their maroon and blue football jackets, a couple of big girls walking behind them, giggling. A colored man with a napkin-covered tray from the hotel moved aside to let us step up on the curb, and the circle of young men around the door shuffled over out of our way, trailing cigarette smoke and the smell of Rose hair oil.

We pushed open the door, the bell tinkling behind us, and Aunt Millie looked up from some cigar boxes she was opening and said, "Why hi, honey. Where y'all been?"

"At Hermann's, Millie, right where I told you we'd be.

Gee, it's nice and warm in here. That wind's getting colder by the minute."

Aunt Millie admired my New Clothes and held Martha May while Mama got her coat off, then said, "Let's have a coke. My treat."

"No," Mama said. *"My* treat. And no arguments, Millie. I guess I can spend fifteen cents on foolishness once in a coon's age without—no, we'd have been here sooner, but Irene Bradshaw waited on us, and—she's a good clerk, I'll give her that, and got right down to business once I convinced her I wasn't there to visit. But I swear, she looks forty if she looks a day. I know I don't look like a kid anymore, either, but she's sure gone downhill from the girl we used to chum around with."

"Well, Irene's got a hard row to hoe, poor girl, being a widow with a child to support and a sickly mama to look after. She works in that store all day and goes home and sews half the night. Makes all her own clothes and every stitch Jane wears and takes in sewing from the public, too. I don't see how she holds up to it."

"I don't see why she does. They live in her mama's house, so she's not out any rent, and she's got a Regular Job."

"Yes, but you know how it is, honey, living in a little town like this, having to keep up appearances. And Irene's ambitious to pave the way for Jane to marry a rich boy— here, you all lay your things over here out of the way." She put Mama's coat and Martha May's cap and sweater on the stool behind her counter and said, "Mavis, don't you want to take your sweater off?"

"No'm."

"I don't blame you, bless your heart. That red looks real good on you."

"At least unbutton it," Mama said. "You'll get too hot in this steam heat."

We went over to the fountain, a long white marble counter with high stools in front of it that turned any way you wanted to go and had a brass rail running beneath them for you to rest your feet on.

Aunt Millie introduced us to Zip and Opaline and gave Zip our order. He was the soda jerk and jack-of-all-trades, he told Mama, and winked at her bold as you please when she handed him three nickels, looking like a picture in a magazine in his white cap and jacket and black bow tie. Opaline was the colored lady who warmed the soup and made the sandwiches and stacked the dirty dishes in a tub under her side of the counter. She petted Martha May and smiled at me and went to wait on some other people while Zip drew our cokes, and when he served them to us, on little paper doilies, mine had a candied cherry in it.

"Oh, you shouldn't have," Mama said. "I only paid for plain ones."

He shrugged and winked again and said, "What the heck? Even Old Man Rathgaber won't miss one cherry. You ain't a kid but once, I always say."

The cokes were a beautiful reddish brown, full of tiny, icy bubbles that stung your nose, and I sipped mine as slow as I could, saving the cherry for last and being careful not to slurp or bend my straw.

"I wish I had a cigarette," Mama said. "Mr. Hermann had to show up right before we left, and damn it if I didn't call him Mr. Papa and ask after Mrs. Mama."

"Well, isn't that what we've always called them?"

"Yes, when we were kids and they were buying friends for Percy, but—"

"Why, Fern. It was only a respectful way of showing affection to our elders. Think of all the parties they gave us, the hayrides and picnics—"

"Yes, just what I said. Buying friends for Percy. And I'm not a kid anymore. I'm grown and married now and have children of my own, and I don't owe them—do you have any cigarettes or not?"

"Mavis, run look in my purse, honey, and bring my

cigarettes and matches. It's there on the shelf under my register."

"He looked like a poor old ghost, and made me so nervous I could hardly keep my mind on what I was doing."

"I know. He wanders in here sometimes, and—thanks, honey."

She and Mama lit their cigarettes and she said, "He didn't mention Percy, did he?"

"No, thank God, and neither did I, I'm here to tell you. What could I have said? 'I'm sorry your son blew his brains out all over the bathroom?'"

"Fern!"

"Well, that's what he did."

"I know, honey, but—"

"Listen, Millie, Will and I had been married over a year when that happened. I was a thousand miles from here."

"You were in El Paso. That's where I wrote you about the funeral."

I didn't remember El Paso. But I did remember stopping at the springs in Balmorhea on the way back from there one Fourth of July. We sat along the edge of the big irrigation canal with a crowd of other people that had pulled off the road, everybody laughing and talking, dangling their feet in the cool water, splashing at each other, dancing in the street that night under strings of colored lights, passing the hat for the three-man band.

"Well, that's close enough to a thousand miles, Millie, believe me, and I didn't have anything to do with it and I wish people would quit hinting around that I did."

"You broke off your engagement to him."

"After three miserable weeks of a mess I never would have got myself into in the first place if Mama and Papa and the Hermanns hadn't tormented me into it. You know that. And when he threatened to kill poor old Fiver Sheridan just for asking me to dance—"

"Poor old Fiver's right. He lit out for San 'Tonia the next day before sun up."

136

"Well, I'll tell you this for sure, Percy was lucky he wasn't dealing with Will Maddox. Will would've called his brag. No, Millie, there was something bad wrong with that boy, even when we were all little kids in grammar school."

"He was a good looking devil, though, and he gave you that gorgeous ring."

"I didn't want his ring. I didn't want him. I didn't want any part of that whole wretched business of the Hermanns setting me up to save something that couldn't be saved, while Mama and Papa were going around seeing dollar signs—lord!"

"They have always had an eye out for a buck, haven't they? But I think Papa worked his way up from such a hard-scrabble life that once he got away and began to make a little money, he just couldn't bring himself to turn loose of any of it."

"That's no excuse for Mama. She never did without anything when she was growing up, and she's as tightfisted as he is."

"Well, maybe coming in between Hallie and Eunice like she did, and both of them making such good marriages—"

"There's nothing wrong with being a barber. And Papa made enough money that we shouldn't have had to—no, they're just stingy down to the marrow, both of them."

"If you think things were tight when we were girls, you should've lived with them like I did after Papa lost the barbershop in '30 and we moved to San 'Tonia and Mama had to start taking in boarders."

"No ma'am! I bless the day Will came through this one-horse burg and took me out of it. I'd have left sooner or later, anyhow. I'd set my mind to that my last year of school when Grandma and Grandpa had to buy my graduation dress."

"I wish I'd had that much gumption, at least after we got to San 'Tonia. Maybe Benny and I would still be together. But every time we mentioned moving to a place of our own, they'd start in about how much cheaper we could live with them, and how much they needed us, and—and then Benny went out for a paper one evening and never came back."

"You had enough gumption to get out of San 'Tonia then. I don't see why you don't have enough to get out of here now. Go to Corpus or Houston or someplace where you can have your own apartment, if it's no more than a light housekeeping room. Get a job where you can meet new people and have a life of your own."

"I just don't seem to have the nerve. I think about it, a lot. But when it comes right down to doing it—"

"I don't know why you're so silly. You don't have to answer to a living soul. How can you stand being stuck in a place where you have to sneak around and fib every time you have a date?"

"Why, Fern. I don't have dates. Benny and I aren't divorced, we're just separated. And I don't call going for an innocent little drive, or having a late supper at some perfectly respectable roadhouse a date."

"I don't care what you call it. That's not the point, anyhow. The point is—oh, don't pay any attention to me. At least you can leave if you ever decide you want to. I'm the one that's stuck."

"Don't say that. You know Will'll send for you all as soon as he can."

"Yes, I know, but—what time is it getting to be? I don't want to keep Dan waiting."

"Oh, you're way early. It's only a quarter of eleven, and he never leaves the pool hall till straight up and down noon. I have to get back to work, but you all are welcome to stay."

Mama jumped up. "You won't get in any trouble for sitting here with us so long, will you?"

"No, no. Mr. Rathgaber doesn't mind if I slip over here for a coke when I'm not busy. He ought not to, the hours I work. But he'll be back from the bank soon and the early lunch crowd'll be coming in and the second push of country people to pick up their medicine, so I need to get back to my counter. You all stay, though, Fern, you're not in the way. Or is Hallie expecting you to wait there?"

"No, we're going down to the depot so Martha May can get down and run around awhile. I'm afraid she might break something in here, and I don't feel up to Hallie today. I love her, and she's good in her way, but she's always pumping me about Will and when he plans to send for us and saying we ought to think about settling down here.

"I'll tell you, Millie, if I'd had any idea this stay was going to drag on the way it has, I never would've come. I don't care if Will did sell all our camping gear, we could've managed somehow. Families ought to stick together regardless. It's better to starve if you have to, than—oh, forget it. Finish that coke, Mavis, we've got to go. I don't want to chance holding Dan up."

I had finished everything but the cherry, including every last grain of the crushed ice, and the only reason I still had my head bent over the glass was I didn't want Mama to notice me and quit talking about Percy. He would've been my daddy if she'd married him, and that would've made Mr. Papa my grandpa. I wondered if he would've let me have things free at Hermann's since it belonged to him. Probably not. My Grandpa Maddox had never let me have anything out of his store. And besides, I didn't want any daddy except the one I had. I just wished he'd hurry up and come get us.

Mama said, "Mavis, we're ready," so I tipped the glass up and let the cherry roll into my mouth, all sticky sweet and chewy, and we told Aunt Millie bye, and walked out into a wind so strong we had to lean back against it to keep our feet. Even then, it pushed us along in gusts that sent us into a kind of stiff-legged run every few steps. People coming toward us were leaning into it, clutching their hats and parcels, screwing up their faces against the flying dust, staggering some, just as we were, and Mama said, "Look at that sky. The bottom's going to drop out any minute."

We crossed East Pecan under low, rolling masses of blue-black clouds, passed the hatchery and the feed store, a vacant lot, the little unpainted shotguns where the town Mexicans lived, and crossed Railroad Avenue to the depot as it suddenly turned pinky-white in the first flash of lightning that cracked like a hundred cannon and shook the ground beneath our feet.

"Run, run," Mama said. "It's going to pour."

A man stood in the depot door, holding it open for us, yelling, "Get in here. Get in here. It's fixing to rain pitchforks and puppy dog tails."

It hit just as we ducked inside, and Mama said, "I never thought we'd make it. Hello, Mr. Bostick. We'd like to wait here for Uncle Dan if it's all right with you."

"Why, you're welcome here any time, Fern. It's good to see you. How you getting along?"

It was quiet out of the wind, dark except for the light coming from the ticket window and the big wood stove at the end of the room between the doors marked 'Ladies' and 'Gents.'

"I've got some coffee back here on the hot plate. How about a cup?"

"Well, I—yes, thank you, I believe I will."

"And the young lady with you?'

"Oh, I'm sorry, Mr. Bostick. I don't know where my manners are today. This is Mavis, my oldest, and this—" she stood Martha May on the floor and took off her cap—"is my baby, Martha May. Would you like a cup of coffee, Mavis?"

The big stove had the room so hot, I even took off my sweater, but the rain made me want some coffee anyhow, so I said, "Yes'm."

Mr. Bostick rubbed his hands together. "Mighty fine. Two coffees coming up. I got canned cream and plenty of sugar, so name your poison."

"Black'll be fine, thanks."

When we laid our wraps neatly across the back of one of the benches, I made sure my handkerchief-wrapped nickel was still stuffed well down in the corner of my pocket, glad I'd been unable to spend it in that greedy moment passing

McCrory's. I had so many nice new things, it was wrong to want something more, especially when Daddy—if I couldn't send it to him, at least I could put it in the collection plate the next day. That way, it would go to some mission in a far-off land to help buy a Bible for a little native boy or girl who didn't have anything.

Mama and Mr. Bostick stood by the window overlooking the loading platform, drinking their coffee and watching the rain. I sat on a bench with my cup, so I could keep an eye on Martha May sidestepping up and down its length, and remembered a tourist cabin we'd come to somewhere late at night after a long, cold drive without any supper. I couldn't remember the name of the town, or what the court looked like, or going from the car to the cabin, only the bright blue hissing flame of the warming stove and Mama waking me up to eat a piece of hot pone.

When the clock struck the half hour, Martha May reached up toward it and said, "Tick tock, hickory dock," and everybody laughed and Mr. Bostick said, "I wasn't much bigger than you, little lady, when the depot was built and that clock was mounted back in '78. They was a German fella set it up. He travelled around this whole country taking care of clocks, for the railroad and the banks, everybody. I remember—"

But I quit listening. Purged of sin or not, I still wanted a train to come in with Daddy on it, or for him to send us a ticket so we could ride one to wherever he was, all dressed up in our good clothes, waving to people along the way.

The front door banged open and Uncle Dan stomped in, his hat dripping rain, his clothes and boots dark with it.

"Come on over here to the stove and warm yourself," Mr. Bostick said. "You look like a orphan of the storm."

"I ain't got time, Clint. We got to get on back to the place in a hurry. This rain's going to be turning into sleet any minute." But he shook hands with Mr. Bostick and took off his hat and slapped it against his leg, while Mama got her coat on and began getting Martha May into her cap and sweater and I finished buttoning mine.

"How'd you find the boys?" Mr. Bostick said.

"Oh, fair to middling. Same old poor-mouthing as usual." He looked all around the room, then, and said, "I thought maybe Henry would come by."

Mr. Bostick cleared his throat and said, "Well, Emmy ain't been too peart this past week."

Uncle Dan started to say something else to him, but looked at Mama instead, and said, "You all ready?"

She said, "Yes," and turned to Mr. Bostick and said, "Thank you kindly for the coffee."

"You're mighty welcome, Fern. You and the girls come back any time."

Uncle Dan held the door for us and we ran out into the rain, Mama holding Martha May's head down on her shoulder, I hugging my sack to my chest, Uncle Dan looking more sour than usual, and by the time we hit the outskirts of town, the rain was beginning to turn white and gritty, sticking along the edges of the windshield wipers.

"Son-of-a-buck," Uncle Dan said. "It's going to freeze sure as shooting."

"Maybe it won't be a hard one," Mama said. "This late in the year it—" but before she could finish, the slush turned to hail, banging and bouncing off the car so loud Martha May covered her ears and the rest of us pulled our heads down into our shoulders. Then it stopped as quick as it had started, changing into a fine sleet so thick we could hardly see the road.

Uncle Dan tapped the brake and shifted into first and said, "Everybody brace theirself," and we went so slow I was scared the car was going to choke down and I wanted to tell him to go faster, to keep moving. That was the first rule of the road, especially when you were in danger of being stranded out in the middle of nowhere, low on gas, maybe, Daddy talking the car on in.

We passed the whitened cedars in front of the Anderson

place and he said, "We ain't got far to go, now, but this windshield's so fogged I can't see nothing. I got to have something else to wipe it off with. My bandana's about soaked." He began tapping the brake again, slewing the rear end around, and I remembered the main reason Daddy always helped the same greenhorns who aggravated him so much was because they put everybody else at risk, too.

I pulled my handkerchief out of my pocket, pressed the missionary nickel for Luck, and handed it over the seat to him. "Here, Uncle Dan," I said. "Use this."

SEVENTEEN

Lost in that long ago snowstorm, in that long ago little girl's sacrificial bid to be the trooper her daddy would've wanted her to be, it took me a second to come back to early summer sunshine and Naomi standing at the screen saying, "Are you still mad?"

"I'm not mad, Naomi, but I do want you to get it clear that when Mama took that paregoric down to the quarters, Grandma and Uncle Dan did try to stop her. You weren't in that hot kitchen that evening. You didn't watch your mama standing up to people who had the power to call disaster down on her. You didn't have to listen to Millie's crying and Dan's cussing and watch Grandma turn into a little stone gnome of disapproval."

"Now Mavis, I can't believe they cared that much about a dose of paregoric."

"Not if it'd been for anyone else, they wouldn't have. But the point is, they didn't care about that baby. Oh, not out of deliberate cruelty. I know that. But they were true, old time farmers, Naomi, and everything was a product to them—plants, animals, people—certainly some Mexican hand or his kid, and once you lost your value as a product, they plowed you under, or put a bullet in your brain, or simply walked away and let nature take its course."

"Don't you think you're being awfully hard on them?"

"No, I think you don't want to hear anything unpleasant about them."

"But you make them sound like monsters."

"No, they were good people according to their own light. God knows what would've happened to us if they hadn't been. But if I live to be a hundred, I'll never forget Mama standing there in that worn-out, washed-out old dress—oh hell. It's the courage in people that breaks your heart."

"Yes. Do you want to eat a bite now?"

"No, I want to go to the cemetery."

"Let's at least finish our tea."

"We can take it with us."

"All right, if that's what you want to do."

"Did you talk to Billy?"

"Yes. He went ahead and bought the option on that condo—now don't fly off the handle again. He said for you not to worry about it. He's got it for thirty days, and if you decide you don't want it at the end of that time, he can flip it and make money on it."

"Well, that's good. I wouldn't want him to take any kind of loss trying to do me a favor. Even if I do wish he'd forget the favors and let me make up my own mind about what I'm going to do."

"The thing is, though, this real estate boom's not going to last forever, Mavis. If you don't make your move soon, you may never be able to unload this place."

"I haven't said yet that I want to unload it. We've lived here—this is my home, Naomi."

"I've heard you say a hundred times you've lived in so many places you never felt really at home anywhere."

"And that's true, if you're talking about *home* home. I left so many bits and pieces of myself along the way—" on April lighted prairies when the grass was first grade green, beside dirt roads where the sundown wind whispered the sand across dead weeds, atop some sun-beat sky-sung rocky hill—"that sometimes at night when Paul was able to sleep

145

awhile, I'd dream of just pitching the cat and one suitcase in the car and heading out."

"That'd be fun, the way Jane Long hates to ride. But why don't you put her in the kennel and go on and do it, if that's what you want?"

"Oh, Naomi. I said it was a dream. I've changed. The world's changed. That's all dead and gone now."

She put more ice in the glasses and refilled them and said, "A trip of some kind might not be a bad idea, though. If you could get someone to look after things here for awhile, the Cantus, maybe, since you say they're such good neighbors—why don't you go to California and visit your Aunt Baby?"

"No. We never were very close, and we haven't even been on speaking terms since she changed her name. When she quit being Mrs. Beryl (Baby) Walker and turned into Ms. Mary (Baby) Walker, that just split the blanket.

"I hate that Ms. crap. There's something so sickeningly coy about it. Why should a woman want to disguise the fact that's she's married? Or has been? Or never was? What's wrong with the old way when your title was public and your private life your own? Why take a mule's name and then go around hinting that you've hopped into your share of beds? Or openly live with some jerk and support him while he's— pardon me for barfing—finding himself? Whose business is it? Who cares?"

"I admit there's an element of prurience in it, but—I didn't know Baby's real name was Mary. You named Mary Fern after her, didn't you? When everybody thought—"

"I never said I'd named her after Grandma. That was something you all assumed on your own hook."

"I'd say it was a natural assumption, wouldn't you?"

"Well, I meant it to honor Grandma, too, if that makes you feel any better, because I knew it would please Mama, but I don't see what difference it makes who she was named after."

"I just never realized you were that fond of Baby."

"I wasn't fond of her. I admired her. She was different from any other woman I'd ever known. Her life seemed so big to me. Flights in the night stuff. Fighting for the right against all odds. She was a kind of hero to me, somebody out of a movie or a book."

"Yet you couldn't forgive her calling herself Ms.?"

"I could have if other things had been different. I wouldn't have liked it. I'd have still thought it cheapened something that ought not to be cheapened, but I'd have accepted it, Baby being Baby.

"By the time she did it, though, I was so bitter about the way she'd treated us when Daddy was dying, that she and everything she stood for, just turned to ashes in my mouth."

"You mean you would've taken money from her when you wouldn't from me?"

"No, no. The bills, keeping the house going, that was our responsibility. We didn't expect anyone to take over any of that. But the little things, the little gestures that would've meant so much to Daddy, to all of us—no, it's all well and good to be out battling on the side of the angels if that's what you feel called to do. But when you get so absorbed in universals you forget your own flesh and blood—

"I was teaching on an emergency certificate, remember, drawing a sub's salary, going to school at night. Paul was teaching at the high school, for the pittance they paid even full time teachers then, working on his master's at night. Billy was still trying to get his business off the ground. Martha May had her hands full with that no account husband of hers and working double shifts waiting tables.

"Our family doctor was good to us, but the specialists— not many of them are ever bashful about asking for their fees, and of course, hospitals never are."

"And I had to just stand by helpless."

"Oh, you helped in a million ways, Naomi. Coming to visit so often, taking him for rides in that flashy convertible, bringing him all those good wines and the special things he liked to eat—roll mops. Lord, how he loved those horrible-looking roll mops.

"And that's what Baby could've done. I realize she couldn't bat back and forth between San Diego and Fort Worth all the time. But she could've come at least once, and she could've sent him some kind of package occasionally, a card, a letter, a five-dollar bill once in awhile. He liked having a little money in his pocket even if he was dying.

"But I guess there's nothing glamorous enough, or earthshaking enough in the day-to-day getting through a long drawn out illness. You know, it's so mundane being worried sick about how you're going to pay the bills and keep the place up and the clothes washed and ironed and meals on the table and the patient comfortable, while you're dragging back and forth to the doctor and the radiology lab and being worn to a nub driving between here and Fort Worth every weekend, frantic that Mama was ruining her health, too, counting pennies all the way—thank God at least I didn't have to worry about money with Paul."

"You wouldn't have had to worry about it with Uncle Will, if you had let me—"

"We couldn't, Naomi. I've told you. There's no use talking about it anymore. They're at peace now, and—let's go."

We walked out to the portecochere where my car was always parked, and she said, "Why don't we move your car and go in mine?"

"No, leave yours in the garage. There's no point in going to all that trouble. But you drive, and don't forget it's a '69 Chevvie, not a new Jag."

"Why don't you buy a new car, Mavis? Sell this one and that old clunker of Paul's and buy yourself some decent transportation, for heaven's sake."

"There's nothing wrong with my car, and I'm going to give Paul's to Raymond Cantu."

"But, Mavis—"

"I am not going to buy a new car."

"*Why?*"

"Because, as Mary Fern says, I have a Depression mind-set. I don't ever spend money when I don't have to."

"But you're giving it away if you just hand a tradable car over to that boy."

"His name's Raymond, Naomi, and he's working and going to school, so he can make good use of it. Don't start nagging me about the cars. You have enough to do to nag me about the house."

We drove out into the hot afternoon, the ice belling in the glasses reminding me of the summer days before Paul left for the navy, when we drove the back roads drinking Lone Star out of iced-down longnecks, listening to country music—

No, what Grandma and Dan cared about was that Mama had gone against their wishes, Biting The Hand That Fed Her, as much a sin in her eyes as theirs, which they well knew, and which was probably the reason they didn't force her to an either/or decision. Because they said if she was willing to set some strange notion they'd never understand above an obligation everyone understood, she had to have some justification for it, though they'd go to their graves wondering what it was.

Outwardly, we went about our lives the way we always had. Inwardly, we walked around on tiptoe, pretending nothing had changed, when everybody knew something had. Mama would never go back on her stand. She had risked too much for it; it meant too much to her; in a way I didn't understand till I was older, it was all she had left, and Hell itself couldn't have snatched it from her. Grandma and Uncle Dan couldn't go back on theirs. That would have meant admitting a whole pattern of life laid down before they were born was wrong, and that was asking more than they could give.

So we went on along inside our miserable Mexican

standoff till about a week later, when Uncle Benny showed up, and the cold war turned into open skirmishing.

I saw the strange car parked out front of the picket fence the minute the bus pulled away, and my heart squeezed down so hard my teeth ached. It had to be Daddy. It wasn't our old car, but it didn't belong to anybody else who came to Grandma's, so it had to be him.

In all my daydreams of that moment, I'd always seen myself running to meet it, fast and light as a dragonfly. But once it was there, I felt tired and heavy, so weighed with a strange, sad shyness, I could hardly put one foot in front of the other.

I opened the front door and heard a man's voice, not Daddy's, coming from the parlor, heard Mama call, "Mavis?" from the kitchen, and realized when Aunt Millie said, "Come on in, honey," that Grandpa must've died, for nothing else would've brought her home at that time of day. I wanted to cry, then, not for him, but for myself.

Aunt Millie was crying. Or had been. Her rouge and lipstick were smeared and her mascara streaked, and she was sitting on the divan next to an uncomfortable looking man I'd never seen before. I wondered why they hadn't sent for Brother Williams at First Baptist where we all belonged, even if I was the only one who ever went. I wondered when it had happened and where the rest of the family was and if I could ever make up another daydream to take the place of the one that had been ruined.

Aunt Millie wiped her eyes and said, "This is your Uncle Benny, honey. Meet Mavis, Benny, Fern's oldest girl."

He cleared his throat and groaned a little somewhere deep inside it and said, "Pleased to make your acquaintance, Mavis."

I knew I ought to answer him. But I felt so mad and cheated, I just turned around and went to the kitchen without saying a word and didn't care whether I had any manners or not. "I was just fixing to come get you," Mama said. "When

I call you, young lady, I want you to come that minute, not whenever the notion strikes you."

"I thought it was Daddy," I said. "When I saw the car, I thought it was Daddy."

Mama looked back down at the shirt she was ironing and said, "Well, it's not, and I want you to stay out of the parlor. Your Aunt Millie and Uncle Benny are talking."

Grandma picked up a cuptowel and popped the wrinkles out and said, "Humph!"

"What kind of an uncle is he?" I said. "A real one?"

Grandma said hmph again and spit into her snuff can and Mama said, "Certainly he's a real uncle. Only like Uncle Frank instead of like Uncle Dan. Because he's your uncle by marriage, not by blood."

"Is he a preacher?"

"Benny? Why, no. What made you think that?"

"He's dressed like one."

"Oh, that's because he's a businessman. From San 'Tonia. Businessmen in big towns wear suits every day."

"I thought—when I saw it wasn't Daddy, I thought—" but I couldn't say I'd thought Grandpa was dead in front of Grandma—"I wanted it to be Daddy."

Mama took the shirt off the board and gave it a shake and laid it back down and began buttoning it. "Your daddy will come for us when he can—no, Martha May, I can't pick you up right now. Go to Mavis."

Grandma took the pile of cuptowels to the safe and said, "I wonder if his highness in yonder is going to stay for supper."

Mama put another shirt on the board and touched her finger to her tongue and then to the iron and said, "I don't know, Grandma. He and Millie have a lot to catch up on, so he may. I'll go see directly."

"Wouldn't be but two words I'd say to him was I Millie—Get Packing! And I'd have met him at the door with them."

Martha May ran back over to Mama and pulled on her

skirt and Mama said, "I told you, Martha May. I can't take you now. Come get her, Mavis, and hold onto her. You all go outside for awhile, why don't you?"

EIGHTEEN

Uncle Benny was gone when we got back to the house. Mama was putting the ironing board away, and Grandma was making biscuits. Aunt Millie stood at the sink peeling potatoes, her face pale and sad looking. Grandpa, who was having such a good day he'd decided to come to the table for supper, was in his chair waiting for Uncle Dan to come in from the field and tell him about the crops. Neither of them said anything, though, after we started eating, and nobody else said anything other than "Thank you for the salt," or "Kindly pass the gravy," the same as they'd been doing the past week, only even more polite.

Not that there ever was a lot of talk at the table. Uncle Dan complained about the market reports or gave the government a good cussing. Grandma wondered where that old turkey hen had hid her nest, or why the Poage's ring had come on the line four times in one day. Aunt Millie told which medicines the sick people they knew were taking and what seemed to help and what didn't. Mama might say something about the weather, or tell Martha May to sit up straight and quit playing with her food. But that was about as close as they ever got to what you could call talk, even when everybody was in a good mood.

When the meal was finally over and everybody but Grandpa was pushing their chairs back into place, Uncle

Dan said, "Well, Millie, I hope your foolishness this after-noon ain't cost you your job."

"Mr. Rathgaber *gave* me the afternoon off, Uncle Dan. Not everybody in the world is stingy-hearted."

He grunted and walked away, and Aunt Millie began scraping and stacking the plates so fast they rattled.

"I've had that set of dishes thirty-five years now," Grandma said, "and I don't aim to see it broke up because you're on a high horse. You just climb down and get ahold of yourself, young lady. That Benny ain't good enough for you and you know it. Give him his marching papers and quit taking out your spite on my plates."

Aunt Millie started crying again and Mama said, "Go on, Millie. I'll tend to the kitchen."

As she ran out of the room, Grandpa yelled, "Now ding-damn it, either them cow's been in the bitterweed or else one of you yahoos is trying to poison me."

Grandma said, "Oh, Buck honey, you know nobody here would harm you, and you know they ain't no bitter-weed in the Little Pasture, and Lovey and Dolly don't never graze nowheres else. It's that medicine you're taking that makes things taste bad." She brushed some crumbs off the front of his shirt and smoothed his hair. "Do you want to go set with Dan awhile, or do you want to go lay down?"

He banged his cane on the floor and said, "I want them cows kept out of the bitterweed, that's what I want. That milk ain't fit for hogs."

"Oh lord, Buck—never mind. I'll see it don't happen again. Fern, you better help me get him to bed. I don't want to disturb Dan."

Mama dried her hands and took one of his arms while Grandma took the other, and they went shuffling out, Grandpa still fussing about the milk. Then Aunt Millie came back in, with her face washed and fresh lipstick on and said, "Where's Fern and Grandma?"

"They took Grandpa to bed."

"Well, I'll finish washing up, then. They'll probably be awhile."

"I'll dry. I've already done my homework."

"That'll be fun, just us two." She poured more hot water in the dishpan and refilled the tea kettle and washed and rinsed slow enough for me to keep up, and finally said, "Are you having a good time at school with all your friends?"

"Yes'm." Grown ups didn't always need the whole truth.

"Making good grades?"

"Yes'm."

"You're smart like Fern." She swished a handful of knives and forks through the rinse water and laid them on the rack. "I bet you have a couple of boyfriends, too."

I shook my head, seeing Maxie Russek, dark-haired, blue-eyed, jaunty-walking, remembering his laughing yell the time I lost my grip on the giant stride and fell on my wrist so hard it hurt all day.

"Oh, everybody likes somebody special. You can tell me."

"No, honest. I don't have a boyfriend." Which was true, because Maxie didn't like me even if I did like him, and if anybody at school ever found that out, my life wouldn't be worth a plugged nickel.

"Well, I thought sure you'd have at least one beau. I always did, and your mama, too. Maybe you read too much, Mavis honey."

We had the dishes done and the floor swept by the time Mama got back. Aunt Millie was undressing Martha May for her sponge bath and I was saving Maxie's life during a fire, or a flood, maybe, and he was telling me how sorry he was he'd treated me so ugly that time on the giant stride.

"Well, we finally got him down," Mama said, "but not without a struggle." She washed Martha May's face and hands. "It's hard to see him so feeble and with his mind so clouded. I know it's just killing Grandma."

Aunt Millie handed her the towel. "Is she still mad at me?"

"She's not mad, Millie. She's just afraid you'll get hurt again. Between Grandpa and Dan, and us and our troubles, it's a wonder the poor old soul's as good natured as she is."

"I know. And I feel like a dirty dog bringing something else in for her to worry about. But she doesn't want me to leave, Fern. She may not want to see me hurt again, but the main thing is, she wants me to stay here. If she had her way, everybody would stay here, forever. Hallie and Eunice and Mama and Lafe—oh, Fern. What do you think? What would you do in my place?"

Mama put Martha May's nightgown on her and said, "I don't like to give that kind of advice, Millie. If something went wrong later on you might blame me for it."

"No, I wouldn't. I'm asking you."

"Well, I think you still care about Benny."

"But he ran out on me."

"You ran out on him first."

"I did no such of a thing."

"Yes, when you wouldn't go with him to a place of your own, that was a kind of running out on him, on your duty to your marriage. Besides, if you didn't want him back, why didn't you get rid of him the minute he showed his face at the drugstore?"

"It was such a surprise—and you may as well know, because it's something else I've got to consider, he's been in jail. He was sorta bumming around the country, and up in Saint Louis they arrested him for vagrancy."

"Ye gods, Millie. That happens to a lot of good men nowadays. Wake up, girl."

"Well, I guess you're right. Anyhow, when he left there, he got hurt pretty bad. He was hopping freights to get back to San 'Tonia, and this railroad bull—"

"Yes, those dirty devils. They knock men in the head for no more than trying to hitch a ride, and some of them don't mind using an iron pipe to do it with, either."

"I don't see why they care if somebody rides in their old boxcars. They're going anyhow. What difference does it make if some poor guy out of work—"

Mama's face turned as white as Martha May's gown and she said, "Hush, Millie. You can't think about things like that. He's here now. That's what counts. He seems to be doing real well, too, dressed so nice and driving a good car and all."

"Yes, his old boss took him back and made him assistant manager at the Handy Dan on Broadway."

"That's mighty close to Mama and Papa."

"No, I'm cured of that. If we do get back together, we're getting our own place the first thing. I won't even tell them we're in town till after we're settled."

"Well—"

"And I could find a job, I know. I'm real lucky about finding work. That's where Benny went looking for me, where I used to work, and they told him I was down here."

"Put some more water on, will you? Mavis has got to wash up and she and Martha May need to get to bed. Us, too. Maybe if you sleep on it—"

"I know you're right about it being as much my fault as Benny's. He kept wanting us to move, to get our own place. We couldn't even—well, we needed our privacy. I'd promise him I'd move, and then when I'd tell Mama—she'd be sitting in the kitchen eating bread and jelly or a bowl of Post Toasties—that's another thing. We didn't eat with the boarders. We ate what Mama called a light supper in the kitchen. Benny worked hard, and so did I, and bread and jelly aren't very filling when you haven't had anything but a sandwich or a bowl of weak soup at noon."

"I know all about being hungry, Millie."

"I know you do, honey."

"Get your elbows," Mama said to me, "they're absolutely rusty."

"You think I ought to take Benny back, don't you?"

"I think you ought to do what you want to do."

"I don't know what I want to do."

"Then sleep on it like I said."

"I don't have time. He's got to leave early in the morning. He can't miss another day's work. He said he hadn't come for me broke. He's got a little money put by, and—I do want my own place, Fern. I don't want to stay with relatives all my life, growing old and—"

"Then for God's sake, Millie, go. What's holding you back?"

"I'm scared. I keep thinking, what if I *can't* get another job? What if Benny gets laid off? What if I have a baby? What if he walks out on me again? I know I have a place here. And I'd miss you, Fern. I don't want to go off and leave you here by yourself."

"Don't put that burden on me, Millie. I wouldn't put it on you. If I had your chance, I'd be out of here like a shot. There's more to life than a full belly—get your gown on, Mavis, and quit dilly-dallying around."

"But you came Home when—"

"Yes, when I wanted to punish Will, I'm ashamed to admit. Because that deal with his papa didn't work out and I knew it wouldn't and he wouldn't listen to me when I tried to warn him. I knew that old man never had any intention of doing right by us, even before he brought that painted up old hussy in to take Will's mama's place, and I couldn't wait to say I told you so. But it was wrong of me to leave, and wrong of Will to let me, because now I don't know whether he wants me back or not."

"Fern!"

"It's the truth. I've been begging him to come get us. I don't care how hard times are. We always managed before and we can do it again. But he keeps putting me off, saying he can't come just yet and he can't send for us, either. Something's bad wrong. He hasn't sent me but fifty cents in nearly a month, and I do know if he had it, he'd send it, out of pride if nothing else.

"He says he's working, and insists he's not sick. I've

asked him that. Of course, the way he's moving around, our letters get delayed, so I don't know what the trouble is. But I'll tell you, Millie, if you really want my advice, you'll get on the phone right now and call the hotel and tell Benny you'll be packed and waiting on the porch when he gets here."

NINETEEN

While we waited at the stop sign for a break in the traffic on I-35, I looked out over the old country cemetery whose metes and bounds forever enclosed all that was left of the most intimate part of my life. Covering a low rise of Black Land Prairie that had once been on the far outskirts of town, it was gradually being surrounded by the new subdivisions and strip shopping centers going up as we had begun more and more to serve as a suburb for a city twenty miles away. Still, I was glad I'd stuck to my decision to bury Paul there. It was the fittest place for him, as it would be for me when my time came to join him.

We crossed the highway into the shade of the dark and ancient cedars lining the narrow drive laid out when all travelers here came in vehicles drawn by horses, and only the well-to-do could afford markers made by masons. And those few were of low-grade marble, their lambs now rounded and blind, the staring angels stained and ragged looking, the fraternal symbols no longer sharp and clear. Many of the older graves were unmarked, but most wore rocks dug from the fields nearby, some naked, some with shallow hand-cut inscriptions smoothing away under the wind and the rain.

Unlike the big new chainstore cemetery on the other side of town, this one was weedy in wet years, brown and bare in dry ones, always littered with styrofoam cups and fast food wrappers thrown from passing cars. But there were no statues of effeminate Christs or disembodied praying hands, no signposts saying Vale of Peace or Valley of Repose, no attempt at all to disguise its stark and necessary function. It was a burial ground, plain and simple, and the people in it were plain and simply dead, even those in the small grave marked

Too Babys
1/26/18

We got out of the car and looked back toward town and I said, "When we first moved here, we lived in a little three-room rent house over yonder on West Oak where the Winn-Dixie is now."

"Yes, I still have a snapshot of you standing on the porch holding Mary Fern when she was about six months old."

"Poor as Job's turkey and happy as if we'd had good sense. I know you thought we were making a mistake to come here, Naomi, but—"

"I just thought Paul would have more opportunities in Austin or some other big town, and of course, I hated that you were forced to drop out of college a year away from graduating."

"I wasn't forced to drop out. We wanted a family. And I did go back."

"But not until Uncle Will got sick and you had to go to work and the school system wouldn't hire you unless you did."

"Well, regardless, I got my degree and I 'made a teacher' as the country folks say—" which was what I'd wanted to be since that long ago day when I'd helped Annie Mattie Mallet teach the pre-primers.

But like the Jews before me—it probably went with being on the road a lot—I was always looking for a sign. And I felt I'd finally received one the day I got off the bus at

161

Grandma's holding my first report card. For the deal I'd made with God and Luck was that if I got good grades on that card, I would be a teacher someday. And except for C's in music and arithmetic, they were all A's—big, heavy, black ones, in Miss Parten's strong and perfect hand.

Mama and Martha May were waiting for me at the foot of the dirt road that led up to the house, and I waved my card triumphantly at them through the thin shimmer of dust the bus raised as it pulled away. They waved back, smiling, and I could see that Mama was getting fat, but I didn't have time to worry about that right then.

I bent down and hugged Martha May and bragged on her scraggly little bouquet of pink evening primroses while Mama studied my card and bragged on it, and then Martha May took off after a butterfly. I turned to Mama, to explain about the C's, and she said, "I have something to report, too." I could tell by the look on her face it was something good, so Grandpa hadn't died and Aunt Millie hadn't come home with her tail between her legs the way Uncle Dan kept saying she would. "I have a letter from your daddy. He's coming for us. Soon."

I felt as dizzy as if I'd just been snapped off the end of a pop-the-whip-line. "When?"

"I don't know for sure, but soon. Here, let's sit down on the edge of the culvert and I'll read it to you—come back, Martha May. We're going to sit here in the shade a minute."

We sat down on the curb of the culvert that drained the wash Naomi and I called Mosquito Creek and Mama took the letter out of her apron pocket. Her stomach *was* pooching out a little, but—she took it out of the envelope and began to read in her reading voice:

"Dear Fern,

"Well sugar, I guess you will be mighty surprised to see the postmark on this letter. I have been here in Beaumont a week today. I would have got off a line to you sooner, but did not want to say anything till I knew for sure this job was going to pan out.

"Honey, I know you have wondered why my letters have been so few and far between, and why I have not sent you any money in so long. Well, it is a long story. I fell off of some skimpy scaffolding when I was in Longview, and broke my right leg. Do *not* worry. I am okay now.

"Talk about Luck. This doctor was driving by when it happened. He took me to his office and fixed me up with a cast and the boys on the job kept me in tobacco and brought me stuff to eat. He is a young man, just getting started in his trade, and a mighty fine one. His name is Doctor Donald Hammond, but I call him Doc.

"As soon as I could hobble around some, he would come get me every day and I would do odd jobs around the place for him. It was the only way I could pay him. He did not ask me to or press me for his bill. He said let it go but I would not. You know I have never believed in riding a good horse to death.

"I mended a couple of chairs for his wife and framed some pictures for her. Little penny ante stuff like that. I wanted to take a real portrait of them, but could not manage the darkroom work. She is a real lady. Always fixed me a good dinner and gave me a pack of tailor mades when she took me back to my car, which I spread around among the boys. It was the least I could do.

"Doc took the cast off of my leg last week and told me if I was willing to go to Beaumont he would call his cousin there and tell him to put me to work. Bill Cheever, one of the boys, decided to come with me and then go on to Houston. He had been living in my car with me and was a big help, so I sure didn't mind giving him a lift. He done most of the driving, because my leg still bothers me some. But do not worry. I am fine, and this cousin of Doc's, Mr. Rettig, that manages this big building, put me right to work.

"I help the building engineer and do not make much, but I have a cot and hotplate in a cubbyhole in the basement, so am not out any money to speak of. I have to wear a uniform, which I do not like, but am not complaining.

"Honey, it hurt me to get your letters asking me to come for you all. I did not have one thin dime and no place for you all to stay. I did not want to tell you about the accident because I know how you worry. But it looks like you would know I would never just put you off for no reason, because—" she read a few lines to herself, her eyes moving fast back and forth across the page, then began to read aloud again— "I am sending you this two dollars. Wish it was more, but I want to get us a place, and I have got my eye on a couple of locations for a studio somewhere down the line if our Luck holds out.

"Well, I will close for now. It has been a real load off of my mind to know you all are in a good place with plenty to eat. I hope someday I can return the favor and pay your folks back. Give the girls a big hug.

"Your loving Will."

She folded the letter and put it back in the envelope and stuck it in her pocket and said, "When you say your prayers tonight, don't forget to ask God to bless all the people who helped your daddy, especially Dr. Hammond and his wife."

"Yes'm. When do you think he'll get here?"

"Well, he'll have to get a payday or two ahead first, but it won't be too long."

"Where is Beaumont?"

"Someplace in East Texas."

"Have we ever been there?"

"Not as a family, but your daddy was there back before we were married. I think it's a pretty goodsized town, though, bigger than Angelo." She stood up and smoothed her apron over her rounding stomach and said, "We'd better be getting on back. Grandpa's had a fairly quiet day today, but you never know." She hugged Martha May and said, "Your daddy's coming. Do you remember Daddy? Say 'Daddy.'"

Martha May broke loose from her and squealed, "Daddy! Daddy!" but I knew she didn't really remember him, not the way he looked or talked or anything. I hardly did myself, except when some sudden sight or sound or smell brought him back to me so sharp and plain.

But thinking of those times made me sad, so as we walked to the house, I tried to imagine what Beaumont would be like. Plenty big if it was bigger than Angelo, with streetcars and picture shows and lots of people and automobiles and tall buildings. We wouldn't live in a camp there, even if it was summer. Our gear was all gone. In an apartment, then, where Martha May and I would have to be quiet all the time.

"What's the matter?" Mama said. "You don't seem very excited about your daddy coming."

The school would be big, too, the teachers different, and the kids. But at least I had a report card to show, and it said straight out that I'd been promoted from the high third to the low fourth, so I wouldn't have to tell my age or read for somebody.

"Oh, I was just thinking about living in a big town again."

"It'll be a change, all right, and I'm looking forward to it. I'm tired of being stuck out here in the sticks—there's Grandma standing on the porch waiting for us—how is he, Grandma?"

"Dozing. But he's awful restless."

"I'll sit with him for awhile."

"No, I only come out here for a minute to get a breath of air and look around the yard a bit. I don't want to leave him any longer than that."

"You ought to let me spell you all I can while I can. We're not going to be here much longer, you know."

But we were there a little over two more months, Grandpa having Taken to His Bed not long after Daddy's letter came, and not dying till the first part of August. Mama wouldn't go off and leave Grandma by herself. She said if Aunt Millie had been there to help with the extra work, she would, but with Millie gone, she just couldn't do it and Will didn't expect her to. Aunt Hallie said if that wasn't a God's blessing, she didn't know what was, and the family would never forget it.

And if Mama ever regretted her decision through those long hot days and nights that kept following each other, despite the constant promise that each one would be the last, she never showed it, sticking to her guns without a whimper till she was honorably relieved by Death, who frees us all.

TWENTY

I slept on a cot in the parlor the last two nights we were there. It was an old one of Uncle Dan's he'd used long ago when he went up on the Navidad to hunt and fish with the other boys, who had turned into old men just as he had, and talked about crops and the weather and notes at the bank when they came to help sit up with Grandpa toward the end.

Except for Mr. Bostick. He always came at night, and after breakfast he'd smoke his cigar and tell us about the olden days when he and his sister Emmy and Uncle Dan were 'pardners' and went everywhere together.

It was hard to imagine Uncle Dan being a 'dashing lad' who could knife-fight Mexican style and dance all night at the fandangos down on the border, then be first place winner at the horse races the next day.

Or to think of him and Mr. Bostick and his now invalid sister riding across the prairies to all the socials for miles around, or taking the excursion train to Corpus with a crowd of other young folks. But they were good stories, especially with the house so quiet and sad the rest of the time, and we were all glad when it was his turn to come.

Uncle Benny and Aunt Millie slept on the three-quarter bed Martha May and I had shared since we first came, and Mama took Martha May into bed with her. I could've crowded in, too, but I wanted to sleep on a cot again if I couldn't spend the night with Naomi. Mama wouldn't let me do that, because Uncle Lafe and Aunt Ada were staying with Aunt Hallie, "And that's company enough," she'd said. "Besides, I want my brood with me at a time like this."

The house had been full of people and food almost from the minute they took Grandpa away, covered with a purple velvet blanket and riding on a table with wheels that the men lifted slow and careful down the steps. There were relatives and neighbors and people from town and people from out of town—Aunt Millie and Uncle Benny getting in late the night Grandpa died, with Uncle Lafe and Aunt Ada not long behind them.

Mama and Papa Dequincey didn't come, though they could've ridden with Aunt Millie and Uncle Benny. Aunt Millie said it was a disgrace and an embarrassment to us in front of the family. But Mama said don't worry about the family, just smooth it over somehow for Grandma's sake, even if you have to make something up, which Aunt Millie did. All I ever heard of the excuse she used was Aunt Eunice saying it sounded lame to her.

Daddy couldn't come to the funeral, either, because his boss couldn't spare him till the building closed down Saturday night. But everybody understood that, and appreciated the wire he sent saying he was sorry and would be in as early Sunday morning as he could. Mama said we'd be packed and ready to go as soon as he ate some breakfast, and Uncle Dan said, "God, Fern, ain't you going to give the man a chance to get a little sleep?"

Mama said, "Will's used to being on the road without sleep, Uncle Dan, and we've got to allow extra time in case of car trouble. He can't afford to jeopardize his job by getting back late."

It was good to see Aunt Millie again, and Uncle Benny, too, but it was Aunt Ada who kept Naomi and me so agitated with excitement we could hardly give them or Uncle Lafe more than a passing glance. Naomi said Aunt Ada played the piano all night after they got in, so loud and thundery it shook the house and she and Aunt Hallie had to stuff cotton in their ears to get to sleep.

"Nobody likes her," she said. "Not even Grandmother. But they all have to play like they do on account of Uncle Lafe. He wouldn't ever come back if they said the least little thing against her. Grandmother says he's besotted by her."

"What's 'besotted?'" I asked.

"'To stupefy with drink; make a drunkard of. To make stupid or foolish. To infatuate.' I looked it up."

"She makes Uncle Dan *drunk?*"

"Yep. With love. That's what 'infatuate' means. 'To inspire or possess with foolish and unreasoning passion, as of love.' I looked that up, too."

"I wish we had a dictionary—listen. Do you know what 'hustle' means? When a lady does it?"

"Shoot, yes. You don't need a dictionary to know that. Besides, dictionaries don't have bad words in them."

"But why is it bad? People say it all the time when they mean hurry up or let's get started or something like that."

"It has a bad meaning, too, though, for when ladies do You-Know-What for money."

"Oh. One time at Papa Maddox's some big boys caught me by myself down at the privies and tried to make me do That. They offered me a nickel and I wouldn't, and then they threatened to turn the privy I was in over and I still wouldn't, and just when they started pushing on it a lady came along and chased them off and took me to her house and washed my face and told me not to tell because it would make a lot of trouble."

"Weren't you scared?"

So scared I cried and begged, and so ashamed I'd never told anybody about it before and wished I hadn't told now, and to change the subject said, "But why doesn't the family like Aunt Ada? She doesn't do anything. She doesn't even talk much."

"They're jealous. At least I think Grandmother is, because Uncle Lafe is her favorite out of all her brothers and sisters and she was going to go to Austin and keep house for him after Grandfather died, but he married Aunt Ada instead."

"Couldn't she have gone and helped him anyhow?"

"No. She says no house is big enough for two women."

"Grandma's is."

"Well, that's what she said. And then my mama and daddy got killed and she had to raise me, so—but I admire Aunt Ada and I intend to grow up to be just like her, don't you?'

"Well —"

"You can if I can. You're smarter than I am in everything but arithmetic."

But I didn't think it had anything to do with being smart. I thought it had to do with having perfect white skin and blue-black hair and gray eyes that turned silver in certain falls of light. That it required high arched feet in slender slippers and lovely, floating dresses and black satin headache bands Aunt Eunice said were a hundred years out of date but what did she know, and lavender cigarettes in an ebony holder banded with silver and jade.

"I've already started," Naomi said. "I'm teaching myself to smoke on her butts."

"Naomi! Are you?"

"I am. I wanted to bring you some so you could learn, too, only I was afraid if I put them in my pocket Grandmother would smell them and kill me. I've had to keep Vicks on my tongue and play like I have a summer cold so she won't smell them on my breath, either. But I would've shared if I could have."

"That's all right."

"Your daddy smokes. Maybe you can learn on his butts when you get to Beaumont. Then when you come back to visit, I'll blow smoke at Lottie and you can blow it at Dottie and they'll be so jealous they'll pee in their pants."

I didn't want to tell her that Bull Durham didn't make good butts and that we'd never come back to Grandma's. I'd asked Mama once not long before Grandpa died, and she said, "No, it would cost too much for the little time we could stay." Then I asked if we might stay for good, the way Grandma wanted us to, but she said, "No, your daddy's not a farmer, and besides, it wouldn't do for him to take orders from Uncle Dan."

"We do."

"That's different. We're women and blood kin."

So when he came we'd leave, and all my secret places, all the flowers I'd learned the names of, the trees I'd watched turn from winter to spring to summer, the birds and the fields, the dusty road, the house, Naomi, would all be gone from me forever. I got up and dressed and tiptoed down the hall where lamplight from the kitchen fell across the floor, wondering why I didn't hear Grandma sifting the grate or opening and closing the oven or making any of the other breakfast sounds she always made this time of morning. But she was just sitting at the table, folding a cuptowel into smaller and smaller squares, smoothing each one as she finished it, pressing the edges with the side of her thumb.

I was glad she had on an everyday dress again, instead of the black silk she'd worn to the funeral the day before. It had made her look like a cross old stranger, Uncle Dan holding one of her arms and Uncle Lafe the other, till she said, "You boys let me be. I ain't going to swoon or run away neither."

She looked up at me and said, "What is it? What's wrong?"

"Nothing, Grandma. I just woke up and saw the lamp was lit and thought it was time to get up."

She looked at the clock and said, "Yes, it's about time for everybody to pile out, I reckon, since your mama's looking to get away early."

I sat down in my chair that wouldn't be mine after this morning, and she said, "I just been setting here thinking about your grandpa. It don't hardly seem possible he's gone."

I knew Heaven was so far away you couldn't see it, but the way she said 'gone' made it sound so far off I felt a little uneasy about it, so I said, "How far away is Heaven?"

"What?"

"How far away is Heaven? Where Grandpa's gone."

"Oh, child," she said, in such a terrible voice I was scared he hadn't gone there at all, and to make sure, said, "That is where he is, isn't it?"

"Yes," she said. "If there is a Heaven, that's where Buck's at, all right."

I fell into a blackness so deep and thick I couldn't breathe, and she said, "Don't look like that, Mavis. You got to learn not to let words spoke in grief or anger mean so much to you. I know you're a high-strung youngun, worse'n Naomi, but you ought to know I ain't a heathen. And you sure ought to know if ever on the face of this earth there was a good man, your grandpa was it.

"Only I don't hold with pearly gates and folks in their nightgowns playing on harps. Buck didn't hold with none of that, either." She took off her glasses and polished them on the hem of her apron. "Buck and me, we saw eye-to-eye on pretty much everything. Married so long there don't seem to be no time in my life when he wasn't with me. No matter how far back I remember, even to when I was a little tyke like Martha May, seems like he was always nearby, waiting for me.

"I believe in the Heaven of the Psalmist, Mavis, green pastures and still waters, and I believe that's where Buck is, young and strong and riding a fine horse—"

Naomi bent over and straightened the little temporary metal marker the funeral home had stuck at the head of the grave, and it irritated me that she was doing something it wasn't her place to do, till the look on her face reminded me she had no grave for Charles, for: Full fathom five her husband lies/Somewhere in the South Pacific.

"I was thinking about Grandma when Grandpa died," I

said, "and Uncle Dan—he was in love with that sickly sister of Mr. Bostick's, wasn't he?"

"Lord, yes. Crazy about her till the day he died."

"Wonder why they didn't marry?"

"All I ever heard was he kept putting off asking her so long, Henry Chester moved in and took her before Dan knew what was happening."

"What was wrong with her? Consumption?"

"Martin Luther always said Henry infected her with gonorrhea, but you know Martin Luther." She started laughing. "I'm sorry, Mavis, but I can't help it. Every time I think of old Martin Luther going through life with the same name as Martin Luther King, it cracks me up."

"Oh, I imagine he dropped the 'Luther' early on, and besides, he wasn't a kid by the time King came along."

"You don't have to be a kid to catch hell over something like that. Not in South Texas, anyhow."

"Well, kid or not, he shouldn't be ashamed of his name, regardless of who else has it. Not that King did anything that didn't need doing, but—"

"Yes, *but*. It dies hard in all of us, doesn't it, Miss Goody Two-shoes?"

"I've never pretended it didn't."

"I know you haven't, and I shouldn't have said that to you."

"Forget it."

"No, I apologize to you and to both Martin Luthers—or to the dead one, anyhow."

"Well, ours at least always had a hide like a rhino, so I'm sure he managed, and I guess he and the rest of that bunch are happy as hogs and rich as Croesus these days."

"With all that oil and real estate? They're swimming in money. I don't want to rush you, Mavis, but I need to rinse out a few things and start packing. I've got to be back in Austin early in the morning, you know."

Yes, I knew. Everyone but me was heading out for, taking off for, going to or along toward—somewhere. Even

Paul. I looked down at the rough mound of fresh dirt, at the tacky little tin marker throbbing in the wind, and understood for the first time in my life what it meant to be the one who was left behind.

TWENTY-ONE

It shamed me now that I hadn't thought about how Grandma must have felt when I left her, or Naomi, or anyone else I'd ever left behind. But my place was wherever my family was, and if it turned out to be Beaumont—

We lived there nearly two years, an unimaginable length of time for us to live in one place, and an unimaginable place, in a lot of ways. It wasn't built at some cross roads on a prairie, or by some small green river half dry most of the time. It was built on low, marshy ground near the Gulf, by a big muddy river that was full all the time. The air was damp and heavy, sour on hot, still days with swamp and refinery odors and miserable with mosquitoes; the sky was narrow and closed in, rainy more often than not; there wasn't a rock within a hundred miles, and instead of our apartment being in a big house with lots of other families, it was only a two-room-share-the-bath half of a regular house owned by a widow lady named Mrs. Linehan, who lived in the other side with her elderly bachelor brother. We only saw him each morning and afternoon as he walked to and from the courthouse, where he went every day in the hopes of drawing jury duty and the dollar a day it paid. We only saw her when we passed in the hall or met on the porch waiting for the postman. Mama said that suited her just fine. The Linehans could tend to their business, and we'd tend to ours.

It suited me, too, because I'd learned long ago it was best to avoid coming to a landlady's attention if you could, the only problem being, I didn't have any business to tend to.

For the most unimaginable thing of all was the kind of kids who lived nearby. They were dark-haired and dark-skinned, but not the same way Mexicans were, and rough-house rude in a way no Mexican could ever be. There were whole big noisy families of them who threw chunks of shell at me and yelled bad words in a language I couldn't understand when I'd tried to make friends with them.

Daddy laughed about it and called me a greenhorn. He said they were just Dagoes, and Beaumont was full of them because it was a port, and port towns were always full of foreigners. But Mama said it wasn't my fault I'd never been around People Like That, a category I soon learned included Greeks and Syrians as well as Italians, and one I didn't know what I was supposed to do with.

Outside of some Indians in Oklahoma, I'd never seen any foreigners before. And I'd never heard anybody in my family use a name for people that wasn't Nice before, either. Except for real old timers, Nice people never said 'nigger,' unless they were designating a certain part of town, and that was done matter-of-factly and without malice. And only real old timers ever said 'spic' or 'greaser', though we all said 'Meskin,' which I wasn't aware of till years later when a college friend even more anxious than I to be accepted in the Halls of Academe called it to my attention. I excused it then as being due to regional pronunciation rather than any wish to be derogatory, as I did 'nigra,' when it took the place of 'darkie' and 'colored'—all attempts at being decent, mis-guided though they might have been. The main thing all that confusion meant to me in my childhood, though, was that I had no one to play with. I taught Martha May Bible verses and nursery rhymes and jump rope chants till she ran and hid under the bed when she saw me coming. I read every discarded newspaper, every letter, flyer, ticket stub, or grocery sack that blew by, every label on every can or bottle or carton laying in the alley, and spent hours every day from the safe distance of the corner, watching the Dago kids play.

Mama was lonesome, too, used as she was to always being around other people. Her only friends were the two ladies next door, Sybil, who was about her age and worked as a waitress downtown, and Mrs. Carter, her mama, an old lady who sometimes didn't know where she was and had to be kept locked in so she wouldn't wander off and get lost.

Mama worried about the house catching on fire with the old lady being trapped inside, till finally she asked Sybil for a key so she could go check on her during the day. Sybil said that would be the biggest relief in the world to her and she'd be glad to pay Mama for her trouble. But Mama said no, she didn't mind popping in every once in awhile to chat a few minutes when Mrs. Carter was all right, or to stay and read the Bible to her till she went to sleep when her mind got fuzzy and she needed calming.

Mama liked them both and said they were as good as gold, but since neither of them had ever been farther away from Beaumont than Voth, where they were from, they were about as interesting to talk to as a fence post.

So whether out of pity for me, or for herself, she got Martha May up from her nap one afternoon and said, "Sybil told me how to get to your school, Mavis. It's not far. Why don't we walk over there, so you'll know the way this fall?"

There were lots of little kids there with their mamas, who sat on the steps watching them and visiting with each other, and lots of kids my age, too. After I made sure none of them were foreigners, I edged my way into the crowd around the merry-go-round to stand by the only other girl there who seemed to be by herself. Her name was Sara Nell Busey and she too was new, since she had just moved to Beaumont from Woodville. We made best friends by the time Mama said we had to go, promising to meet at the school every afternoon it wasn't raining. And if that wasn't Luck enough, Daddy came home the following Friday night and said, "You'll never guess in a million years who I ran into today."

"Don't tell me Jules and Evelyn have turned up. I thought they were going to California."

Daddy laughed. "No, not them, but California's got something to do with it."

"Baby?"

"Baby. In the flesh. It was the damnedest thing. I'd been up on the ladder changing a bulb in the lobby, coming down careful so I wouldn't drop it. They're big as basketballs and slick as goose grease and—well, anyhow, I stepped down just as this lady walked by and we bumped into each other. I started to say excuse me, ma'am, and there she was, big as life, saying, 'Will?'"

"I just can't believe it."

"Neither could we for a minute. My boss came by about then and I introduced them and he told me to take off awhile and get reaquainted with my sister. So I gave him the bulb and we went in the coffee shop and—"

"Supper's ready and everybody's hungry, Will. Let's sit down and you can tell us all about it while we eat. I want to know how they are and what they're doing here and the whole kit and caboodle. I've never been so surprised in my life."

"So that's the story," Daddy said at last. "Beryl just got ants in his pants like he always does and wanted to move on."

"I thought they were so crazy about California?"

"They are, they are. Baby says it's the coming place to be. But Beryl, he wanted to come back to Texas, and being a topnotch salesman, he got a job right off the bat at the Pontiac dealer's here, and—"

"Did they stop off in Angelo?"

"Umm—yeah."

"What did Baby think of your papa's new wife?"

"We didn't go into that much."

"Well I hope you told her how he did you."

"Damn it, Fern, can't you never let nothing go? What's past is past, and we're out of it, and—" he looked down at his name on the pocket of his uniform—" and Baby was a lot more unhappy about seeing me in this monkey suit than she was about any of the Old Man's foolishness, I can tell you for sure."

"If you think I take any pleasure out of seeing you do work that's beneath you to keep a roof over our heads and food on the table, you're wrong. My bitterness against your papa is on your account far more than it is on mine."

"I know that. But—"

"And if you want to go back on the road—"

"No. We agreed before we ever got to Angelo that that part of our life was over. The road ain't like it used to be, anyhow. You seen for yourownself what it was turning into those last couple of years. And it's getting meaner and harder all the time. When you all was at your grandma's, I— well, it ain't no place for a man with a family no more if there's any way on earth he can stay off of it.

"But that don't mean the door's closed. There's still op- portunities around. That's why I hung onto my camera and the rest of my equipment, when there was plenty of times I was tempted to sell it for—never mind. I been putting a little by, two bits here, half a dollar there, building us up a stake. I don't plan to spend the rest of my life doing what I'm doing now. I'll be back in my own trade one of these days, and not too far in the future, neither."

"Kidnapping? Even a town this size wouldn't last—"

"No. A studio. That's what I'm aiming for."

"Oh, Will!"

"Now you think about it. Beaumont's a pretty thriving town. It's got the port and the refineries and lumber and a lot of little towns nearby people come in from on paydays, cot- ton farmers and rice growers, scrub ranchers. I been doing some scouting around on my dinner hour, and there's some good locations for rent at a reasonable price."

"I thought you said there were a couple of studios here already."

"Well sure, Fern. I expect competition. This ain't Russia."

"But, Will—"

"Now I ain't going into this half-cocked. I'm going to start out working on the side, picking up appointments at night, Sunday afternoons—"

"You tried that in Angelo."

"This here's a horse of a whole nother color. I ain't bound to that building fourteen hours a day like I was to the store. I'm beginning to get acquainted around town some. There's plenty of people know my janitor job's just a stop-gap. And Baby's going to see if she can't get me some sittings with some of her friends. I wouldn't be a bit surprised if when they get here tomorrow night—"

"You didn't tell me they were coming tomorrow night! I don't know what I'll fix for supper. They're used to—"

"She said you wasn't to worry about that. They'll swing by niggertown and pick up some barbecue."

"They *must* be doing all right."

"Well, a good salesman can always make a little money, and Baby's working, too. They can't stay long, she said. They got a meeting or a party or something they got to go on to."

"I don't care. I'll be glad to see them for however long they can stay. I just wish—"

"What?"

"That Baby wouldn't come flying in stirring up things and putting ideas in your head."

"If you're talking about the studio, don't lay the blame for that at Baby's door. You know how long I been planning on that. I took this piss-ant job here so we could be a family again while I got back on my feet. But I've had a place of my own in mind ever since I knew our time on the road was done, and I'm going to have it, I don't care what it takes."

Though what it ended up taking—

"*You'd better* pull over, Naomi," I said. "I think I'm going to be sick."

"What?"

"Stop the car, damn it. I'm going to throw up."

I got out and fought the dry heaves till I thought my toenails would come up, and she came around to stand by me, saying, "I don't doubt you're sick. You haven't eaten enough to amount to—"

"It's not that. I've been thinking about Beaumont."

"Oh hell, Mavis, that can't make you sick. Here." She handed me a Kleenex and I wiped my mouth and blew my nose and said, "Yes it can."

"Enough to make you *vomit?*"

"No, Naomi. I just thought that was a fun idea."

"Well I'm sorry that I'm not able to understand why that place affects you the way it does."

"Of course you can't. You never lived there. I'm okay now, let's get back to the house."

She pulled out onto the highway, dragging the clutch, and said, "I still think the main thing you need is something hot and nourishing in your stomach, and not any warmed over funeral food, either. Yes, I know, everybody's been wonderful, and they've brought stuff in by the truckload, but—let's go out to eat tonight. Play redneck somewhere. Eat barbecue and drink beer and listen to honky-tonk music."

"God, Naomi."

"I mean it. As bad as I need to get on home, I'm not leaving here till you prove to me you're going to be all right all the way."

"And *that* would prove it?"

"It'd help."

"Naomi, I'm not suicidal, if that's what's worrying you. People like us—" and I didn't say present company excluded if I did think it for one bitter instant—"hang onto life for all it's worth."

"You know that I know that you don't have to blow your brains out or stick your head in the oven in order to kill yourself."

No, I wanted to say, you can drink yourself to death or pop pills till you croak or screw around in so many beds— but the glare off the gravel shoulder reminded me of the white stones mentioned in Revelations that each of the faithful will receive at the end of time, with a new name inscribed on it, their true name only they and God will know.

Or at least that was the way I'd understood it the day I came across it at Grandma's when I was looking up my Sunday School scripture for the week. And having found just such a stone a few days earlier, a flat, perfect oval the size of a bird's egg, as purely white and smooth as crystallized milk, I immediately believed I'd found my Heavenly stone, which waited only for the inscription of my Heavenly name.

I wished I could hide it in the shoebox I used to keep on the ledge above the back seat, with my Sunday School pamphlets and paper dolls and the nickel matchbox that held the broken bits of colored glass I called my jewels. But it had been left behind in Angelo. So I hid it in my most secret place, the notch where the cross beams that supported the rain water cistern met, and set out to find one for Naomi.

I kicked over and hand sifted through every inch of chert and pea gravel around the mailbox, where I'd found mine, and put Naomi herself to the task the following Sunday afternoon. We found carnelian colored pebbles, caramel colored pebbles, plain brown ones, white ones stained with iron, chert pitted black, and chips of pink granite glistening with mica. But no second Heavenly stone.

The sun was beginning to go down when we gave it up and went back to the cistern, and crouching there in the cool, dark green sweetness of crushed mint, I said maybe God would put my name on one side and hers on the other. But she said, "Never mind, Mavis, if there can't be but one, I'm glad it's yours."

So what I did say was, "If it'll make you feel better, I'll

182

do my best to gag down some beer and barbecue. But not around here. I don't want to listen to any more condolences or know somebody's saying look at her drinking beer the day after she buried her husband she must not care very much."

"Where do you want to go, then? Waco?"

"No."

"Austin? We could be there in—"

"No, Naomi, I don't want to go to Austin. You and Billy'd start in on me about staying a few days, and—let's just head out and see what turns up."

"Fine. I don't care where we go so long as it has a gravel parking lot and red plastic booths and Bob Wills on the jukebox."

"Well, I think it's silly, but I said I'd do it, so I will. We'll have to go by the house first, though. I have to bring Jane Long in and shower and change clothes."

"You've already showered once today. Does thinking about Beaumont really mess you up so bad you have to go through some kind of purifying ritual afterwards?"

"Don't be ridiculous. I want to freshen up, that's all. You always try to make more out of something than—"

"No, I'm just trying to understand. Beaumont wasn't the only place you all had a hard time in. What makes it so different?"

"Because I was a little kid in the other places, and when you're little, if you have good parents and everybody else in your limited bailiwick lives the same way you do—I was growing out of that stage by the time we hit Beaumont. Those months at Grandma's, when I didn't have the road to fence off the real world, made me see things in a way I'd never seen them before."

"If you can call Robb's Prairie the real world."

"Well, it was as close as I'd ever come—oh, Beaumont wasn't so terrible in the beginning—not after the first shock wore off, anyhow."

183

Because in the beginning and after the first shock wore off, I had a best friend, a library card, a Sunday School class, and visits from Aunt Baby and Uncle Beryl, who paid my way to the Organ Club every Saturday. I rode into town with Daddy those mornings, then walked to Aunt Baby's on Sabine Pass, where my nickel waited for me in her mailbox.

Since I always got there early, I sat on the steps till it was time to start back down to the Jefferson, pretending I lived there in a Real apartment house, a big, two-story place, with front porches on both floors supported by tall columns. There were rocking chairs on the downstairs porch, and potted plants, and on sunny days, a canary in his cage out for an airing. I could hear talk through the open windows, radios playing, a vacuum cleaner going, and sometimes got to see someone come hurrying out to a waiting taxi.

On the way back to the theater, I always stopped off for a few minutes at the little park above the turning basin to watch the distant freighters riding the muddy water, all their age and ugliness disappearing into wonder at the length of their journeys and the strangeness of their destinations. I could see Hotel Dieu from there, too, the nuns walking by in pairs, their black habits flowing behind them in the damp breeze. I knew they were wicked, that they burned people at the stake and buried little babies at midnight in secret, hidden graves. But I thought they were beautiful, too, just as I thought some of the Dago girls were beautiful, and worried that God might punish me for finding such dangerous people attractive.

Like all the other kids, I was at the show before the doors opened, milling around in the crowd looking for Sara Nell or somebody else I knew. Waiting to be pushed into the lobby's dimly-lighted marvel of thick carpet and ivory-colored statues and tapestry-covered benches; into the smell of popcorn and candy; on into the vast darkness of the theater itself, where all the random noise turned into screaming cheers when the spotlights hit the organ pit and the great instrument rose with thundering magic, its music louder than a thousand clapping hands and stomping feet.

But of all the things I had, my school was the best. It was the last one I'd ever be in love with, though I didn't know that then, thinking only it was mighty strange that after all the years of being shuffled from grade to grade because I didn't have a report card, once I did have one, I still wasn't put where I belonged after the first day.

Not knowing, in my ignorant innocence, that double promotion was simply a means of bumping a bunch of kids from a grade that was too crowded up to one that wasn't, I took it for the privilege and honor the teacher said it was, and went along to the office for the principal's final decision as proudly as the other little dupes.

She studied my card and said while I was weak in arithmetic, my other grades were excellent, and she felt sure a smart girl like me would do well in the fifth if I'd apply myself to my numbers.

And of course I said yes ma'am I would, despite knowing I'd never been able to shift the functions of numbers from grade to grade the way I'd been able to shift the functions of words. But it wasn't my place to disagree with a principal, even if I'd been able to see the results. Besides, who wouldn't want to be a fifth grader, whatever the cost.

They were the Big Kids, their authority established before the first bell on the first day, and when we were joined to their exalted rank in a special assembly, where we were charged with the responibility of running errands, leading the Pledge of Allegiance, and, holy of holies, serving as monitors, in the basement on rainy days and the playground on clear ones, our word the Law, surely, I thought, my cup runneth over.

TWENTY-TWO

But it didn't run over with milk and honey all the time. By the first of October, even I could see Martin Luther had been right about one thing—Mama *was* going to have a baby. And while I didn't mind having a new little sister or brother, I couldn't understand how it had happened. Because not long before Aunt Millie had left Grandma's, I'd heard Mama tell her, "I just *can't* have another baby, Millie. I just *can't.*"

Aunt Millie said, "Oh Fern, you wouldn't—"

"Here? God, no. How could I?"

"Not *any*where, honey. You know Evelyn and that doctor boyfriend of hers saved your life that time in Colorado."

"They did more than that. They kept Will from knowing I'd deliberately—" then she saw I was listening and didn't say anything else. But I distinctly remembered she'd said she couldn't, and here she was doing it, and the problem was, Mrs. Linehan did mind. She said a new baby meant a lot of extra washing and ironing that would run her bills up, and she didn't appreciate it one bit.

Daddy was back in the picture business by then, taking sittings in his spare time, mostly of friends of Aunt Baby's. He said it gave him a chance to build up a clientele while his Regular Job paid the rent and kept beans on the table. But that bothered Mrs. Linehan, too, because he had to use the kitchen for a darkroom. She said the chemicals were ruining her pipes and making her sick. I liked being around a dark-room again, though. It reminded me of nights on the road when the glow of the red lantern and the smell of hypo meant our Luck was good.

Not caring about anybody's opinion but his own, Daddy went straight ahead with his business, as did Mama with hers, and Billy was born on a cold, rainy night in November that Martha May and I spent by ourselves in Aunt Baby's apartment. She had to be with Mama, and Uncle Beryl, after depositing us, had to fetch the doctor and stay with Daddy.

Martha May was too impressed with her new status as a Big Girl to act scared. But I'd been a Big Girl myself too long not to know that just because you didn't act scared didn't mean you weren't, even if Mama had assured me doctors spent more time helping babies into the world than they did helping old folks out of it.

I turned the radio on to keep us company, low enough that it wouldn't bother anybody, and turned the lights out to save electricity. Then we sat on the bed in the dark, listening to Rudy Vallee through the static and watching the rain fall against the streetlight on the corner till we went to sleep.

Aunt Baby woke us up at daybreak saying, "Your mama's doing fine, and you have a new baby brother named William Beryl."

I knew Beryl would be the baby's middle name. Mama had promised it would be, boy or girl, when Uncle Beryl asked her to name it after him.

"They'll never have kids of their own," she'd told Daddy, "and he's a good man. They're both good people. I know they're flighty in some ways, and I know they're mixed up in things you don't approve of, but they've been a godsend to us."

"Why, hell, we was doing all right before they showed up."

"Yes, but—"

"I don't care who you name the baby for, Fern. I just want you to be okay and me to get my business going. I want us to have a place to ourselves, too, a house out in the country, maybe, where we can have a garden and a few chickens and begin to put down some roots."

"Here?"

"Here's as good a place as any. If Beryl and Baby are serious about staking me—"

But as the winter went on, crazy as they seemed to be about Billy, and anxious as they said they were to see Daddy established in his own studio, they came by less and less often. They made a lot of overnight trips out of town, Uncle Beryl going in one direction and Aunt Baby in another. And they went to lots of big meetings and parties downtown, some of them so important they wore evening clothes and looked like movie stars when they ran by for a few minutes on the way.

Most of the time there was still lots of talk and laughter when they did come, but they seldom stayed long enough to eat supper anymore, or to play a game of penny ante with kitchen matches the way they had at first. And sometimes, after I was in bed, I could hear all of them except Mama arguing. The next day at breakfast Daddy would look so mad and Mama would be so quiet, I began to feel like something was getting ready to happen that would turn our Luck bad again.

Daddy's picture business stayed slow, even around Christmas, when he usually did pretty well. He said it was because he didn't have a studio where people could drop in any time, the way city people were used to doing. Mama said it was because the Depression was getting worse, and I guessed she was right, because the day after New Year's, Daddy had to take a cut in pay at his Regular Job.

"No use blaming Rettig," he said. "He had to take his cut, too. Everybody from building superintendent on down to the elevator operators took one. It was either that or lay some of us off, and being as how most of us are family men—"

That night after the light was out, Mama said she could

hardly make ends meet as it was, and with even less in the pot, she was afraid we'd start getting behind in our rent. Daddy said he was doing the best he could and things were bound to get better and it was time to get some sleep. But when I went to sleep myself, he was still sitting on the edge of the bed, staring out the window.

Sometime later, the light coming back on woke me up to movement in the room and hushed voices, Mama saying, "Don't wake up the kids. We'll go in the kitchen and I'll light the stove in there. You all must be freezing."

But before Daddy turned the light off, I saw Aunt Baby in her black evening gown and silver fox fur, and a man and a lady I didn't know in regular working clothes. When Mama pulled the door to behind them, there was enough of a crack left between it and the facing that I could see through to the kitchen by kneeling on the foot of my bed.

Mama and Daddy stood to one side, Daddy putting on his shirt, Mama wrapped in their quilt. Aunt Baby sat at the table, and the man and the lady warmed their hands over the burners.

Daddy said, "Now what's this all about, Baby?"

"Just what I told you, Will. I was driving my friends here to Port Arthur, and—"

"Dressed like that?"

"Well, I was at a party at the Edson."

"And these folks just happened to come by and ask you for a lift."

The man looked at his cap and the lady looked at the floor and Mama looked back and forth between Daddy and Aunt Baby, her face tight.

"Yes. Why not? I said we were friends."

"Then the cops got after you for speeding and you decided to outrun them."

"That's about the size of it. I'm afraid now if I get back out on the street they'll spot my car and fine me no telling how much, and—"

Daddy straightened up real fast and mad and said,

"What kind of a greenhorn do you take me for, Baby? You never tried to outrun the Law on account of a speeding ticket."

"Well, I'd had a little too much to drink, too."

"You seem sober enough now."

She laughed. "Being chased by the cops does that for you."

"You might as well can the malarkey. I want the truth."

"Look, Will, all I want you to do is lend me your car so I can get these folks to Port Arthur."

"Where'd you ditch your car?"

"In an alley a couple of blocks over." She turned to Mama. "No one followed us, Fern. I wouldn't have come here if I hadn't been sure of that. You know I'd never do anything to get Will fired or blacklisted."

"Not on purpose you wouldn't, Baby, but—"

"They've got your license number," Daddy said. "They'll trace your car."

"My car will be reported stolen. There are a dozen people at that party who will swear I never set foot out of the hotel till I walked outside and found it gone. All I want is to get hold of a different car so I can take these people to Port Arthur."

"I think the best thing to do is for me to take you all—just be quiet and listen, Baby. I don't want to hear no more of your cock and bull stories. You ain't running from the Law. You're running from a carload of union busters that'd just as soon beat you to a pulp as look at you. I knew this damn organizing and running around with a bunch of Reds would get you in trouble."

Aunt Baby stood up. "Trying to help working people earn a living wage doesn't make a person a Red, Will. If you don't want to help me, just say so."

"It don't matter what I want. With Beryl not here, I'm responsible for you, and I don't aim to see you get hurt if I can help it. Let me get my coat on."

She looked hard at him a minute and said, "The Law *is*

involved, Will. I want you to know that in case you'd like to change your mind."

Mama said, "Will?"

But he was already starting for the door. "Don't worry," he said. "They're looking for Baby's car, not a old hoopy like mine. I'll be back in a couple of hours."

I retched in spite of myself and Naomi said, "What's the matter? Are you going to be sick again?"

I swallowed my nausea and said, "Oh, no. I was just thinking about that night Daddy took Baby and her buddies down to Port Arthur when they were running from the cops and the company goons, that's all."

"But it's making you sick again, isn't it? I don't know why you persist in thinking about something you know is going to tear you up."

"I guess because I'm still trying to understand how Baby, for all her crap, could've put us in such a position. I only got the story in fits and starts over the years, so I've never known for sure what they tried to do that night—burn some place or bomb it or what."

"But Baby wasn't involved in that part of it, Mavis."

"No, her job was to take those two organizers or terrorists or whatever they were to Port Arthur, if they got in a bind, and get back to her party and establish her alibi."

"Well, since the company people got wind of it and had their goons there waiting—"

"But instead of those idiots dumping their car and heading for the bus station or somewhere, they ran straight to Baby at the hotel, which was a dumb thing to do with the goon squad and the cops both hot on their trail."

"She was supposed to get them out of town, Mavis. Naturally they went to her."

"Yes, only she shouldn't have—oh, what difference does it make? Daddy delivered them to Port Arthur with whole hides and got her back to the hotel before her party broke up. There was an article in the paper the next day about her 'stolen' car. With a picture of her giving the Dago kids who found it and called the police a reward, and an expression of her gratitude for the quick return of her automobile, which had been taken from the parking lot of a well-known hotel, etc., etc. When I think of the danger she put Daddy in—"

"Mavis, there's no point in dwelling on something that didn't happen."

"But what if they *had* been caught? What if Daddy'd been beat up? Or killed? Or put in jail? Losing his job over her little escapade was bad enough."

"You don't know he was laid off because of that—yes, I understand it happened only a couple of days after what you call Baby's escapade, but you've said yourself they'd already started cutting salaries."

"I didn't know it then. I still thought she was wonderful. I thought Daddy was just being hard on her the way I had to be hard on Martha May sometimes. But Mama knew. When they lit out back to California a couple of weeks later, and Baby gave Daddy fifty dollars to open a studio with, Mama called it blood money. And that's damned near what it was."

She turned in the driveway and cut the engine and said, "Well, it ended up okay and that's what counts."

I picked up the phone that was ringing as we opened the door, and when I heard Billy's voice, I started crying. For him, for me, for Mama and Daddy and Martha May, for Paul when we were young and made love standing knee deep in Village Creek one hot afternoon, laughing in the loving that the baby we were making would have little webs between its toes, a faery child.

Naomi took the phone and said, "She needs a good cry. She'll be all right. No, no, I promise you I won't leave till I'm sure she is," and I thought, "You'll have one hell of a wait, girl," and heard Jane Long banging against the screen wanting in and said, "Tell him I'll call him back later."

"She'll talk to you after while, Bill, sometime tonight

when we get back from supper. I don't know where yet, someplace on the road—where are you going, Mavis?"

"To let Jane Long in. You know what the Old Man always said, everybody's got to eat."

TWENTY-THREE

I hated to go eat without showering and changing my clothes, but I settled for washing my face and brushing my teeth, because I didn't want to get Naomi started again on something she didn't know anything about. She tried to understand. But her life was so far removed from the kind of experiences being sieved through my memory, it was impossible for her to grasp what we endured that last long year in Beaumont.

To her, it simply formed another chapter in the continuing adventure she conceived our life to have been. She knew it was filled with insecurity and hardship. It wouldn't have qualified as adventure otherwise. But her ignorance of what it really meant to be poor, certainly her ignorance of what it meant to go from being poor as a matter of course to being poor as a matter of some lack within yourself, allowed her to imagine our life very differently from the way it was.

Just as my ignorance of the world outside the road, only slightly dented by our insulated stay at Grandma's, had allowed me to imagine it differently from the way it was, even as I lived it. Protected by all Daddy's Regular Job had stood for, I didn't know till it was gone that being poor was something to be ashamed of. Or that the physical deprivations we'd suffered in the old world of the road, where it was taken for granted that everybody did the best he could with the Luck he drew, would become, in that new world we entered not long before we left Mrs. Linehan's, privations of the spirit from which the heart could never wholly heal.

Daddy had gone back to kidnapping when he lost his Regular Job, saying that was the trade he knew and what he should've stuck to in the first place, instead of flunkying at some job he'd never have got anywhere in if they'd kept him on for forty years. But business was so bad he wasn't making much more than enough to buy film and paper for the few orders he did get and enough gas to keep the car running so he could go out and try again the next day.

About a week before Aunt Baby came to what we thought was going to be our rescue, when we were behind in our rent again, and I was coming home at dinner to a piece of cold pone I only realized years later Mama was saving for me out of her own breakfast, she asked Daddy if he didn't think maybe he ought to find another Regular Job until things picked up a little.

"Hell, Fern," he said. "You make it sound like jobs are out there just waiting for somebody to come along and claim them."

"No, Will. I know better than that. But they say the WPA is hiring."

"I told you the one time I tried that I wouldn't never go begging hat in hand for another government job. I meant it then and I mean it now. Sink or swim, hell'll freeze over before I make that mistake again."

Mama didn't say anything else, but that Sunday afternoon when we went next door for hers and Sybil's weekly get-together, she offered to make a deal with Sybil to do up her uniforms.

It was my job during those visits to sit next to Mrs. Carter and read her a chapter from the Bible so Mama and Sybil could drink their coffee and talk in peace. I always listened to them while I read, because I had to read so slow to please Mrs. Carter, and to pause so long after every verse for her to tell me what it meant when I already knew, I had to have something to do.

"Oh, Fern," Sybil said. "They're an awful job. That's why I send them out, even if I do have to walk back and forth to work to help pay for it."

"I know they have to look just so, and if I don't do them to suit you—"

"It's not that I think you wouldn't do a good job, girl. It's just that all that heavy starching and ironing's a real pain."

"I'm not going to make any bones about it, Sybil. I need the money."

"I wish you'd let me pay you for the time you spend with Mama. I've offered before, remember."

"And I've told you before. I couldn't take money for that. That's just being neighborly."

"Well, I've never had any other neighbor willing to do it."

"I don't know why, we get along fine—does a quarter apiece sound fair? Caps included, of course. I wouldn't ask that much, but I'd have to buy starch."

"I pay the laundry thirty-five cents a set, and I think you ought to get the same."

"No. A quarter's fine. Six-bits a week sounds like a fortune to me."

"If you take them in the morning, can you have one back to me by Tuesday? I can't wear a set but two days."

"I'll have them both back to you tomorrow night if it doesn't rain, and if it does, by Tuesday for sure if I have to dry them in front of the oven."

"Well, if you're bound and determined."

"I am. Only I don't want Will or Mrs. Linehan to know. You hear me, Mavis?"

I said, "Yes, ma'am," before I thought, then saw by the look she gave me she'd known I was listening all along. But I didn't see that it mattered. Mrs. Carter was happy hearing what she couldn't read for herself anymore, plus getting to preach sermons to me, so—

"It's none of Mrs. Linehan's business what I do, and I'll tell your daddy in my own time, understand?"

But they both found out before she finished ironing the second uniform. Daddy because he came home to dinner to print up a rush order, and Mrs. Linehan because Mama couldn't hide what she had to hang on the line, even by sandwiching the uniforms lengthwise between Billy's diapers, a pitiful little ruse only someone as guileless, and as driven, as Mama, would've attempted. And one the mere memory of, fifty odd years later, left me shaking with grief and rage.

Daddy came in all happy and excited about his order, a good one he said he had to get out right away, and Mama, happy and excited for him at the same time she was trying to cover up the evidence of what she thought of as her own secret good news, said she'd have the kitchen cleared out in a jiffy. But before she could move the uniforms, one stiff and shining on a hanger over the door, the other just stretched out on the ironing board, he saw them and said in a funny kind of voice, "I'm glad you got Sybil for a friend, Fern, and I don't mind you doing little favors for her and her mama. They're good people. But I call doing up somebody's clothes for them, if they ain't flat on their back sick, more of a favor than one friend's got a right to ask of another."

I could tell she wanted to fib to him, the way I always wanted to do when I'd done something that was going to get me in trouble. But she just rolled the uniform on the board back up to keep it damp, and said, "I'm not doing this as a favor, Will. I'm doing it for the money Sybil's going to pay me."

He looked at her like he hated her—Mama!—and said, "That's a hell of a note, going behind my back to—"

"I was going to tell you. Later. I wanted it to be a surprise."

"Well it's a goddamn good one, I'll say that, to come home and find my wife taking in washing like some old colored mammy, or some back alley Irish widow-woman."

"I was only trying to help, Will. To bring in a little money."

"I don't give a damn about the money. I don't give a damn if we all starve. I'm not going to be shamed by—"

"No, because you're not the one who has to send Mavis back to school every day with nothing to eat but a piece of cold pone and a drink of water, or—"

"What the hell do you think I eat for my dinner out there batting up and down the roads? No, goddamn it, you take them uniforms back over to Sybil's as fast as you can trot, and Mavis, you get yourself back to school before I— I'm disgusted with you, complaining to your mama like a—"

But I didn't wait to hear the rest of it, or to explain that I hadn't complained to Mama about anything. I just ran. And when I got home from school that afternoon, he was gone and so were the uniforms, and Martha May was hiding under the bed because she'd wet her pants.

"See if you can coax her out," Mama said. "I've got such a headache, I don't feel like fooling with her anymore."

It took ten minutes of hard talking and the promise we'd walk down to Magnolia and watch the streetcars to get her to come out and change her underwear. Even then, she kept sniffling till I told her if she was going back on her word, I'd go back on mine.

By the time we reached the row of shotguns the only colored people in the neighborhood lived in, damp clouds began to roll in on a cold wind heavy with the threat of rain.

"Listen," I said, "don't you want to go back now? I think it's fixing to rain again." Which it did about every other day, except for when it set in and poured for a week at a stretch. I got sopping wet going to and from school and the house smelled musty and we learned another unimaginable thing—that the periodic deluges our West Texas minds had interpreted as meaning it was an exceptionally good year for rain, were normal for Beaumont all the time.

"No. I want to see the streetcars. You promised, Mavis."

"All right. But you remember you promised to tell Mama the next time you need to go to the bathroom."

"I didn't know I needed to go. It just started peeing before I could stop it."

"Well, try to be more careful next time, and hurry up. It's getting colder by the minute."

We half ran the rest of the way, into a fine, blowing mist that shimmered black on the wet streets and feathered the colors of the traffic light on Magnolia opposite the little corner grocery store where we stopped under the overhang.

"Mavis?" Martha May said, "I really didn't mean to pee in my pants."

"I know you didn't, Martha May."

"I'm not a baby."

"No, Billy's the baby now."

"Did Mama do something bad today, too?"

"No! Mama never did anything bad in her life." My theory being that any house Mama burned needed burning.

"Then why did Daddy get so mad at her?"

"I don't know." I hadn't been able to think of anything else all afternoon, but I still didn't know. I'd told Sara Nell about it, and she said all the daddies she ever heard of always acted like that. But *my* daddy?

"Here it comes!" Martha May said, dancing up and down, waving and smiling as it passed. The motorman clanged the bell for her and waved back, and she said, "All the way to the zoo and beyond," because I'd told her once that was where the line went, and maybe someday we'd take that ride ourselves.

When we couldn't see it any longer, she said, "Could we wait for one more, Mavis? Please?"

"No. We've got to go now."

I expected her to fuss, but she didn't, so we hurried back through the early twilight, with the mist turning into a thin drizzle, and hardly got in the house good before Daddy came in, too.

He handed Mama a sack and said, "I picked up some nice salt pork for supper," like it was nothing unusual for him to be bringing meat home.

"All right," Mama said in the same careless way. "I'll go put it on as soon as I finish drying Martha May's hair."

"It's good and lean, too," he said, "just the way you like it."

Not looking at him, Mama said, "That's fine, Will," and Martha May ducked out from under the towel and said, "What's salt pork?"

I hoped everybody would laugh and we'd be happy again the way we used to be when we got something special to eat. But nobody did, and just as she started to ask again, Aunt Baby opened the door and stuck her head in and said, "Anybody home?"

"Yes, come on in," Mama said. "I'm just fixing to finish getting supper ready." Then in the polite voice she used with strangers, "Y'all are welcome to stay."

"No," Aunt Baby said. "We just stopped off to say good-by. We're packed and on our way, but we want to be sure Will's set up in his own place before we go." She handed Daddy a fifty dollar bill, and Uncle Beryl pulled a pint of bourbon out of his overcoat pocket to celebrate with, and Mama said, "Thank God," in such a way I didn't know whether she meant for the money or the whiskey or that they were leaving.

As we walked out to the portecochere, Naomi said, "I moved the cars around so we could take mine, if that's all right with you. I didn't think you'd want to drive, and I don't feel like wrestling your old heap on the highway."

"Your car's fine," I said, in the same offhand manner I always used in speaking of her cars. Not through any desire to rob her of whatever pleasure my approval of what she drove might give her, but to forbid myself, as much as possible, any pleasure in the looks of a car—a rule I'd held to since that evening soon after we'd moved from Mrs. Linehan's out to what Daddy called the country, but what didn't look like any country I'd ever seen before.

I was hanging around a few doors down watching some kids play, when Daddy went by on the way home. One of the boys laughed and said, "Look at that old car. I wouldn't give you a plugged nickel for it." Everybody else laughed, too, and another boy said, "Ready for the boneyard. Good by, old Paint."

I wanted their approval so much, I didn't have the courage to say it was our car and give them a good cussing. But the shame of that lapse in honor burned such a hole in my spirit, I assumed from that time on the penance of trying never to allow any car to mean anything to me beyond its function as a form of transportation.

Long after Paul and I could've afforded to buy, if not anything in Naomi's class, at least a top of the line Buick or Olds every three years, I'd insisted we stick to the economy models of economy makes, and that we drive them till the wheels fell off. Which they were about to do on my old Chevy, and of course Naomi didn't mind saying so, any more than she minded pointing out every flaw in my house.

"Well," she said. "If you're ready."

"Yes. I don't know why I keep standing here. I guess I'm like Grandma was when Grandpa died. She said she kept thinking she had to go see about him, give him his medicine—no, that's a lie. I don't feel like I need to do anything for Paul. I *know* I'll never do anything for him again, ever, and you know what? Right now I don't even care. My God, Naomi, what's the matter with me? We were married all those years. We had a child. We truly loved each other."

"It's called shock, Mavis. Surely you've been through it enough times to know that."

"Yes, but—I nearly grieved myself to death over Daddy and Martha May, and when Mama died, I wanted to run down the street naked. I wanted to beat my hands with a ball peen hammer—"

"I think we ought to go."

"Yeah, when all else fails, hit the road."

"Oh, Mavis."

"No, I mean it. Let's go."

We got into her new Jag, black and gleaming as a midnight pond, and sank down into the creamy leather seats rich as warm spring nights and gardenia corsages and dancing at the Blackstone to 'Stardust' and 'Deep Purple' and 'Racing With the Moon,' and backed out into that last sad light that ends the day, when the sun is almost down and the wind drops and the most distant mourning of a dove, the farthest whine of a truck or whistle of a train, makes the heart ache with defeated longing. I felt I was abandoning Paul, Mary Fern as a little girl, the house, my whole life there, to the coming night.

It was early in the morning, though, when we left Mrs. Linehan's, hot and humid for February, even in Beaumont. All of us but Daddy stood around on the sidewalk while Sybil stopped on her way to work to say goodbye.

"I sure do hate to see you all go," she said, "and, Fern, I feel real bad that Will got upset about the uniforms. I wouldn't have caused any trouble between you two for anything."

"It wasn't your fault," Mama said. "I asked you for the job, you didn't ask me."

"Still and all—"

"Forget it, Sybil. It was just one of those things that didn't work out."

"Yes, but for you to go on and do them up so pretty and not let me pay you."

"I couldn't leave you in a bind just because Will and I didn't see eye to eye."

"All the same—well, we're really going to miss you, girl. You've been such a blessing to Mama."

"I'll miss you all, too. I really didn't want to move right now, but—"

But Mrs. Linehan had asked us to. She hardly let Aunt Baby and Uncle Beryl get off the porch before she came knocking on the door, self-righteous with the ammunition she'd been saving all day. She said the extra utilities a new baby took was bad enough, but what with Daddy turning the kitchen into a workshop and Mama taking in washing for the neighbors and her having to wait for her rent all the time, it was just more than a poor old widow-woman could put up with and she'd thank us to find ourselves another place.

Daddy said that was fine with him. He'd been wanting to move his family to a place of their own, and he'd spotted a house that very week that filled the bill, and she was mistaken about the washing. His wife was only doing a favor for a friend, and she'd get every last cent of her rent as soon as he got his new studio off the ground—which he never did do, permanently, and which Mama knew he wouldn't, because she tried to get him to go on kidnapping awhile longer and use some of Aunt Baby's money to pay the rent up to date.

"That's all she really wants, Will, her rent money. We're so close to everything here, and Mavis is so wrapped up in her school."

"No. I need every dime of that money to get my studio open and running. That's what Baby gave it to me for, and that's what I aim to use it for. Once that's done, I'll be glad to pay her what I owe her. But when I do, I intend to remind her of all the free handyman work I done around here, fixing steps and replacing shingles and glazing windows. Hell, if the truth was told, she owes me."

And if the truth was told, Mama *had* taken in washing. Or tried to. I still didn't understand why it had made Daddy so mad, or why he'd felt forced to lie about it, not knowing then that when it was a question of saving your hide or saving your pride, grownups weren't a whole lot different from kids. Though I did know, in Daddy's case, at any rate, it was never hide that counted.

"I know she's a tightfisted old ingrate," Mama said, "but she does have bills to meet, and where would we find another place we can afford and set you up in a studio at the same time?"

"I wasn't just whistling Dixie when I said I'd already found a house, Fern. I've had my eye on it for some time. It's out in the country, with a big yard—and the plain fact is, kidnapping's going the way of the road. A fella in my trade's got to have a studio to pull in the people that got jobs and money to spend."

"Maybe so, but I don't think now's the time or Beaumont's the place."

"Hellfire, Fern. The times are the same everywhere, and as long as a town's got something to draw on besides cotton and cattle—this chance to get some of the good things in life ain't just for me. It's for all of us. Like this little house. We wouldn't have some damn landlady snooping over our shoulders every minute, and—it ain't no palace, but we would be out in the country."

What I expected was some kind of combination of West Texas and Robb's Prairie. What I got was a loose straggle of ordinary, edge-of-town houses strung out along a narrow shell road fronted on both sides by rainfilled bar ditches and backed on both sides by lowering, living walls of black-green trees.

Daddy turned in over a plank-bridged culvert in front of a sad little yellow house with a rusting screened porch in front and a leaning gray privy in back.

He said, "Here we are, folks," in his normal, every day voice, and got out and paced around as natural as if he were choosing a place to pitch the tent.

The rest of us stood there in the knee-high weeds, listening to the trees talk in unknown tongues, sweating in the heat rising from the wet ground, too stunned at the face of our exile to move or speak till he said, "Well, mamacita, what do you think?"

Mama walked toward the steps in a kind of floating slow motion and said, "I think I better sweep it out good before we move anything in. Give it a good soap and water scrubbing."

"Then let's hop to it. Mavis, you watch the kids for your mama while I start unloading. I want to get back in to town and get my own place ready for Saturday's business in the morning."

I hadn't minded leaving Mrs. Linehan. She didn't even come out to see us off and wish us Luck. But my school, the place I had there, my friends, the library, the Organ Club— Mama stopped at the top of the steps and said, "I don't want Billy down on that wet grass, Mavis. You all better come on in here on the porch while I sweep out the house. Martha May, come hold the door for your sister."

And as she turned away from us, her face full into the sun, the deep line that had formed between her eyes the day of the fuss over Sybil's uniforms, flattened out white and shiny as an old scar.

TWENTY-FOUR

Naomi turned north on I-35 and headed up that old 98th meridian Walter Prescott Webb made famous forty lifetimes ago, and said, "Are you about ready to tell me where we're going?"

"Why, I don't know. I thought we said we'd just drive till we saw something that struck our fancy."

"Yes, but surely you have a place in mind."

"No, this is your party, remember."

"It's your party, too, Mavis, unless you really would rather go back home and wallow in self-pity."

"No!" Not no, I didn't want to quit feeling sorry for myself, but no, I didn't want to get off the road. "Let me think a minute. We'll have to turn off somewhere and go into a town. The kind of place we're looking for won't be on the highway. And the problem is, it's been so long since I've been up this way, I can't remember which of these little burgs is dry and which isn't."

I checked the speedometer, eighty without a tremor, and wished Daddy could've owned a car like this, once in his life, anyhow. He'd driven good cars before the Depression, and a good one during the war when he was making money. But never a really fine one like this. And what a fool he would've thought I was, to still be clutching those ancient rags of guilt to my bosom. "This is a marvellous piece of machinery," I said. "A beautiful car," and felt Naomi's quick stare across the side of my face.

"Why don't you drive it for Uncle Will?" she said.

But I wasn't able to go that far. "Not now. Maybe coming back. I tell you what. We're about twenty minutes out of Hillsboro, if the Highway Patrol doesn't stop us first. We might spot something there."

"Okay. You call it." She pulled out around a line of trucks and said, "Have you been giving any thought to what we talked about today?"

"You mean moving to Austin? No."

"No, certainly not. You're too wrapped up in thinking about Beaumont and how unhappy you were there."

'Unhappy' wasn't the right word. I didn't know the right word to describe how I felt that Monday morning when I left the little yellow house for yet another new school. Maybe I'd been off the road so long I'd forgotten how to walk away without regret. Or maybe I'd been sent out to suffer trial by ordeal one time too many. But for whatever reason, that quality that had carried me through every fear and anxiety every new school ever offered, gathered itself for one more try, looked down that long shell road, took one last tired breath, and went drifting off into the waiting trees.

I went, of course. That day and all the other days of what was left of that term. But I never did any homework, never answered a question in class, never even opened my arithmetic book unless I knew the teacher was watching me.

Daddy never noticed I'd quit bringing books and papers home. He took it for granted that anyone with the opportunity to get an education would take advantage of it. And he was so absorbed in his studio, so busy trying to make a living, so deep in his own daydream . . . Mama worried about it, though. I could see it in her eyes sometimes when I was rocking Billy while she ironed, or talking Martha May into taking her dose of sulfur and molasses. But Mama's energies were strained in nursing Billy, in putting something on the table, in keeping us in clean clothes.

"It wasn't all unhappiness, Naomi," I said. "We had some good times, too, after those first lean weeks. Even with the Depression still clinging on, it looked for awhile like Daddy's studio was going to make it after all. If the economy hadn't taken another downturn, if he hadn't hurt that leg he broke back when he was in Longview, if hard work and sacrifice had been enough—"

"And if this is your idea of the good times—"

"No, I'm trying to tell you. Toward the end of that summer, we finally began pulling out of the stretch in Starvation Alley we'd been serving. We were paying the rent on time, eating all the beans and pone we could hold, even talking about hooking up to electricity and buying a radio for Christmas.

"We had good neighbors in the Foshees, and I'd finally made a best friend—poor, weird, wicked little Delphine Hutto. She was as much of an outcast misfit as I was. But she helped me get over my fear of the woods. She was used to real bayou country, where wolves and alligators and God knows what all lived in those days, and still do, I suppose, if there're any pockets of them left civilization hasn't been able to find and destroy. Our little strip of woods didn't mean squat to her. She wasn't scared of anything, anyhow, not even snakes.

"She said her grandpa's pigs kept his place in Louisiana free of them, and any they missed, she and her cousin Aylard—I don't know which used to turn my stomach the worst, the pigs eating the snakes, or her holding one's head down with a forked stick while Aylard chopped it to bits with his knife as he pulled the coils off her arm."

"For God's sake, Mavis!"

"I forgot. You've heard that story before."

"Yes, and I don't care to hear it again, especially not when I've got my mouth set for a plate of hot links."

"It does tend to spoil your appetite for pork, doesn't it? But what I'm trying to tell you, is—"

"That you had a short reprieve between the time things

went from bad to worse, which you've told me about before, and for which I'm grateful and wish you'd concentrate on more if you have to think about those days at all. The Hillsboro exit's coming up. Shall I take it?"

"Could we go on to Fort Worth?"

"Yes, if that's what you want to do."

"I was hoping Buster's might still be there."

"I think that's a long shot, but I don't care where we go so long as I don't have to listen to any more Beaumont horror stories."

"I'm sorry I've been boring you."

"You're not boring me, Mavis, you're worrying me. All this remembrance of things past business is unhealthy."

"I just wanted to let you know that I *do* think about the good times, too, that's all."

"I know, but you don't think about them with joy, Mavis, you think about them with regret. And even so, if I thought going through all this *Gemutlichkeit,* or whatever it is, would help you make an intelligent decision—"

"One you'd approve of, you mean?"

"Oh hell. You're impossible."

"No, I'm only trying to understand what made the bottom drop out that autumn. I know the Depression hadn't been whipped, and that the fall-out from the Dust Bowl was just reaching its peak. But there had to be some money circulating, with all the government programs that were operating, and all the preparations for the Centennial the next year. About the first of November, though, when Daddy's Christmas business should've been picking up, everything just went to pot again.

"Several of our neighbors lost their jobs and had to move. All the men at the plant where Curly Foshee worked had their hours cut. But we had a good Thanksgiving. Curly said he was starving to death for meat, so he borrowed a shotgun from somebody, one of his relatives, I guess. He didn't know how to shoot, which was unusual for a Cajun. They're all big hunters and fishermen. But he didn't. So

Daddy bought the shells and they drove out to some rice field somewhere late that Wednesday evening, and Daddy brought down enough of those red-winged blackbirds to feed an army."

"Stop. Stop. You're rattling like a gatling gun yourself."

"I'm just concentrating on the fun times the way you told me to."

"You call eating blackbirds for Thanksgiving fun?"

"Sure. If you'd been as hungry as we were—Mama browned them good and stirred in some onions and a little flour and filled the pot with water. The birds were mostly bone and buckshot, but that gravy! Rose had brought over about half a washtub full of rice, and we all sat there stuffed to the gills, warm and out of the rain. It was like a potluck. We loved it."

"Mavis, I'm glad that—"

"Then after Christmas, Daddy hurt his leg. I don't even remember how he did it. It just looked like a bad scrape when he got home that night. Mama doctored it with coal oil, but—"

"Mavis. Wait."

"That's all we had in those days. Coal oil and castor oil and sulfur and molasses. If they couldn't cure what ailed you, you were sunk. But everything developed into something bad in that godforsaken hole. If you walked through wet grass, you got dew poisoning. If you scratched a mosquito bite, you got impetigo. If you rubbed your eyes, you got pink eye. And staph went for the jugular on everything else. Those were just names, though. The truth was, we were all half-dead from malnutrition."

"Mavis, I just cannot listen to anymore of that stuff tonight. And I can't see that it's helping you to be thinking about it. The only thing that's going to help you now is for you to think about your future and how you're going to handle it. The past has been handled, there's nothing we can do about it. So please, put it behind you. Let it go."

"I can't."

"You can if you want to bad enough."

"You know nobody's ever free of the past, Naomi."

"Maybe not, but I also know you don't have to sit around and drown yourself in it, either."

We were running through true night, then, past the closed-down outposts of little bypassed towns and cotton fields and fencerows left to Johnson grass and bois d'arc, across hollow bridges above dry creek beds where dark billows of lost trees rose and fell in the night wind, through miles of starlit pastures into the exploding novas of truck stops and last chance package stores.

But it wasn't the same, anymore than it had been the same when we left Beaumont for San Antonio, toward the end of that last, desperate winter when even hope seemed dead and frozen.

TWENTY-FIVE

It was the pony man who saved us. Well, actually, it was Aunt Millie. But it was the pony man who kept us going at the same time he forced things to a head by taking us for what little we had.

Pony men were beneath kidnappers in the old hierarchy, just as kidnappers ranked beneath men who owned their own studios. They were usually old men, failed kidnappers, finishing men fired from some big chain, a few topnotchers felled by drink or women or cards. Drifters and loners, they travelled around the country with a Shetland pony, a red bandana, a small-sized Stetson and cut-down paint-hide chaps, taking photographs of children seated on the pony in the drugstore-cowboy regalia of their parents' picture-show daydreams.

Like most road people, they holed up in some town during the winter, some hick place where they could find pasture for their pony and maybe pick up a little business among the crowds when some two-bit carnival or tent show came through. So that one who would come by working the far edges of a big town like Beaumont was the last thing we expected.

But by one came, late in the afternoon of the day Daddy had finally had to give in and go to the doctor with his leg. The doctor said he'd have to stay off it completely. No standing, no walking, no driving, no weight on it at all.

We were sitting in the kitchen, Daddy staring at his propped up leg, his face as hard and bony looking as it'd been the time they found the drowned man and the little boys; Mama squeezing her hands bloodless to keep from wringing them; I wondering if anybody was ever going to say anything again, or move again, or if we'd all sit there silently till we turned into pillars of salt like Lot's wife.

Then Martha May came in from the porch and said, "There's a man in the yard, with a camera and a little bitty horse, and he wants to speak to the lady of the house."

Mama added water to the coffee pot and set it to boiling, Daddy offered his Bull Durham, and Pony Jack told how he was flat busted at his sister's over in Burr's Point, a little community a couple of miles down the road from us, with a ruined tire and tube on the trailer he hauled Star in. He said he'd been trying to work his way up to Dallas to get in on some of the money that'd be floating around there when the Centennial Exposition opened in April, but his Luck was about as poor as he'd ever seen it outside of West Texas. He got out every day it wasn't raining, and worked some neighborhood he and Star could foot it to and back without wearing their hooves plumb to the ground. But he *was* wearing out his welcome at his sister's, and if he could just get him a little stake together to tide him over till the weather broke—

"There wouldn't be no wages," Daddy said. "I ain't been doing much more than keeping my head above water here lately. But you'd have food, and tobacco money, and there's plenty of room in the back to stake Star. I'd expect you to drive my car, and I'd buy the gas. I ain't looking for no miracles. But if you can just keep the doors open till I can get back on this leg, when business does pick up, I'll see you get a fair cut."

So Pony Jack came to live with us. But not till Daddy had coughed up a dollar and six-bits of the money he'd put back for his studio rent to buy a new tire and tube, and not till Billy and Martha May had their picture made on the pony, Billy in the saddle, Martha May behind him, holding him.

I'd already had my pony picture made, a long time ago—one of several prints I treasured that got lost in the shuffle of one move or another through the years. But the one of Martha May and Billy in front of the little yellow house was still on my dresser, in the gray cardboard folder with 'Maddox Studio' stamped on it.

When our Luck had made that brief turn for the better just as I was going into junior high, I'd hoped a fresh start in another new school would turn my Luck, too. And it might have if the family Luck had held—no, scratch the Luck. I couldn't have survived Mr. Mulholland if I'd been wearing diamonds to school, which I thought I was in a way, that first morning.

I had a new dress to start in, a new pair of shoes, a best friend, a full belly, and a timid tremble of desire to win back the place I'd once held. Not as a playground monitor or errand runner or leader of the Pledge. I knew those things were gone forever. But simply as a good pupil who loved school and was happy in it. A modest little desire, shot with doubt and trepidation, that gave up the ghost without a struggle five minutes into the second period.

Mr. Mulholland helped coach football at the high school and taught all the arithmetic classes at the junior high, which was located on the same grounds. All the boys called him 'Coach,' as did the important girls, the pretty and popular ones, whose big sisters were cheerleaders or band members at the high school.

He printed his name on the blackboard in big capital letters, 'Coach Everett Mulholland,' then turned around and gave us a long, terrible looking-over before going into what he called his 'First of the Year Pep Talk.'

He said everything in life was like a football game and that went double for school. He said you built up your *de*-fense by studying, and moved the ball on *of*-fense when you went to the board or took a test. He was the coach and the quarterback, too, and we were the team. Some of us would be varsity players who could always be counted on to carry the ball over the goal for a touchdown. Some would be hard hitters who could block a kick or move the ball for a first down. And some of us would be nothing but benchwarmers, too dumb and too lazy to play *de*-fense or *of*-fense, either, and we—oh yes, I knew my place immediately—would be the ones who let the team down, both at school and in the game of life. But he could promise us that by the time he was through with us, we'd wish we were the kind of players we ought to be.

We had board drill, which he called 'scrimmage,' every day. He'd send a 'squad' to the board, always including a few benchwarmers, and though I prayed with enough fervor to move mountains, my turn came around as regularly as everyone else's. We stood at the ready, chalk in hand, till he called the 'signals,' which was the statement of the problem, then he yelled, "Hup! Hup! Now run, you yellow-bellied sapsuckers, run!" and whoever finished first scored.

If that had been all there was to it, if the rest of us could've gone on back to our seats after the touchdown hero had been applauded—but, no. We had to stand there till he finished explaining where we had messed up, starting with those who had made the most yardage. After a little half-friendly sarcasm and a pat on the back for effort, they sat down all fired up and ready to run again.

Next came those who had made it to the fifty yard line, or who had at least managed to begin a faltering run in that direction. They got everything from a tongue-lashing that would've melted a steam locomotive to an appointment with the paddle.

Last came those of us who had done little more than get the 'signals' on the board, or who, as often happened to me, were too paralyzed to do anything but stand there staring at the chalk tray in a blind and violent jumble of dread. We got pity, usually collectively, though sometimes, just as we thought our suffering was over and done, he'd single out

someone in our raggedy-ass little ranks for a dose of per-
sonal pity all his own.

So when I started home on mid-term report card day
near the last of January, when the playlike spring had shriv-
eled back into winter, with a cold rain blowing hard enough
to keep the exhausts pumping and the windshield wipers
tocking on the cars that waited for the important kids, I
wasn't surprised that I'd failed arithmetic. I was only surprised at how big and how red an F looked. Never having
gotten one before, not even at the end of the last term when
I'd been passed on to junior high on probation, I'd somehow
imagined it would be the same size and color as the other
grades, none of which gave me any cause for pride.

I had salvaged B's in spelling and reading, because I
made 100's on my written work. But because I couldn't
spell out loud anymore, or answer reading questions out
loud, without stuttering, that teacher had soon quit calling on
me, due, she said, to my lack of desire to take part in class
discussion.

Delphine's grades were worse than mine, but she didn't
care how bad her grades were. It didn't bother her to have to
sit on the back row or to be reprimanded for not having her
homework. What did bother her was Mr. Mulholland's
brand of pity, and it bothered her to the point of hatred.

One day at noon, after I'd been pitied so thoroughly that
morning I couldn't keep my lunch down, she said, "You
won't have to worry about that old shithook much longer,
girl. I already got word to Aylard, and when he gets here,
Mr. Coach Everett Mulholland's going to have hisself such a
bad accident, he'll be took care of from now on."

I'd always been a little bit scared of Delphine. Not that
she'd pull my hair or twist my arm or do any of the other
hateful things even so-called friends sometimes did in a
flash of half-playful cruelty. She never started any kind of
meanness with anybody. Nor that she'd ever fly into the
same killing rage against me I'd seen her pour on girls a
head taller than she was for making fun of her clothes or the

216

way she talked—who was I to make fun of anybody? I was an object of ridicule myself.

But sometimes when we were alone in the woods, when her eyes went droopy and her lips got wet and thick, I was afraid she'd hurt me in some way I wasn't quite able to imagine, and I'd run for the nearest sign of civilization as fast as I could go, and wait for her to turn back into her regular self.

"What do you mean, he'll have an accident? What kind of accident?"

"Foo, I don't know. Maybe his brakes'll go out on him. Maybe his house'll catch fire in the middle of the night. Maybe he'll just disappear and won't nobody know what happened to him."

I wanted Mr. Mulholland to disappear as much as anybody, but I meant by moving away or going over to the high school full time, not— "Aylard wouldn't do anything real bad, would he?"

"Ain't Mr. Mulholland done real bad things to me?"

"Well, yes, but—" and I fell back on the final authority this side of God— "what would your mama and daddy say?"

She laughed. "They won't know nothing about it. Me and Cousin Aylard tend to our own business our own-selves."

I had a sudden vision of Delphine and a shadowy Aylard wrapped together in a gasping tangle of sweat and spit amid the grunting of pigs and the smell of something burning, and leaned over and finished emptying my stomach.

"If you tell on us," she said, "something bad will happen to you, too, even if we are friends. So you better keep your mouth shut."

TWENTY-SIX

I knew I ought to tell somebody, no matter what. But I couldn't have faced Mr. Mulholland to've saved my own life. And at home, while hope had revived, our Luck continued to remain so near the same as it had been, I didn't want to add to Mama's and Daddy's worries.

Pony Jack came in most evenings that first week shaking his head, saying, "Not a dime, Will. Just ain't no traffic." A couple of evenings he did hand over a dollar and some change, and on Saturday, so late we were about ready for bed, three dollars.

"I know it ain't much," he said, "for such a long hard day, but it was the best I could do."

The next morning after he went to his sister's for Sunday dinner, she apparently liking him better since he no longer lived with her, Mama said, "Something's wrong, Will. I know Jack's not the photographer you are, or the salesman, either. But we've ended up with less than seven dollars for a whole week's work. We can't live on that, all six of us. I'm ashamed of the short rations I'm putting on the table now, and what with two rents to pay and gasoline to buy, we simply can't make it."

"He just ain't got the hang of it yet, Fern, that's all. He'll catch on. I been going over things with him, giving him some tips. And you got to remember I wasn't doing so hot myself there before I banged up this leg."

"Yes, but four or five dollars more a week and one less mouth to feed and buy tobacco for, not to mention oats for that damned pony, makes a big difference."

"He's got to keep Star fed up. She's his livelihood."

"Well it looks to me like there's enough grass and weeds around here to furnish graze for a whole herd of ponies."

"You know this old water-soaked grass ain't got any nourishment in it. I'm surprised at you, Fern. I never knew you to be stingy before, with man or beast."

"I'm not stingy, Will. But it's hard to buy oats for a pony when you can't buy—that's not the point, anyhow. There's just something going on I don't feel right about. I don't trust him and that's that."

"Ain't he always conducted hisself like a gentleman?"

"Yes, but—"

"Does he ever complain about what you set before him or act dissatisfied about sleeping in his bedroll on the kitchen floor?"

"No, Will, I'm not arguing any of that. He's quiet and clean and well-mannered, and I know he leaves for work early and comes in late. But something's rotten in Denmark. I feel it in my bones."

"The man can't go out and drag people in off the street and make them let him take their picture. He's keeping the doors open for me, and he took the rent in to Mr. Bergson and explained why it was late, so we got another month's grace there. This ain't going on forever, Fern. I'm going to be able to work myself in another week from what Dr. Broussard said when Curly carried me in Friday."

"Dr. Broussard never said you'd be back at work in a week, Will."

"Well, the same thing."

"No, it's not the same thing. Just because he said your leg's healing faster and better than he thought it would doesn't mean he wants you taking any chances with it."

"I don't see how me riding in with Jack along toward

219

the end of the week and sitting there doing a little retouching, or passing a few proofs could hurt anything."

"No. I don't want you risking it."

"Well, Fern, if you don't want me to work, and you
don't want to cut Jack any slack, what do you want?"

Mama blushed and threw her head up and said, "I want
three cents for a stamp so I can write Millie. I haven't got a
letter off to her in ages."

"My God, Fern, is that what you been raising all this
cain about? I never have tried to keep you from writing your
sister, have I? Go get your letter wrote and Jack can buy a
stamp and mail it for you in the morning."

"No. Curly'll be working tomorrow. I'll let him take it
in for me. He goes right by the post office."

Jack brought in so little during the next week, that on
Friday Daddy made himself a cane out of a limb Curly cut
for him. He began hobbling around the house, touching his
bad leg to the floor instead of hopping as he'd been doing,
and when Saturday came and Jack handed in even less than
he had the week before, Daddy said, "That settles it. I'm going in to work Monday if it harelips the world. Jack can do
the driving and the darkroom work, but I'm going to wait on
customers and handle the camera."

"I don't think you're ready for that much standing yet,"
Mama said, "even with your cane. What will Dr. Broussard
say?"

"It ain't Dr. Broussard's business going down the drain.
It's mine. You might as well hush, Fern, because when
Monday morning rolls around, I'm going to work. Me and
Jack together'll turn this thing around, pronto."

But Pony Jack woke us up the next morning putting his
stuff in his car, and when Daddy asked him what was going
on, he said it was just time for him to be hitting the road
again. He said there wasn't so much business Daddy
couldn't take care of it alone. He appreciated the job and the
hospitality, but—and before Mama could put the coffee on,

he was pulling out of the driveway, Star bouncing along behind in her trailer.

"I knew he wasn't anything but a no account gypsy the minute I laid eyes on him," Mama said. "If it wasn't for your leg, I'd say we're well shed of him. But I was depending on him sticking it long enough for your leg to get better."

"No use going on about it," Daddy said. "People are what they are. I can manage. Hell, I've managed worse things than this." But he had a quiet, studying look on his face all day.

I went home at noon on the days it didn't rain. Not that that made any difference in what I had for dinner, pone being pone, no matter how it's served. But I liked to get away from school any time I had the chance, especially on one of the warm, sunny days that made you think it was already spring, like that Monday when Daddy went back to work. I couldn't enjoy it as much as I usually did, for trying to figure out how I could warn Mr. Mulholland without getting my own family's house burned down, and for worrying about what I was going to say at the end of the week when I had to show Mama my report card.

I'd tried to prepare her several days ago, but I didn't know enough about football to explain it right. When I finished, she said, "Honey, I can't make heads or tails out of a word you've said."

But Daddy said, "It's plenty plain to me. You've got to get your mind off of football, young lady, and back on your lessons where it belongs."

So I wasn't any easier in my conscience on either score when I opened the back door to the smell of pone frying and the sound of Mama laughing at something Martha May said. I was just sitting down, praying that everything would be all right somehow, when we heard Daddy come in the front.

Mama said, "Why, Will, what on earth—" and stopped. His face was white, his eyes blue enough and hard enough to bore holes through a two by four.

"Well, Fern," he said, "you called that shot. The son of

a bitch aced me as slick as if I was the rawest greenhorn that ever came down the pike. He never paid the rent, he never took a picture or passed a proof, he never done nothing but play poker all over town with my money, and my studio's kaput."

"Sit down, Will. Let me pour you some coffee."

"I don't want no damn coffee. I want to get my hands around that lying old bastard's throat, that's what I want."

"But he stole *fifty* dollars from us, Will, in rent alone." She went on reluctantly. Only poor trash ran to the Law with their problems, "Couldn't we call the police?"

"It'd just be my word against his. No, he's in Dallas by now, with a fat bankroll he snookered me out of so smooth—"

"I don't understand. He came in every evening talking business, and he brought you some money."

"What he did was, he took the fifty I give him to pay Mr. Bergson and used part of it as a stake in his first game. From then on—I checked a bunch of games around town. They knew him, all right, even places where the ante's a dollar. What he brought back here was some of his winnings, or money he held back to dribble out to me so I'd keep thinking everything was on the up and up. But he never went near the studio.

"When I walked up to the door this morning, not a sample in the window, my name gone, people I never saw inside—it's a damn bail bond office now. I hustled around to see Mr. Bergson, and the long and the short of it is, since he never got his rent and never heard nothing from me and nobody was showing up to open, he didn't know what happened. He's got his living to make, too, so when he had a chance to rent to a paying client, he took it.

"He was mighty white about everything, though. Had my camera and all my equipment stored in the back of his own place. Said he knew I wasn't the kind of a man that could go off and leave the tools of his trade without some kind of reason, so he was going to hold everything safe till he got some word from me. He even helped me load it in the car and offered me another location, on trust. Said he knew I was good for it. Hah!"

"You didn't take it?"

"No, Fern. I'd be two month's rent in the hole before I even started, and it's in a dead part of town not ten people a day go by. If I couldn't make it in a good location, I sure couldn't make it there. I'll just have to go back to kidnapping. That's all I can do."

"But your leg, Will. It'll never hold up to all that driving and walking."

"It'll hold up to whatever it's got to hold up to. We can't just sit here and starve."

Mama looked at him the way she'd looked at Grandma when they'd argued about the paregoric and said, "Then I'll do your calling for you, and pass proofs and deliver orders."

"What?"

"Why not? I'm not an idiot, Will. I know how to meet the public, and I certainly know something about the picture business after all these years. It'd cut the strain on your leg in half."

"But what about the kids?"

"If Rose'll keep Martha May till Mavis gets home from school, and I feel sure she will, we'll take Billy with us. I'll fix him a pallet on the floor in the back, and when he needs to nurse you can pull over somewhere and I'll nurse him. We could give it a try for a few days."

So Mama went to work with Daddy every morning the rest of that week, and I came home to a house made strange by its emptiness every afternoon. I lit the burner under the beans Mama had got up early enough to have half cooked before she left, lit the other one to knock some of the chill off the kitchen, then lit the little round coal oil heater in the room that served as Mama's and Daddy's bedroom and living room for all of us. When I was sure every burner was the right height and color, I went across to Rose's to get Martha May, and we spent the rest of the afternoon sitting by the front window watching the cars go by, waiting for the one that would bring us that other part of ourselves.

As I crossed the tracks, the rain that had been mostly blowing drizzle when I left school, turned to a fine, stinging sleet that sent me running for the shelter of the woods, the report card with its bright red F sliding around under my sweater, Delphine's news that morning of Aylard's imminent arrival sliding around in my conscience.

I was stopped at the last bend in the narrow trail by a bunch of the big gray cattle Delphine called 'Brimmers.' They stood there like mountains, steam rising from their humped bodies, moisture shining along the curves of their horns, their soft, dark eyes pearled by the reflected light of sleet sifting through the leaves and branches. There was no way around them. The trail was hedged tight by great, dense thickets of blackberry and Cherokee rose. But I had to get by. Martha May was waiting for me.

I breathed as deep as my tight chest would let me, then edged in among them quietly, slipping sideways between their stolid, smoking bodies, and went on down the trail to the bobwire fence, glassy now with ice. I could see lamplight in the kitchen window, and was glad the bad weather had driven Mama and Daddy home early; glad the house wouldn't be empty; glad I could show them the card and get it over with; glad that somewhere in the middle of the Brahmas I'd quit caring what happened to Mr. Mulholland. If God wanted him saved, He'd have to do it Himself. I sure couldn't.

I crawled under the fence as the sleet turned into snow, and hurried across the whirling white world of the backyard, past the leaning shadow of the privy, down the beat-out path dark yet under the bending arch of weighted weeds that slapped wetly at my legs. I went up the glazed-over steps with my toes curled to keep from slipping, crossed the shallow porch streaked with ice pellets, and opened the back door to real light, warm and yellow, to talk and laughter, to the good Luck look on Mama's and Daddy's faces, to Martha May saying, "We're moving to San An-ton-i-o."

TWENTY-SEVEN

"This sudden run to Fort Worth," Naomi said as we entered the city limits. "You're not thinking of moving up here, are you?"

"Lord, no. If I were going to move, and I'm not saying I am, so don't start, it wouldn't be to Fort Worth. It's a good town, and I have a lot of happy memories there, but I have a lot of sad ones, too."

"Then why are you so dead set against Austin? You don't have any sad memories there. And you've got to move somewhere, that's all there is to it. We're not kids anymore, Mavis. I know you have a lot of friends and good neighbors, but that's not the same as being near your family as you get older. It worries me to think about you living alone in that big old house."

"You live alone."

"In a complex full of people, with Billy a mile away, and Mary Fern and the boys in town half the time, twenty minutes away if I did need them? We're all close enough to be able to check on each other and help each other when we need to."

"I don't need any help, Naomi, and besides, I may not be alone long myself. I may go get Millie and bring her home to live with me."

"Oh my God, Mavis."

"What?"

"I don't care if you do bite my head off for saying it, the last thing you need right now is someone else sick and dying to take care of."

"That's a hell of a thing to say. And you don't know she's in that kind of shape."

"She must've been in pretty bad shape to give her kids power of attorney and let them put her in a nursing home."

"Even so, she was awfully good to us. I'd like to repay part of what we owe her, if I can."

"Owe her, my foot. You all were good to her, too, don't forget. It was Uncle Will who put up the money for her and Benny to open their first Big Ben's and co-signed the note that let them expand when they were ready to. They never would've had their own chain of stores and made the money they made if he hadn't bankrolled them."

"Well, he had it to give, then. He was raking it in with both hands during the war."

"But afterwards? When Kodak flooded the world with cheap cameras and he got sick and things went to hell for him? Where was Millie then?"

"She did what she could. Losing Benny to that sudden heart attack put their own business in danger."

"No, she did what her kids let her do, and it was damned little. Admit it."

"All right. I admit I was disappointed that she didn't go see Mama and Daddy very often after Daddy got sick and things turned bad for them. But I still think—"

"And you'll be disappointed again, my dear. Those kids aren't going to let you get anywhere near Millie and her money."

"Oh, Naomi! Surely they know I'm not after Millie's money."

"No, surely they don't. They think everybody else is as greedy as they are. They're scared of you."

"That's just plain silly."

"Not from their point of view."

"You're wrong."

"No, I'm not. I promise you, they are not going to let you take her off where they think you'll have some kind of undue influence over her. I'm not too sure they'll even let you visit her."

"Now that's insane."

"Is it? Haven't you always said they treated you all like strangers?"

"Well, it's true we've never been close. But we weren't raised near each other, remember, and there's such a difference in our ages. Maybe they feel I haven't done much for Millie this past year, though God knows I wrote and called when I could."

"It's a sleeping dog you'd do well to let lie."

"I just don't like to think of her being in a nursing home. I couldn't stand it if she were neglected."

"She's not neglected. They at least put her in the best place in San Antonio, so I'm sure she's well cared for. Think about your own life for a change and strike out for new pastures—"

Yes, and when your Luck runs out there, move on down the road to the next place. I wished I could remember moving to Fort Worth the way I remembered moving to San Antonio, but I couldn't. Fort Worth was nothing but a word marking the end of something I didn't want to face, till we were already in a tourist court on East Lancaster waiting for Daddy to find us a house. While San Antonio, like the Heavenly City itself, sprang into being the instant Martha May called its name that snowy afternoon, becoming, by the time I went to sleep that night, more real than the house around me, the final, shining bead in a rosary of rivers and towns and old campgrounds sung through memories Mama and Daddy chanted far into the night.

And like the pilgrims we were, we headed out for its holy environs before dawn two days after Millie's letter came. The snow was long gone, the old car loaded down to the last bounce in its old springs, Billy in Mama's lap,

Martha May and I wedged into the half of the back seat the camera allowed us, everything else packed into the places assigned long ago, secured, as were we all, by a smart new rope and a magic old knot.

Mama had tried to get Daddy to sell his equipment. She said the big studio where Aunt Millie had got him a Regular Job would have everything anyhow, so why hang onto a bunch of stuff he'd never use again. But he said he would use it again. He said, "Luck don't never make its final turn till they haul you off in a hearse. There's always another chance waiting somewhere down the road, and when mine comes, I aim to be ready for it."

"What do you call what we've just been handed?"

"I call it a way out, Fern, and I'm damn grateful for it. But I've had a taste of owning my own place now, and working for the other fella's going to be hard to do."

"These people are hiring you sight unseen, Will, making you the photographer, the *manager* of one of their busiest studios. If that's not enough of a chance, I don't know what would be."

"They ain't exactly buying a pig in a poke. I'm known in the trade. Somebody there's heard my name, seen some of my work. I don't care how good a friends they are with Millie, they wouldn't turn one of their studios over to the first guy in off the street like I done."

"Oh, Will."

"No use pussyfooting around about it. I burned my butt, now I got to sit on the blister. But this job will give us a chance to get back on our feet, put some money aside, and when the time's ripe—"

"I can't think that far ahead. I can't think of anything but how glad I am to be shaking the dust of this place off our feet."

"Aw, Beaumont's not a bad town. If I hadn't bunged up this leg, we might've done okay there."

"Don't talk to me. It's the opposite end of the stick from Angelo as far as I'm concerned, and they could both sink in the middle of the ocean for all I'd care. This is a really good job, Will, and San 'Tonia's a really good town—I know, I know. It's my fault we've avoided it like the plague since Mama and Papa moved there. But they're not going to bother us, I assure you. I've made up my mind to that.

"Though I will say, shabby as they've treated us, I don't think if they'd owned a grocery store they'd have stood by and let us be forced to ask for Relief the way your papa did. I don't blame you for it, Will. I know it hurt you worse than it did me. But I'll never forgive Mr. Maddox for it, not in this world or the next."

It shocked me sick to hear Mama talk about The Secret out loud, to remember that day, Daddy at the table saying, "I'd rather steal, goddamn it, or see us all in our graves."

"Which is where we're going to be, Will, if we don't get something to eat soon, and you being in the pen wouldn't help. If it was just you and me, I wouldn't do it, either, but we have the children to think about. I'm going now, Nina Caldwell's waiting downstairs to take me."

As she walked out the door carrying Martha May, Daddy's head went down on his arms, and I understood that having to ask for Relief was something so terrible it could make a grown man, your own daddy, sob like a wind-broke horse and put a witch's mask on your mama's face as she cooked the supper Daddy said he wouldn't eat.

"Yes you will," she said, "You owe it to me for what this day's cost me."

And he did. But when those groceries, the funny looking cans and boxes without regular labels, began to run low, Mama wrote Aunt Millie and she sent us the money to ride the Travel Bureau to Grandma's house in Robb's Prairie, just as she'd sent us money this time to get to San Antonio in our own car.

We stopped often so Daddy could get out and rest his leg. He didn't want to. He said at the rate we were going, we'd never get through Houston and across the Brazos by nightfall.

"You *have* to pet that leg, Will. Dr. Broussard warned you that infection could get stirred up again. He said—"

"Damn it, I know what he said. But he ain't the one making our living. I am."

"He was mighty good to us."

"I know that, too. And I'm obliged to him. But Millie didn't send us this money so I could sit on my behind till Dr. Broussard give me the nod. She sent it so we could get to San 'Tonia and I could get to work."

"Yes, Will, but we don't have to drive straight through."

"I said I'd stop ever once in awhile, Fern, and that's what I'm doing. But between petting this bum leg and petting this old car—I don't want to get there all crippled up anymore than you want me to. When I walk into that studio Monday morning—but we got to get at least halfway today. Farther if we can."

It was almost dark when we pulled in under the porch of a boarded up grocery store-filling station on the far side of Sealy. The cold wind, damp with the smell of the river, creaked the rusting sign that said 'Casey's One Stop,' and rattled a loose section of corrugated tin nailed around the collapsing corner of a wood fence that staggered down one side of the lot. Cast off parts lumped up out of the dead weeds like fallen tombstones in some old, forgotten cemetery, and the lone pump, as rusty as the sign, sat canted to one side without its hose.

We stood there a minute, hunched against the chill, then Daddy started pulling boards off the fence, and Mama said, "You girls better go pee-pee, then you can watch Billy for me while I go."

We were still in the trees, where full night had already settled, the only light left a pale glimmer down the narrow strip of road and in the puny dent the station clearing made among the thick growth of pines and hardwood.

"Hurry up," I told Martha May. "And turn loose of me."

"I'm scared of snakes."

"There aren't any snakes out now. It's still winter. Here, behind this bush'll do. And turn loose of me, I said. You can't pull your dress up and your pants down without using both hands."

"Where do they all go?"

"I don't know, Martha May. Down a hole someplace."

"You go first. There might be one left over."

"You squat yourself this minute, young lady. I'm tired of fooling with you. Now come on, we'll go together."

We faced into the trees and brush, not wanting that waiting darkness at our backs, straining to hurry, flinching at the plop of something striking water somewhere in the blackness in front of us.

Martha May jumped up. "I'm through," she said. *"You* hurry up. It's scary here."

"There's nothing to be scared of," I said, but I ran right beside her all the way back to the clearing and the fire Daddy had built against a log he'd pulled in from the edge of the woods.

"I've got the beans and the water jug out, Mavis. While Martha May watches Billy, you climb in the back and get what I need for the pone. I'll get it on before I run to the bushes."

We didn't have a regular chuck box like we used to, just a plain cardboard one from the Red and White. But the groceries were packed the way they'd always been, so I knew exactly where to reach, even in the darkness inside the car. And when I raised back up, I saw things the way they used to be out the frame of the window. Daddy watching Mama set the bean pot on the bed of coals he'd raked out for her, Martha May-me and Billy-Martha May playing pattycake on the quilt, the firelight warming the night. Then it all turned back into the ordinary now of what we were at that moment, tired and hungry and strangely out of place where we'd once been at home.

"It seems funny to be without the tent," Mama said, "and so quiet with just us here all by ourselves. I keep thinking somebody ought to come by to get acquainted, or to ask about the road. I've got that night we spent at the ford on my mind, when Jules and Evelyn showed up, and that girl, what was her name? The one travelling with her kids and her mama, the one we had the big potluck with?"

"I don't remember."

"Oh Will, sure you do. You got her a job with that friend of yours that had the fried pie business."

"I know who you're talking about, Fern, but I can't recall her name."

"Johnnie," I said. "Her name was Johnnie."

"That's right, Johnnie," Mama said. "I wonder where they are now?"

"No telling. You want a smoke?"

"I believe I do. Then I'll get these dishes washed up and give the kids a lick and a promise and get them bedded down. I wish we didn't have to sleep in the car, though. It's so crowded, I'm worried you won't be able to rest your leg."

"My leg'll be okay. I'm going to roll up in a quilt and sleep out here so you and Billy can have the seat to yourselves."

"You don't need to do that. You'll freeze."

"I won't be out here long enough. I plan to be back on the road by about three o'clock."

"After the day we just put in?"

"That's the whole point. We been fighting it since before daylight, and I don't figure we've averaged more'n twenty miles an hour. What with resting this leg and fixing two flats and getting hung up in Houston—boy, there's a town that's growing. I wish I'd gone on there instead of to Beaumont when I left Longview. Maybe—"

"You didn't have a job waiting in Houston, Will. Besides, there's always a maybe."

"Yes, and some of them pan out. Maybe if I hadn't held to my promise to stay out of boom towns, we'd have already made our pile and been sitting on easy street right now."

"And maybe you'd have been shot or stabbed to death

and Mavis would've been run over by some drunk mule skinner."

"You always look for the worst."

"And I'm usually right. Oh, let's don't fuss. We made our choices and did the best we could. I just thank the Lord we're on our way to better times now."

TWENTY-EIGHT

And true to his word, Daddy headed us out toward better times them while it was still so deep dark the lantern looked like the last light left in the world, and so cold our feet were numb when we climbed out at Mama's call, Martha May whiny with sleep, my right arm aching from the weight of her head against it all night.

There was no fire to huddle up to. "I don't want to take the time to fool with one," Daddy said. "You all stir around and get your blood to moving and you won't be so cold."

"But what about breakfast, Will? The girls need something in their stomachs."

"We'll eat on down the road. With any Luck, we ought to be in Schulenburg, maybe Flatonia, by daybreak. Mavis, you and Martha May go tend to your business and climb right back in so we can get rolling."

When Mama finished nursing Billy, she licked her thumb and wiped the milk stain from around his mouth and said, "I do wish we could clean up some. I don't want to get in to Millie's looking like the wrath of God."

"We'll stop at a filling station in Eagle Lake or somewhere. I got to gas up and air the tires, and I want to grab a quick shave myself. I ain't going to let us pull in to Millie's looking like a bunch of sheepherders."

We drove through shifting layers of fog till well after we crossed the Colorado, gassed and cleaned up at a station in Glidden because nobody was open in Eagle Lake, watched the sun rise over our breakfast fire outside of Schulenburg, and didn't stop again till we hit Luling.

Mama didn't want to stop there. She said they didn't call Luling the meanest town in Texas for nothing, which Daddy well knew, and the only reason he wanted to stop there was to look up his old crony. But Daddy said the boom had been over for years and Luling was as civilized as any-place now, and yes, he did want to see Buford if he was still in business, which he was, at a big combination filling sta-tion and garage called 'Buford's Magnolia,' right on the highway.

Daddy parked the car off away from the pumps, head-ing it into a picket fence that divided the station lot from the house next door, and went in to see his friend. Mama said Martha May and I could get out to stretch our legs, but we had to stay where she could see us every minute. We walked up and down in front of the fence on *real* gravel, made out of *real* rocks, and watched the lady next door come out to sweep her porch, singing 'Love Lifted Me' while she worked.

The wind was dry, smelling of gas and oil and trainsmoke, dust and cottonseed and last year's stubble, pee-wet mud and manure from the feedlot across from us where cattle were being prodded into a truck. Freight cars being bumped down the line rattled and banged, tires sang and ploppity-plopped down the highway, the gravel crunched brown and red and caramel coffee under our feet, and above us, great miles of sky opened out over the tracks and trees and buildings and I knew I was almost Home.

"You all come get in the car," Mama called. "I think your daddy's finally coming to see whether somebody's cut our throats or not."

She always got mad when he kept us waiting, and he al-ways did keep us waiting. But he looked so young when he turned from the station door laughing, walking toward us fast the way he used to, without any limp at all, that I thought it would put her in a good mood again instead of putting tears in her eyes.

But she smiled when he got in and said, "Well, how's Buford?"

"Going great guns. Got a good crew, a garage full of work in there, and a brand new wrecker on order. Doing a good gas business—he asked about you, Fern. I think you might at least have gone in and said hello to the man."

"I didn't want to wake the baby."

"He saved my hide once, don't forget."

"Yes, I owe him for that. But he owes me for ever putting you in such a dangerous position to start with."

"You talk like he tied me up and drug me along."

"He was older than you. He influenced you."

"No, goddamn it, he didn't. I was a grown man."

"You were nothing but a wild buck of a boy."

"With a wife and baby?"

"We were all babies back then, Will, with about as much sense as a bunch of geese."

"I had enough sense to know if I could've roughnecked a few more months, I'd have had the stake to open my own studio the way Buford opened his station."

"You weren't ready to settle down then, and you know it."

"For a place of my own I would've been."

"You think that now, but—well, *I* had enough sense to know many more fights over pipes and fittings and whatever it was you all were constantly fighting over—"

"You *had* to fight then, for everything you got around here. Or fight to hold onto it. That was the only way you could keep your rig going. We was just taking care of our own."

"And I was just taking care of *my* own. I didn't want you hurt bad or killed or turned into some kind of thug."

"Why, Buford wasn't no thug."

"No, Will, I don't say he was. And whatever sins the poor devil was guilty of, he's paid for dearly from the seat of that wheelchair all these years. But I do say that was a dead end kind of life. We never saved a penny in any boom town we ever worked. It cost too much to live. And that could've been you, brought home to me on a gate torn off of somebody's fence."

"And would've been, if Buford hadn't—"

"I said I owe him, and I'm glad his business is prospering and doing well. It certainly cost him and Ruby enough. But I couldn't live that kind of life. Having to tie Mavis to the porch railing while I did my housework, and—"

Daddy laughed. "Do you remember that, Mavis?"

"Nossir." Only men and mules and trucks, yelling and cussing, mud and dust, and black-red nights smoky with piano music and burning gas stacks.

"Your mama couldn't trust you to stay on the porch and play, and if she kept you in and locked the screen, you'd climb up on a chair when she wasn't looking and push open the hook and—"

"And just go wandering off while I nearly went crazy. You were a good little girl, Mavis, but you did have itchy feet."

Daddy laughed again and said, "Well, she come by them honest."

"I wonder what time it's getting to be?" Mama said. "I sure would like to be in and settled by dinnertime."

"Well, we ought to make it by then, if the tires hold out. I been pushing along at a steady thirty all morning, and so far, so good. But we got to go by Millie's first to find out where our place is, and if you all get to visiting—"

"I thought we could visit a little while we eat," Aunt Millie said.

"Well, we'd really like to get on in our own place and get settled," Mama said. "I can throw something together later."

"No, now honey, I've got tea made, and I'll just call Benny and get him to bring some hamburgers home."

"What's a hamburger?" Martha May said, and everybody but me laughed. It embarrassed me for her to be such a little greenhorn, but I didn't like for her to be laughed at in a strange place, either. It wasn't her fault she didn't know what something she'd never seen was. I took her in the kitchen to explain, feeling out of place and uneasy around an Aunt Millie suddenly rich. Not only could she just pick up her own telephone and call her husband to bring something as expensive as hamburgers home for dinner, she lived in a fancy apartment with painted walls and shiny new linoleum and strings of crepe paper sweetpeas hanging in the bedroom door like sleeping butterflies.

I felt more at home, though, by the time we finished eating and Uncle Benny had to go back to work. He was the manager of his store now, and Sunday was the day he had to make sure his assistant manager cleaned out the meat and dairy cases and scrubbed the vegetable racks while he brought his books and orders up to date. He shook hands with Daddy again, and told Mama to stop by and see him any time she was in the store, and then Mama and Aunt Millie cleared the table and we got back in the car to go to our own place, Aunt Millie sitting in the front so she could show Daddy where to go.

We went down her street one block and crossed Broadway, a big wide busy street where Uncle Benny's store was, along with used car lots and cafes and all kinds of businesses, down another block past a house with a sign out front in the shape of a hand that had 'Madam Melba's' painted on it, and Aunt Millie said, "Turn right here, Will. It's just a couple of more blocks, on your left."

It looked like all the apartment houses we'd ever lived in rolled into one. Two-storied, multi-porched, sprawling with odd, added-on rooms and outside stairways and a row of sheds tacked together at the back, it was the kind of house where cars would always be coming and going, worked on, checked over, bragged about or cussed, leaned on, sat in, traded off in despair, taken home in triumph or resignation, named, blamed, and cherished. Where clothes would always be blowing on the lines; somebody always sweeping a porch or a walk, airing bedding or babies or old folks, sitting at a window reading or sewing or watching people go by, stopping to chat, running in to borrow something, flirting, fussing, being mad or sad or glad. Where life in all its sweetness and terror hummed through the walls and passageways to echo along the blood like summer thunder.

TWENTY-NINE

"Lord," Naomi said, "looks like we're the only signs of life in this place. The whole downtown's dead as a doorknob."

"It always has been after dark. You're too used to living in a college town."

"Fort Worth has colleges."

"But it's not a college *town*."

"It wasn't always a *ghost* town, either. It was crowded with people during the war, day and night. You couldn't stir them with a stick."

"Yes, but once the war ended, everybody went back to the old custom of rolling up the sidewalks at six o'clock. You don't remember it like that, because when you came up here then—well, the world had changed. Our lives had changed. We had more important things to think about than running around having a good time."

"But oh, didn't we have some great ones while it lasted? Remember before Paul left for the navy, when I'd come stay with you, and Charles'd manage to hitch a ride in from Hensley? We used to hit a dozen places a night—private parties, the Clover Club, the old 400, all the hotels. Remember the silver dollars stuck in the bar at the Pirate's Cave, and the conga line that time at the Casino when Charles led us— well, as you say, it was a different town then."

"Everything was different then."

"Yes. Even us."

"Especially us. Especially me, anyhow. Oh, I don't know, Naomi. It's not just the grief, though God knows there's been enough of that to go around. Or even the passage of time and the toll it takes. It's that—there's not any *poetry* in life anymore. Everything's as dull as grits."

"You don't have to eat everything that's set in front of you, you know."

"I guess I was taught too well to clean my plate when I was little. But I've about reached the point where I've swallowed all I can stand."

"Which is another good reason for you to move to Austin."

"Where poetry runs rampant, I suppose?"

"Yes, in some parts of town it still does. I know you're right about all the development. That monstrosity of a freeway's a horror, and some of the new buildings going up are ugly enough to make a buzzard puke. The traffic's a headache and they're destroying the aquifer—but there're still some of the old places left, the old ways, the river."

It wasn't the Colorado I longed for, though. It was the San Antonio, in the days when it was yet a piece of the wet and the wilderness poets sing about, instead of an expendable piece of real estate for the vultures to turn a buck on—

Vertie and I took the shortcut along the river every day on our way to and from school, along a path that led down to the low bank from a machine shop's sideyard on St. Mary's and came up at the bridge on Guadalupe where the praline factory stood.

Mists rose above the water those first chilly mornings, shining with refracted light, grayed shreds of it drifting through the underbrush. Beading spider webs and grass blades, dripping from leaves, it settled in the breaks and hollows, closing over sections of the path, hiding all the far bank except for the sunlit tops of the tallest trees, wrapping us in such a stilled remoteness we were dazzled when we came up out of it into the city on its way to work.

In the afternoons the shortcut was a wide, greeny-gold, open-skied tunnel of moving leaf and light and water, from which we could catch glimpses of the backyards of houses and businesses across the upper banks of both sides. Piles of brickbats and other scrap were scattered around off the path, partly covered by new grass and tangles of wild morning-glory, while flies buzzed over human excrement behind certain bushes and silence hung above the leavings of some solitary hobo's camp—doused ashes, an empty can, a man-sized wallow in the weeds, the ribbon thin ripple of a trot line strung too shallow.

We always stopped a few minutes at the big cottonwood that leaned out over a little cut in the bank where silver minnows swam above beds of green moss and metallic blue dragonflies skimmed in and out of the shadows.

"It's already Friday," Vertie said at the end of that first week. "Is your mama going to let you go or not?"

"She just says maybe."

"Good grief, girl, it only costs a nickel."

Vertie could afford to be cavalier about money. She was an only child and her mother had a good job with the WPA. I couldn't. Not that Daddy didn't have a good job, too, but we were a big family and had lots of old debts to pay.

Even if she was spoiled to having her own way, though, she was my best friend and the first person I met the day we moved in. Except for Mrs. Thirkle, who was hanging clothes when I took Martha May and Billy outside so Mama and Daddy and Aunt Millie could get the car unloaded and the apartment set up.

She was a skinny, wrinkled little old lady, with black frizzy hair that turned purple when she moved into the sun that bounced and burned around the rings on her fingers like a dozen tiny Fourth of July sparklers going off at once.

She said, "Hidy," her smile showing big yellow teeth that would've been scary if her eyes hadn't been so friendly.

We walked over to meet her, slowly because of Billy, our feet whispering through the drifts of last year's leaves under the big pecan tree.

"You all belong to the new family moving in?"

"Yes'm."

"I thought so. I met your Aunt Millie when she took the place for your folks, and she said there'd be three younguns. I only got one chick, myself, my boy Beau. That's him yonder, helping your daddy unload."

I looked down the driveway. Daddy had the rope off, coiling it around the crook of his arm, laughing. A grown boy was standing on the long box, reaching for the top mattress. He was laughing, too, the sun bright on his light blond hair.

"I'm Mrs. Thirkle," she said. "We live in front of you all, me and my boy Beau and his wife Boots, on the other side of the bathroom we'll be sharing."

"Our last name's Maddox. I'm Mavis Marie, only I'm just called Mavis, and this is Martha May, she goes by both names, and the baby's William Beryl, but we call him Billy."

"My, them's a mouthful of names, ain't they?" She pinned another shirt on the line, her rings blazing again. "Your aunt said y'all come here from Beaumont?"

That was called 'pumping,' which grown ups weren't supposed to do to children, though most of them did, so children were taught to answer them respectfully without telling them anything that wasn't any of their business.

"Well," I said, " we're kind of from all over."

"I never been to Beaumont myself, but it's got a pretty name. Is it a good town?"

"It was all right, I guess."

"Well, you'll like San 'Tonia, I bet. Most everybody does."

I said, "Yes'm," watching her rings shoot flame again.

"I see you're admiring my jewels," she said.

I felt my face go hot. "Yes'm."

She laughed. "Lord, child, you ain't done nothing impolite. I'd feel insulted if you didn't notice them. They're my fortune, all I got left in the world to tide me over old age and hard times. 'Course I got Beau, a big, strong boy, but my Late Husband he didn't want me depending on nobody, so he bought these here rings for me back when we was bootlegging in Oklahoma. You all ever been there?"

"Yes'm, when I was little."

"Well, like they say, it's a good place to be from."

I didn't know that was supposed to be a joke. It sounded like a simple statement of fact to me, so I said, "Yes'm" again and bent down to pick Billy up out of the leaves Martha May had piled around him, my eye catching the ice card in our back kitchen window. The number 25 looked very black and neat on the clean whiteness of the new card, and I wanted Mrs. Thirkle to see it, too, to know we were going to have regular ice delivery like other regular people.

But she didn't seem to notice it, so I said, "Is tomorrow the day the iceman comes?"

She picked up her basket and said, "Yep. Every Monday and Friday. But I'd be glad to give your mama room in my box tonight if she's worried about something spoiling."

"Oh no, ma'am, thank you just the same. I was only wondering." Which was a lie, because I knew exactly when he came.

"You need to get your ice card up for tomorrow," Aunt Millie had said. "He only comes on Mondays and Fridays."

"Oh, I don't think I'll be ordering any ice just yet," Mama said. "Later on, when it starts getting hot, I will. On Fridays, anyhow, so we can have ice tea with our Sunday dinner. Oh my God, Millie. I haven't had an ice box in so long I won't know how to act, and this nice apartment—"

"You really like it, honey?"

"Do I? That big bedroom, and this roomy kitchen, an ice box, a gas stove. I'm going to get Will to set the girls' bed right here in the kitchen under those back windows."

"That's a good place. And you don't have to worry

about the bedsteads. Mama and I came down here and went over every crack and crevice with a turkey feather dipped in coal oil."

Mama raised her eyebrows at Aunt Millie, like she was surprised Mama Dequincey had helped, then turned away and said, "That latticed-in back porch'll make a perfect place to wash, and we have an indoor toilet. I tell you, it's like dying and waking up in Heaven compared to—Mavis, why don't you take Martha May and Billy outside awhile so Millie and I can get this kitchen in order in peace."

"Couldn't I put up the ice card first? Please? Just this one time. I promise I won't ask again."

"Let her, Fern, I'll pay for it."

"No. You and Benny have paid for enough. I guess it'll be all right, Mavis, but just this one time, remember. I don't want you bothering me about it again till things settle down and I can get my bearings. All this prosperity at once is— run on, now, and keep Martha May out of trouble."

But Martha May was too scared of the newness of everything to cause any trouble. She stayed close to me even while she was picking up leaves to pile around Billy, and when Mrs. Thirkle went back in the house, she said, "Is this a Nice place, Mavis?"

"Yes, it's very Nice."

"Am I going to like it here?"

"Sure you are. We have a real bathroom and an ice box and there're lots of kids to play with."

"I don't see any."

"They're here, though. Notice how the grass is tramped down and the limbs are broken off those oleander bushes? And didn't you see the skates under the front steps and the little tea set in the corner of the stairs when we first went in?"

And right then Vertie came out on the back steps and said, "Hi. Y'all the new guys?"

She made me acquainted with the other kids as they turned up, showed me the way to school, and gave me a tour of the vacant lot down the street where all kinds of good stuff was dumped in a pit in the back—wall paper sample books for paperdoll clothes, beautiful pieces of bubbly blue glass to look through, and strips and chunks of scrap metal you could sell at the junkyard on Saturday mornings if you could beat the boys to it.

"See, they mostly dump stuff late Friday evening about dark," she said, "because it's against the law or something. Sometimes there's plenty to go around even if you don't get there till after breakfast Saturday. But sometimes the boys camp out down there on Friday nights and hog it all for theirselves and cart it off in Little Jesse's red wagon before anybody else has a chance to get any.

"If you can finagle a nickel out of your mama this Saturday, then next week we'll go real early and I'll help you get enough scrap to pay your own way and maybe have some left over for a soda pop. I made fifteen whole cents one time, and with the nickel Mama gave me, I went to the show and drank a strawberry Nehi and ate two Baby Ruths and a bag of popcorn and got sick as a dog. Mama said it served me right for being such a glutton, but I don't care, I'd do it again I had so much fun."

We went along a different stretch of the river on our way to the picture show, in a different direction from school. It took us down behind the vacant lot, past the back of the deserted tortilla factory, and below a little bluff that marked the far edge of Grandma and Grandpa Dequincey's backyard. Not that we called them 'Grandma' and 'Grandpa.' We had to say 'Mama' and 'Papa' Dequincey the one time we went as a family to see them. They were such strangers to us, and so different from us, I thought maybe Mama had been secretly adopted and was glad she only took Billy with her when she walked down to see them occasionally after we got settled.

Vertie wanted to know if the reason we weren't a close family was because my grandpa had put his hand in my bloomers, which nearly made me faint. But she said that was why her mama and daddy got a divorce. That her grandpa did that to her and her daddy wouldn't do anything about it so she and her mama left.

I didn't know whether to believe such a thing or not, it sounded so impossible. And I didn't know whether to hope Vertie was fibbing or hope she wasn't, because best friends were supposed to always tell each other the truth. But still. An old man? Your own grandpa?

Right before we went under the bridge that marked the real beginning of downtown, we passed the back of the Georgia Pines, where Boots worked as a waitress and made almost as much money as Beau, who drove a beer truck, as legal as the Law was long, Mrs. Thirkle said, which must keep her Late Husband spinning in his grave, him being such a well known bootlegger and so good at his trade.

We climbed up the bank at the City Auditorium, where Vertie said we could cut through and use the bathroom and get a drink of water. I was scared that first time we'd get in trouble, going in such a fancy building, but she said, "It's the *City* Auditorium, silly. That means anybody can go in it, any time they want to. Didn't you have a City Auditorium in Beaumont?"

"I don't know. We had a library, though, that looked just like a castle, and after we moved kind of out in the country, they sent a bookmobile to the schoolyard every other week the whole summer and let us check out five books at a time."

"That's one thing I don't like about you, Mavis, all that reading. My mama says it's not healthy to have your nose stuck in a book all the time."

"I don't read all the time. And besides, *my* mama says a good book is your best friend."

"I thought I was your best friend."

I could see Naomi standing there saying, "We're not relatives. We're blood first cousins and eternal best friends," and I felt so lonesome for her I could only whisper my lying "Yes," to Vertie's "Well? Am I your best friend or not?"

Then we took off toward the State, where we would trade our nickels for the black and white fantasies of the silver screen when it truly was silver, and bliss lay in every direction.

THIRTY

Naomi pulled up at a red light and said, "Hell, I can't tell if I'm going in the right direction or not. They've got this town so screwed up with construction and one-way streets, I don't know where I am."

"You should've turned off on 30 or stayed on 35 to Belknap instead of going through the middle of town."

"I think you're right. I'm lost as a goose."

"No, we're okay. I may not recognize many of these new buildings, but I can tell where we are by the street names. Go straight on. You can hit Belknap from here."

"If I can get through."

"Well try it for heaven's sake. If you can't, we can always get to Henderson some other way. They can't have completely closed off one whole side of town."

"All right. I don't guess there's anything else to do, if your heart's just set on Buster's."

"You said you wanted to play redneck, Naomi, and I can't think of a better place. If it's still open. I don't know. It may've burned down by now."

"Or been turned into a MacDonald's."

"Well, if it is, I'm sure we can find some other joint. Fort Worth's full of them."

"But we don't know where they are anymore."

"So instead of circling the block like you've been doing the last ten minutes, why don't we go on out there and see if it's still standing? If I'm going to do this thing, I want to do it right. I want to listen to 'San Antonio Rose' on a juke box and drink beer so cold it cracks my teeth and—"

"Will wonders never cease. I do believe you're glad you came."

"Yes, I'm glad."

"Okay. I promised you beer and barbecue and Bob Wills, and that's what you're going to get. Only don't pin your hopes on Buster's too strong. Remember God can't hide away little dibs and dabs of the world the way it used to be just because you think He ought to."

"Thanks for the lesson in theology, Naomi."

"I'm sorry. But I'm getting tired of this morbid quest for the past you're so hell bent on."

"I'm not on any morbid quest. I'm just trying to—I guess, figure out where I've been and where I ought to go. What I ought to do."

"I know what you ought to do. You ought to sell that old house and come to Austin and—look. We've got what? Ten, maybe fifteen years left, if we're lucky, before we break a hip and die of pneumonia, or go ga-ga and have to be locked up. Spending those years just rotting away—"

"Is that how you see my life? A rotting away?"

"Well, sitting on the back steps every morning staring out into the dark isn't exactly what I'd call healthy."

"I told you why I do that. And I work like a Turk most of the other twenty-three and a half hours every day, taking care of—taking care of things."

"But you don't *have* Paul to take care of anymore. You don't have anything left to take care of but that old house."

"I don't want to talk about Paul right now. I can't even think about him yet. And I'm tired of hearing you call my home that old house. I've tried to explain to you—"

"And I've tried to explain to you. Holding onto that big house, all the furniture, the pictures, the papers, all the crap and corruption you've accumulated all these years. I never walk into that place without feeling that Grandmother or

251

Grandma or Aunt Fern, one, is going to materialize out of the walls.

"You've simply got to get out from under all that. Come on to Austin and get an apartment, if you don't want that condo of Billy's. Or a house if you just have to have a yard to mess around in. But something small that's new and easy to keep up.

"Go back to teaching, to Woman Clubbing, to your work with the Historical Commission. Meet some new people, think some new thoughts, go some new places."

"Yes, yes, where the grass is always etc., etc."

"Sometimes it is, you know."

"And sometimes it isn't. I spent the first twelve years of my life riding that hobby horse, don't forget. More, actually. Paul and I did our share of moving around before we finally settled down in—there's Belknap. We ran right into it, just the way I knew we would. Take a left now and hook a right on Henderson and we're on our way."

She was quiet just long enough to make me think I was going to have a few minutes' peace, waiting till we crossed the Trinity to start again, saying, "Some of the new places were better than the old ones, though, now weren't they?"

"Yes, Naomi. San Antonio was, and I guess a cool corner of Hell would beat Angelo or the boonies of Beaumont, but—"

"Then how do you know Austin wouldn't be—"

"Just the place I had in mind?"

"Well, if not exactly that—"

"No, because exactly that doesn't exist. Not even in memory."

For not even in memory did any one place rest whole and complete in itself. Each carried the husk of the last and the seed of the next as it moved down the road of its own time: dirt, dust, mud, rock, gravel, shell, hottop, pavement; section road, farm to market, four-lane highway. And each led, whatever camp or town or city it passed through, to a noon stop somewhere under endless sky, where Billy not yet

born sat on the quilt by Martha May, while I listened to the
wind singing in the light wires and Mama and Daddy leaned
against the fender sharing a smoke—

"Shoot. I'm out of cigarettes. Pull in that 7-11 up yonder and let me hop out and get some."

"I have plenty."

"No, I want my own. It won't take a minute."

"All right. If that jasper ahead there will move over."

That was once her favorite pejorative, learned from the
pulp westerns we used to sneak into Uncle Dan's room to
read on long Sunday afternoons when the weather was bad.
A room that was always cold, always smelled of Lifebuoy
and bourbon and Muriel cigars, and always terrified our tres-
passing little souls into a frenzy of guilty delight.

"I haven't heard you call anybody a jasper in I don't
know how long."

"I haven't even thought of it in I don't know how long.
I guess it's all this—oh, Mavis."

"I don't know, Naomi. I'm not sure I could stand another move—"

"Yes, Millie," Mama said, "it is hard to pick up and
move again, and when Will first told me, I plain didn't think
I could stand it. But he feels like it's the kind of chance he
may never get again."

"I thought you all were happy here."

"We are. We love San 'Tonia. And lord knows we've
done better here than anywhere else we've been since we
first married and times were good for everybody. But you
know how Will is about having a place of his own, and with
this opportunity to buy a going concern, I just can't fight
him on it."

"If it's such a going concern, how come that guy's so
willing to turn loose of it?"

"Because he's got California fever, Millie, like half the
rest of the world. I've already told you that. He says he can
make twice the money out there he can here."

"Well, I think he's some kind of crook out to take your money, like that Pony Jack Will set such store by before he robbed him blind."

"No, this fella's on the up and up, with a good name in the trade and a solid business. Will checked into all that with a fine-tooth comb when he went to Fort Worth to look the place over. We're not total fools, Millie."

"I never said you were."

"Well you've said everything but."

"No, honey, I'm just scared that—if you all were broke, or couldn't make it any other way, I could understand. But Will's *got* a job. A good one."

"Yes. I know."

"And he's well thought of. Why goodness, Fern, in no more than a little over a year he's been raised to $27.50 a week. That's a lot of money to walk away from."

"I know that, too. Better than you do, I expect. But he makes ten or twelve times that for the owners. Which he doesn't begrudge the least little bit. It's their business. They're entitled to the profits. All Will wants is a chance to do the same thing for himself, and I don't see why you're carrying on about it like this."

"Because I feel like you deserve a chance, too, that's why. You're my sister, Fern, and I don't want to see you spend the rest of your life going through—I know Will's a good man. I know his intentions are good. But honey, to make you pull up stakes again and start off on another wild goose chase that won't amount to a hill of beans—"

"Don't say that! You'll sour our Luck."

"But, Fern—"

"I mean it, Millie. Not another word. I'm not going to play like giving up what we have here is easy for me. It's not. I haven't slept worth a fig since Will first began talking about this deal. But he's the breadwinner, and he's worked—I never realized how hard he did work till those last few days in Beaumont when I was calling and passing proofs for him.

"I don't know how he held up to it all those years, knocking on doors day after day, with people—let me tell you something. Plenty of people had just as soon slam the door in your face as look at you. Or stand there eyeballing you like you're some kind of bum or something—oh, don't start crying.

"There were a lot of good people, too. Some that couldn't buy anything, no matter how bad they might want to, but would at least treat you like a human being. Some that would ask you in for a cup of coffee, and some I know gave me orders because they felt sorry for me—well, it's all water under the bridge now, and I promise you, we aren't going back to that.

"Will'll have his own place, be established. The Depression seems to be easing off some, and we've got a pretty respectable little nest-egg saved."

"I hope you're right, honey. You know I do. But I can't help worrying. What if—"

"He's got his heart set on it, Millie, and his mind made up. There's nothing I can do."

Except what we always did. Load up the car, light out down the road, leave all the people and places we knew behind.

"And Fort Worth's a good town. It's not as big as San 'Tonia, or near as pretty, but there's money there. And Will's going to get us a place of our own as soon as he can, where we can have a garden and some chickens and—"

And a milk cow and a snazzy little roadster and a new school where I wouldn't know anybody. A new neighborhood, new church, new picture show, new everything.

"Well," Aunt Millie said. "You know if you ever do need anything—"

But I didn't want to hear any more of that old story I'd already heard too many times before, so I got up and walked out as quiet as I could and eased the door to behind me.

THIRTY-ONE

I stood on the back porch, in the late afternoon sun, listening to the birds homing in to their roosts in the big pecan, wondering how much time I had left. Probably not enough to find out if Owen really did like me, the way Vertie said he did. Certainly not enough to finish my last year in a junior high where I had friends and my grades were good again. Nor enough to learn how Beau's trial would end, or whether Mrs. Thirkle would ever get her rings back.

"Well, the lawyer says I can redeem them," she'd told us. "If I can rake up the cash by thirty days after the verdict's in, which I got about as much a chance at as a snowball in Hell."

"I'm awfully sorry," Mama said. "They were such beautiful stones."

"The best money could buy. My Late Husband always said, don't never put your hard-earned cash into no cheap hunk of glass you can't get nothing for if you ever need to sell it. 'Course he never figured on some son-of-a-bitching, pardon my French, lawyer getting them all. And if Beau'd just had enough sense to make small runs, a couple of cases in the trunk of his car, stead of trying to truck it in with some trigger-happy ex-con of a partner—why, I asked him. Why?

"His daddy always told him, don't never use a gun against a peace officer of no kind. If you can't outrun them, pay them off or pay your fine, or do your time if you have to, but don't never get mixed up in no shooting with the Law."

"But, Mrs. Thirkle. The police know it wasn't Beau that killed that deputy. Surely—"

"They know he rented the truck, Mrs. Maddox, and bought the booze and was doing the driving. Inside a dry county." She drew in a deep breath, then, and began to recite the damning part of the charge as it had been read in court. We all knew it by heart, she'd repeated it so many times. When Mama asked her in for coffee of a morning, when the ladies sat on the back steps to visit in the afternoons, when you passed her in the hall or met her on the porch—'" The defendant was in the company of a known felon, during the progress of a crime in which the arresting officer was shot to death.' You think they're going to have any mercy on my boy because he was too dumb to listen to his dead daddy?"

She got skinnier and more wrinkled up looking every day, and Boots didn't smile or cut up anymore or look as much like one half of what Mama called the Gold Dust Twins. Not because Boots and Beau looked like the little pickaninnies on the box, but because they used to always be together when they weren't working, laughing and dancing around without a care in the world. But I thought the name mainly suited them because they were both a golden color all over, their hair, their skin, even their eyes.

Boots was still so pretty people really did turn around and look at her twice when she walked by, but she was dulled down somehow after Beau's arrest, and worked so many double shifts we hardly got to see her except for a few minutes on Sunday mornings when we were leaving for Sunday School.

Sometimes she'd give us a nickel apiece to put in the collection plate, or a mint to keep our breath nice, but sometimes she'd just stand there in the hall in her red silk kimono, hugging herself, not even seeing us.

Before Beau got in trouble, any time Vertie and I were

going along that stretch of the river, we'd climb up to the back door of the Georgia Pines and stand in the shade of the overhang, as far away from the flies around the garbage cans as we could get, and wait for Boots to come out for a smoke break. She'd laugh and talk and tease us about boys and do funny imitations of her boss, who was a transplanted cracker, she said, that couldn't go back home on account of something called 'an outstanding warrant,' so he'd named his beer joint for his favorite tree, and stayed lit higher than any Georgia pine she ever heard of, ever since.

But afterwards, she didn't take many breaks. She said she had to make every dime she could, because the whole family depended on her now, and if she got fired, or her tips went down, she didn't know what they'd do.

Well, I'd never know how it turned out. Or have the river to prowl up and down anymore. Or hear the boys calling the Tarzan yell back and forth across the long sweet twilights when the cars came in from work, the men walking jaunty and gay, knowing their suppers were waiting, their families glad to see them.

I walked on over to the corner between the back fence and the shed row where Martha May was teaching Billy to make a play-like campground the way I'd taught her a long time ago, as a means of keeping those days as alive in her memory as they were in mine.

She had the loose dirt patted down, the roads smoothed out with the side of her hand, a little trench lined with twigs for the river, Billy's little cast-iron car parked by two canvas-colored sycamore leaves propped together.

"That's our tent," she said. "It's going to be the biggest one."

"I never said our tent was the biggest, Martha May. I said it was the Nicest."

"Well I want mine to be the biggest, too."

They'd put a lot of work into it. Or at least Martha May had. Billy had mostly watched and fetched, I figured, being still so little. But he was quiet, and careful not to step on anything, and I hated knowing it would be smashed to bits before morning.

"You all've done a good job," I said, wishing for a minute it was a real camp on the real road, where you knew you were going to be moving all the time and were too young to expect anything else—or want anything else.

"It's not finished yet. Go get some more big leaves, Billy. We got to put up the rest of the tents."

"I wouldn't try to do any more now," I said. "It's almost suppertime."

"We have to have more than one tent, Mavis. This is a big campground, and it's all mine and Billy's, and if anybody messes it up, they'll be plenty sorry."

But after supper, when the dishes were done and the family talk finished, when the grownups leaned back to read the paper or went to sit on the front porch to visit while the little kids chased lightning bugs, the Big Kids went around to the back and climbed up on the shed roof. We talked and sang, poked easy fun, told corny jokes, and in the trembling silences, moved hesitantly to the edge of an awareness so tentative, we only recognized it for what it was by the strangeness of the fears and longings some note or phrase in the music, some texture of the wind, stirred to aching life in a region of our selves only now making itself known.

We sang 'Red River Valley' and 'Streets of Laredo,' and once in awhile, 'The Prisoner's Song,' till we remembered about Beau and changed to something else, Owen's harmonica leading us off into some other song that might be sad but wouldn't be about somebody in jail.

Once the rush to the shed roof began, I wouldn't be able to keep the campground safe. There were too many of us, there was too much pushing and shoving, it was too dark to see where you were going, even if you cared.

"Well," I said, "the fairies might come here to play tonight. You can't tell. And if there's a lot of them—"

"Oh, Mavis! I don't believe in fairies anymore."

"Why, Martha May Maddox!"

"Well, I don't." And before I could warn her that Billy was standing there with his hands full of leaves, "I don't even believe in Santa Claus anymore."

"Do you realize your baby brother is listening to every word you're saying?"

"He won't understand. He's too little."

"No, he's not. He's nearly three, Martha May, and he understands a lot more than you think. You're getting too big for your britches, Miss Priss-ike."

"No, I'm just too big to believe in fairy tales. Goodness, Mavis, I'll be starting the first grade this coming fall."

Yes, and I'd be starting high school. But not in San 'Tonia. Not with kids I knew, friends already made, a place already paid for. "Well then, since you're so smart, young lady, I guess you've already figured out that you won't be going to Ben McCulloch when you start."

"Why I most certainly will. Ben McCulloch's my school. You took me over there and showed it to me."

"It *was* your school. But it's not anymore. We're moving."

I'd always corrected Martha May, and fussed at her a lot. I was the oldest. That was my job. But I'd never tried to cut her down to the size of my own misery before, and her head kept making little bobbing jerks back from the shock of it that never quit shaming me, that I saw over and over again the day she was killed in the accident her drunk-driver husband walked away from with nothing more than cuts and bruises.

"Listen," I apologized, "I thought you already knew. Haven't you heard Mama and Daddy talking about it all week?"

"Yes, but they said *might,* Mavis, *might.* I thought might meant maybe."

"It does, Martha May. But if they say 'might' or 'maybe' when they're talking about moving—"

"I don't want to move."

"Neither do I, but we're going to. And soon, from what I heard Mama telling Aunt Millie while ago."

She snatched the leaves out of Billy's hands and crumbled them to bits and flung them out over her campground in a miniature dust storm, then began kicking and stomping everything to pieces—the roads, the river, the trees, the tent. I knew she would never build another one, that I would never build another one, that Billy would never know how to build one. And there was nothing I could do about it but stand there watching her put a deliberate and final end to the last tangible reminder of that part of our life I had loved best and found it hardest to give up.

THIRTY-TWO

At the end of another part of my life, with the decision as to where I'd spend what was left of the next already made, I stood in line in a strange store, in what amounted to a strange town, waiting for the Irani or Pakistani, or whatever he was, to give me my cigarettes.

Not in the warm light and mixed smells of jumbled shelves in the old corner grocery that served between the weekly trips to Leonard's. Those stores were as dead as the big, cumbersome camera Daddy had manipulated from a fixed tripod, giving like way to maneuverability and high speed.

The cowboy types were the same, the truck drivers, manual laborers, the work-worn, hard-used women, the sweet-hungry kids. But the canned beer came in neat cardboard cartons and the open camaraderie of the pinball machine had been replaced by hooded TV screens where solitary warriors fought solitary battles in the privacy of their own darknesses. Credit cards paid for the self-pumped gas, and the flashy little radio behind the counter pumped a brand of country music different from anything the Light Crust Doughboys ever played.

The whatever-he-was handed me the cigarettes, at last, along with my change and that California-silly have a nice day that had begun to substitute for a genuine thank you. I made myself smile at him, more cordially than I would have

262

at one of my own kind, in apology for the resentment I still felt for foreigners—and yankees, who were also invading us in droves. Well, the poor bastards were just trying to find a place for themselves the same as everybody else, and I wished them Luck at it, so long as it didn't end up being too close to mine.

Stuffing the change, and the cigarettes I no longer wanted, in my purse, I walked out into the faded neon glory of that stretch of the Jacksboro Highway once called Blood Alley and now Chamber-of-Commerced into Miracle Mile; to the car where Naomi waited to destroy, with the good intentions of a well-meaning adult, rather than with the hurt rage of a disappointed child, not a play-like campground and what it represented, but a real house and all it represented.

I knew saving it meant risking the loss of peace and approval among the people I depended on, as saving her conscience had meant for Mama during that long ago fight over the paregoric. And just as she had first counted her cost, so had I counted mine, and considered it as nothing against giving up the last place left to me I could call home.

But as I got in the car, prepared to make my stand and pay my price, Naomi said, "Ready?"

And the joy that word triggered, inside the memory of a time when we aimed ourselves at the place we had in mind without regard for obstacle or opinion, counting always on the ultimate goodness of our Luck, released me into the sure hope that I would cross my river, if not to cheers and whistles, at least to the steady accord of a tested friend.

"Let her rip," I said.

She stared at me a minute. "You're all right?"

"Oh yes. I'm pretty bruised and beat up, and I know the worst part of losing Paul is still ahead of me. But I think the vital organs can limp on awhile yet."

She pulled back out onto the highway, easing the car along the next few blocks as slowly as the traffic would allow, and we both saw Buster's sign at the same time, in the same yellow letters on the same black background, lighted by the same three-hundred watt goose neck incandescents.

She turned into the lot, the gravel crunching under the tires, and said, "Well, what do you think?"

"It looks the same on the outside." The same cracking stucco, the same curtained plate-glass windows streaked with the same dirt, the one on the right still centered with the word 'Beer' spelled out in the same blue neon script, the same smoke drifting up from the pit at the back, the same sound of cars and trucks whining by behind us. But it was the one-dimensional sameness of a photograph. All the familiar features were there, even to the look in the eyes. But of flesh and blood and bone there was none.

"Come on," she said. "Let's go for it. This many pickups can't be wrong."

"Wait."

She knew what I was going to say, old mind-reader that she was, before I opened my mouth. But I wanted it put into words that would forever put it to rest.

"Before we—celebrate, blood first cousin and eternal best friend, I want you to know I have listened to you today, and I know you always have my best interests at heart. So I promise you I am going to call someone in to get the house back in shape, and I am going to make it down to Austin often. I'll probably even stay with you this fall. I'd like to be back on campus awhile, I think, and take a couple of courses to get my mind to working again. And I am going to San 'Tonia and see Millie if it takes a court order to do it. But I'm not moving. I can't carry the weight of one more place left behind."

She touched my arm, so lightly and briefly I might only have imagined it, and said, "All right. Then let's go do what we came for."

We got out of the car as the door to Buster's opened and a couple coming out bringing the sound of Hank Snow singing 'Moving On' with them, and we started laughing, moving toward the reflections coming to meet us in the window, not Mama and Martha May and me of long ago, just Naomi and me of now, two old ladies, whose laughter looked like weeping.